BEHIND THE RAKE'S WICKED WAGER

Sarah Mallory

MILLS & BOON

First published in Great Britain 2013
by Mills & Boon, an imprint of Harlequin (UK) Limited.
Harlequin (UK) Limited, Eton House, 18-24 Paradise Road, Richmond, Surrey TW9 1SR

© Sarah Mallory 2013

ISBN: 978 0 263 89803 3

Harlequin (UK) policy is to use papers that are natural, renewable and recyclable products and made from wood grown in sustainable forests. The logging and manufacturing process conform to the legal environmental regulations of the country of origin.

Printed and bound in Spain
by Blackprint CPI, Barcelona

Sarah Mallory was born in Bristol, and now lives in an old farmhouse on the edge of the Pennines with her husband and family. She left grammar school at sixteen to work in companies as varied as stockbrokers, marine engineers, insurance brokers, biscuit manufacturers and even a quarrying company. Her first book was published shortly after the birth of her daughter. She has published more than a dozen books under the pen-name of Melinda Hammond, winning the Reviewers' Choice Award from Singletitles.com for *Dance for a Diamond* and the Historical Novel Society's Editors' Choice for *Gentlemen in Question*. In 2012, her Sarah Mallory novel THE DANGEROUS LORD DARRINGTON won the Romantic Novelists' Association's RONA Rose Award.

Previous novels by the same author:

THE WICKED BARON
MORE THAN A GOVERNESS
  (part of *On Mothering Sunday*)
WICKED CAPTAIN, WAYWARD WIFE
THE EARL'S RUNAWAY BRIDE
DISGRACE AND DESIRE
TO CATCH A HUSBAND…
SNOWBOUND WITH THE NOTORIOUS RAKE
  (part of *An Improper Regency Christmas*)
THE DANGEROUS LORD DARRINGTON
BENEATH THE MAJOR'S SCARS*

*The Notorious Coale Brothers

**Look for Sarah Mallory's
THE ILLEGITIMATE MONTAGUE
part of *Castonbury Park* Regency mini-series
available now**

**Did you know that some of these novels
are also available as eBooks?
Visit www.millsandboon.co.uk**

For P and S, my own twin heroes.

Chapter One

'Well, well, Lord Markham, have you ever seen such a bonny child?'

Jasper Coale, Viscount Markham, looked down at the baby lying in its crib and was at a loss for words. Thankfully, his sister-in-law came to his aid.

'Fie now, Lady Andrews, when was a man ever interested in babies? I suspect the viscount is merely glad that his little godson is not screaming the house down, as he was doing during the ceremony.' Zelah gazed down fondly at her baby son. 'Fortunately the journey back from the church has rocked him off to sleep.'

The christening of Dominic and Zelah's second child had been a major event and the little church at Lesserton was crowded for the ceremony. Afterwards, Dominic laid on a feast at

the White Hart for the tenants and villagers to
enjoy, while family and close friends were invited to Rooks Tower for an elegant and sub-
stantial repast. Zelah had the satisfaction of
seeing her rooms overflowing with guests, despite the threat of snow which was always a
concern during the early months of the year.
She suspected no small part of the inducement
to the local families to leave their firesides was
the knowledge that no lesser person than Viscount Markham would be present.

Jasper had been unable to attend the christening of his niece Arabella some eighteen months
earlier, but Zelah and Dominic had asked him
to stand godfather for their new-born son, and
only the direst winter weather would have kept
him away.

The fires at Rooks Tower were banked up,
the table almost groaned with the banquet it was
required to support and the wine flowed freely.
Jasper was sure the neighbourhood would be
talking about the Coales' hospitality for months
to come. Most of the guests were gathered in the
yellow salon, but Jasper had wandered across
to join Zelah in the study where the baby was
sleeping, watched over by his devoted nurse.
Sir Arthur and Lady Andrews had followed
him into the room, brimming with good humour thanks to the abundant quantities of wine
and food.

'I admit I have nothing but praise for my god-son while he is sleeping,' said Jasper, glancing down into the crib.

'It makes me quite broody,' declared Lady Andrews, causing her husband to guffaw loudly.

'Now, now, my dear, our breeding days are well past, thank the Lord!'

'I am well aware of that, sir.' The lady turned her bright gaze upon Jasper. 'But what of you, Lord Markham? I am sure, seeing your brother's felicity, you must envy him his happy state.'

Jasper's smile froze. Glancing across the crib, he saw the sudden alarm in Zelah's dark eyes. He must respond quickly, lest they notice how pale she had grown. But even as he sought for the words his sister-in-law recovered with a laughing rejoinder.

'Having spent the past two weeks here with his niece and godson, Lord Markham is more likely to value his freedom!' She tucked her hand in his arm. 'If you will excuse us, Sir Arthur, Lady Andrews, I must carry the viscount away now to speak to my sister before she leaves us…'

'I commend your quick thinking,' he murmured as they crossed the hall.

'I had to do something,' she responded quietly. 'I did not want you to snub them for their impertinence. They are good people, and mean well.'

'Mean well—!' He smothered an exclamation and after a moment continued, 'I beg your pardon, but it seems these days the whole world is eager to marry me off. I cannot look at a woman without her family hearing wedding bells.'

She chuckled. 'Surely it has always been thus. 'Tis merely that you are more aware of it now.'

'Perhaps you are right. I thought by leaving London I should have some respite from the incessant gossip and conjecture.'

Zelah gave a soft laugh and squeezed his arm.

'You are nigh on thirty years old, my lord. Society considers it time you settled down and produced an heir.'

'Society can go hang. I will not marry without love, and you know you are the only woman—'

Zelah stopped. 'Hush, Jasper, someone may hear you.'

'What if they do?' He smiled down at her. 'Dominic knows you refused me, it matters not what anyone else thinks.'

Zelah shook her head at him, trying to joke him out of his uncharacteristic seriousness.

'For shame, my lord, what of your reputation as the wicked flirt no woman can resist? It would be sadly dented if word got out that you had been rejected.'

He looked down at her, wondering how it was that of all the women he had met, the only one he had ever wanted to marry should prefer his twin.

'So it would,' he said, raising her fingers to his lips. 'Then let it be our secret, that you are the woman who broke my heart.'

Zelah blushed and shook her head at him.

'Fie, Jasper, I may have bruised your heart a little, but it is not broken, I am sure. I am not the woman for you. I believe there is another, somewhere, far more suited to you, my lord.'

'Well, I have not found her yet, and it is not for want of looking,' he quipped lightly.

'Mayhap love will come upon you when you least expect it,' she responded. 'As it did with me and Dominic.'

Jasper's heart clenched at the soft light that shone in her eyes when she spoke of his brother. It tightened even more as he observed her delighted smile at the sound of her husband's voice.

'What is this, sir, dallying with my wife again?'

She turned, in no way discomposed at being discovered tête-à-tête with the irresistible viscount, but that was because she knew herself innocent of any impropriety. She had never succumbed to his charms, thought Jasper, with a rueful inward smile. That had always been part of the attraction. She held out her hand to her husband.

Marriage suited Dominic. The damaged soldier who had returned from the Peninsula, barely alive, was now a contented family man and respected landowner, the horrific scars on his face and body lessened by the constant application of the salves and soothing balms Zelah prepared for him.

'Lady Andrews has been telling Jasper it is time he married,' said Zelah, her laughing glance flicking between them.

'Aye, so it is,' growled Dominic, the smile in his hard eyes belying his gruff tone. 'Put the female population out of its misery. My friends in town tell me at least three more silly chits sank into a decline when you left London at the end of the Season.'

Jasper spread his hands. 'If they wish to flirt with me, Dom, who am I to say them nay? As for marriage, I have no plans to settle down yet.'

'Well, you should,' retorted his twin bluntly. 'You need an heir. *I* do not want the title. I am happy enough here at Rooks Tower.' His arm slid around Zelah and he pulled her close. 'Come, love. Your sister is about to set off for West Barton and wishes to take her leave of you.'

'Ah, yes, we were on our way to say goodbye to Maria and Reginald, and little Nicky, too. I doubt we shall see my nephew again before he goes off to school in Exeter.' She sighed. 'We shall miss him dreadfully, shall we not, Dom?'

'*Little Nicky* is now a strapping eleven-year-old and so full of mischief he is in serious danger of being throttled by my gamekeeper,' retorted her fond husband.

'Ripe and ready for a spree, is he?' Jasper grinned, remembering his own boyhood, shared with his twin. 'Then by all means pack him off to school.'

He allowed Zelah to take his arm again.

'So you intend to leave us tomorrow,' she remarked as they walked towards the yellow salon. 'Back to London?'

'No, Bristol. To Hotwells.'

'Hotwells?' Dominic gave a bark of laughter. 'Never tell me you are going to visit Gloriana Barnabus.'

'I am indeed,' replied Jasper. 'I had a letter from her before Christmas, begging me to call upon her.'

'What a splendid name,' declared Zelah. 'Is she as colourful as she sounds?'

'No,' growled Dominic. 'She is some sort of distant cousin, a fading widow who enjoys the poorest of health. Did she say why she is so anxious to see you after all these years?'

'Not a word, though I suspect it is to do with her son Gerald. Probably wants me to sponsor his entry into Parliament, or some such.'

Dominic shrugged as he stood back for his twin and his wife to enter the yellow salon.

'Well, dancing attendance upon Gloriana will keep you out of mischief for a while.'

Zelah cast a considering glance up at her brother-in-law.

'I am not so sure, my love. With that handsome face and his wicked charm, I fear Lord Markham will get into mischief anywhere!'

Jasper set off from Rooks Tower the following morning, driving himself in his curricle with only his groom beside him and his trunk securely strapped behind. Dominic and Zelah were there to see him off, looking the picture of domestic felicity. He did not begrudge his twin his happiness, but despite Zelah's words he could not believe he would ever be so fortunate. He had met so many women, flirted with hundreds, but not one save Zelah had ever touched his heart. With a sigh he settled himself more comfortably in the seat and concentrated on the winding road. He would have to marry at some point and provide an heir, but not yet, not yet.

Miss Susannah Prentess wandered into the morning room of her Bath residence to find her aunt sitting at a small gilded table whose top was littered with papers. She had a pen in hand and was currently engaged in adding up a column of figures, so she did not look up when her niece addressed her.

'How much did we make last night, ma'am?'

Mrs Wilby finished her calculations and wrote a neat tally at the bottom of the sheet before replying.

'Almost two hundred pounds, and once we have taken off the costs, supper, candles and the like, I think we shall clear one-fifty easily. Very satisfying, when one thinks it is not yet March.'

Susannah regarded her with admiration.

'How glad I am you discovered a talent for business, Aunt Maude.'

A blush tinted Mrs Wilby's faded cheek.

'Nonsense, it is merely common sense and a grasp of figures, my love, something which you have inherited, also.'

'And thank goodness for that. It certainly helps when it comes to fleecing our guests.'

'Susannah, we do not *fleece* anyone! It is merely that we are better at measuring the odds.' The blush was replaced by a more indignant rose. 'You make it sound as if we run a gaming house, which is something I could *never* condone.'

Susannah was quick to reassure her.

'No, no, of course not, I was teasing you. We merely invite our friends here for an evening of cards, and if they lose a few shillings—'

'Or guineas!'

'Or guineas,' she conceded, her eyes twinkling, 'then so much the better for us.'

Aunt Maude looked at her uncertainly, then clasped her hands and burst out, 'But I cannot like it, my love. To be making money in such a way—'

'We do not make very much, Aunt, and *some* of our guests go away the richer for the evening.'

'Yes, but overall—oh, my dear, I cannot think that it is right, and I know our neighbours here in the Royal Crescent do not approve.'

'Pho, a few valetudinarian spoil-sports. Our card parties are very select.' She sank down on to a sofa. 'I agree, Royal Crescent would not be my first choice of a place to live, but Uncle's will was quite explicit, I cannot touch my fortune or sell this house until I am five and twenty. Another two years.'

'You could let it out, and we could find something smaller...'

The wistful note was not lost on Susannah, but she shook her head, saying firmly, 'No, this house suits my requirements very well. The location lends our parties a certain distinction.' She added mischievously, 'Besides, I am a great heiress, and Royal Crescent is perfectly in keeping with my status.'

Aunt Maude looked down, gazing intently at the nails of one white hand.

'I thought, when you asked me to come and

live with you, it was so that you could go about a little.'

'But I do go about, Aunt. Why, what with the Pump Room and the theatre, the balls and assemblies, we go about a great deal.'

'But I thought you wanted to find a husband.'

Susannah laughed at that.

'No, no, that was never my intention. I am very happy with my single state, thank you.'

'But at three-and-twenty you are in danger of becoming an old maid.'

'Then that is what I shall do,' she replied, amused. 'Or mayhap I shall accept an offer from one of the charming young men who grace our card parties.'

'If only you would,' sighed Mrs Wilby.

'Mr Barnabus proposed to me yesterday.' She saw her aunt's hopeful look and quickly shook her head. 'I refused him, of course. I tried very hard not to let it come to a proposal, but he would not be gainsaid.'

'Oh dear, was he very disappointed?'

'Yes, but he will get over it.'

'I hope to goodness he does not try to end it all, like poor Mr Edmonds.'

Susannah laughed.

'I hope you do not think my refusing Jamie Edmonds had anything to do with his falling into the river.'

'I heard he jumped from Bath Bridge…'

'My dear Aunt, he was drinking in some low tavern near the quay, as young men are wont to do, and then tried to walk the parapet on the bridge, missed his footing and tumbled off on to a coal barge.' Her lips twitched at the look of disappointment on her aunt's face. 'I know it to be true, Aunt, because Jamie told me himself, when I next saw him in Milsom Street.'

'But everyone said—'

'I know what everyone *said*, but that particular rumour was spread by one of Mr Edmonds's friends, Mr Warwick. He was angry because I would not take an IOU from him last week and sent him home before supper.'

'Ay, yes, I remember Mr Warwick.' Mrs Wilby nodded. 'It was quite clear that he was drinking too much and was in no fit state to be in a respectable establishment.'

'And in no fit state to play at cards, which is more to the point,' added Susannah. 'But he did make me a very handsome apology later, so he is forgiven.' She jumped up. 'But enough of this. I am for the Pump Room, then back via Duffields, to find something to read. Will you come with me?'

'Gladly. I hope we shall find old friends at the Pump Room to converse with.'

Susannah's eyes twinkled wickedly.

'And *I* hope we shall find new friends to invite to our next card party!'

Chapter Two

The damp February weather made for a dirty journey north, but Jasper spent only one night on the road and arrived at Mrs Barnabus's house at Hotwells shortly after mid-day. He was ushered in by a butler whose sombre mien led him to wonder if he had maligned his relative, and she was in fact at death's door. However, when he was shown into the elegant drawing room, Mrs Barnabus appeared to be in her usual state of health. She came forwards to meet him, hands held out and shawls trailing from her thin shoulders.

'Markham, my dear cousin, how good of you to call.' Her voice was as frail as her person, but Jasper knew there was a will of iron inside the waif-like body. He took the hand held out to him and kissed it punctiliously. The fingers curled around his hand like claws. 'So good of you to come out of your way, when you know I have no room to put you up here.'

'Yes, wasn't it?' he replied cheerfully.

She sank on to the sofa, trying to pull him down with her, but he freed himself and drew up a chair.

'You are on your way back to London, Markham?'

'Yes. I hope to reach Corsham tonight. Well, Gloriana, what can I do for you?'

Her sigh was audible.

'So like your dear father.'

'Devil a bit, madam. He wouldn't have put himself out to come here at all. He would have sent a servant to find out what it was you wanted.'

Gloriana looked a trifle discomposed at this but she recovered quickly and gave him a wan smile.

'In looks, my dear boy, in looks. And how is your poor, scarred soldier-brother?'

The epithet grated on Jasper but he concealed it.

'Dominic is prospering. And very happy with his growing family. Now, Gloriana, tell me why you have summoned me here.'

The widow wrung her hands and uttered dramatically, 'It is Gerald.'

'I thought as much. What has the boy done?'

This cool response drew a reproachful look from the widow.

'So charming yet so implacable.' She sighed. 'No wonder you break so many hearts.'

'Not intentionally, ma'am, I assure you.' He took out his watch. 'I am sorry to hurry you, Gloriana, but my curricle is waiting and I do not want to keep the horses standing too long in this cold weather. Tell me about Gerald.'

'Your manners, Markham, leave a lot to be desired.'

'But a moment ago you were telling me I was charming.'

Mrs Barnabus struggled with herself. She would have liked to give the viscount a sharp set-down but she wanted his help, and she was very much afraid if she ordered him to apologise or be on his way, he would choose the latter option. The fact that he was well aware of her inner turmoil did nothing to improve her temper. She forgot her plaintive tone and spoke curtly.

'He has formed a disastrous attachment.'

Jasper's black brows rose.

'Really? That does not sound like Gerald. When I've met him in town I have always thought him a level-headed young buck.'

Apart from a faint moue of distaste she ignored his description of her beloved son.

'That is why I am so concerned. He came to

see me before Christmas, extolling the virtues of this woman—a very paragon she sounded!—but I took little notice. He has always been a sensible boy and I thought his infatuation would soon burn itself out. Then one of my acquaintances wrote to tell me that this…this *female* holds regular card parties. I am told she won a considerable sum of money from Gerald. Two hundred guineas!'

'A mere nothing. He could lose more than that in a sitting at White's.'

'Perhaps, but my acquaintance says all Bath was talking of it.'

'Bath!' Jasper laughed. 'He has become enamoured of a lady from *Bath*? Is she an invalid or old enough to be his grandmama?'

'It may not be quite as fashionable as it was, but there are still any number of people who like to visit there,' replied Mrs Barnabus, affronted by his humour. 'I should go there myself, if the waters here were not more beneficial for those like myself who are prone to consumptive symptoms.'

'Well perhaps you should go there anyway, to find out just what Gerald is about.'

'He will not listen to me. He is one-and-twenty now, and in charge of his own fortune. Besides, I could not possibly travel such a distance.'

'It is barely fifteen miles, Cousin.'

'And I would be so knocked up I should be in

no fit state to help my poor son.' She sank back on the sofa and waved her vinaigrette under her nose, weakened merely by the thought of such a journey. 'No, Markham, as head of the family, it is up to you to rescue Gerald from the clutches of this—this harpy.'

'My dear ma'am, we have no evidence that there is anything wrong with the woman at all, save that she has beaten Gerald at cards. And even that is not to be wondered at. If I remember rightly he was never that sharp.'

Gloriana's eyes snapped angrily.

'You are too cruel, Markham. The boy is almost ten years your junior and lacks your worldly experience. And now, when I ask, nay, *beg* you to help him, you can do nothing but jest.' She broke off, dragging a wisp of lace from her pocket and dabbing at her eyes.

Jasper regarded her in exasperation as he saw his dinner at the Hare and Hounds slipping away. However, beneath his insouciant exterior he was quite fond of Gerald, so he gave in with a faint shrug.

'Very well, ma'am, I can as easily stop at Bath tonight as at Corsham. I will seek out Gerald and find out just what is afoot.'

Gently brushing aside her grateful effusions and the belated offer of a glass of ratafia, Jasper took his leave of Gloriana and headed for York House.

* * *

He arrived at the busy Bath hotel before five o'clock, in good time to bespeak rooms and dinner. Then, having changed his travel clothes for the coat and knee-breeches that were still the required evening dress for Bath, he sallied forth in search of Gerald Barnabus.

Susannah looked around the drawing room with satisfaction. It was filling up nicely and most of the little card tables were occupied.

'Another good turn-out.'

Susannah heard the murmur and found Kate Logan at her side. Kate was a widow and past her thirtieth year, although she looked younger and her stylish gown of bronze satin with its matching turban drew many a gentleman's eye. Susannah knew Kate was well aware of her attraction and used it to advantage at the card table, although she never succumbed to any gentleman's advances. She continued now in her habitual slow drawl, 'There is a ball at the Lower Rooms tonight, so doubtless many will take themselves off there at ten and then we can get down to business.'

Susannah shushed her with a look and said in a voice of mock severity, 'There is no *business* here, Mrs Logan. We merely invite a few friends to enjoy a game of cards.'

Kate gave a knowing smile.

'That is what I meant, Susannah.'

'Of course,' added Susannah innocently, 'some of our guests might lose a few guineas at our tables, but that is hardly to be wondered at, after all.' She glanced at her friend, trying to keep her countenance, but failed miserably, and her peal of laughter made several heads turn. 'Oh dear, now I have made people stare. Go away, Kate, before I forget myself again. Look, my aunt is waving to you to make a fourth at whist.'

'And she is sitting down with Mr and Mrs Anstruther, who spend so much time bickering that they invariably lose. Very well, I shall go, and I see old Major Crommelly is coming over, no doubt to engage you for a game of picquet, which is his pretext to get you to himself and subject you to the most fulsome compliments.'

'He may positively shower me with compliments as long as he is happy to play for pound points,' chuckled Susannah, turning to greet the elderly gentleman who was approaching her.

It was well over an hour later that she rose from the table, refusing the major's suggestion that they should play another hand.

'But, my dear Miss Prentess, the night is yet young.'

'It is indeed, but I have other guests to attend, Major, and cannot let you monopolise me.'

She softened her words with a smile and went off to join her aunt, whom she found bubbling with excitement.

'Susannah, I am so glad you are come, I was determined to interrupt your game if you had not finished when you did.'

'My dear ma'am, what has occurred to put you into a spin?'

'Mr Barnabus has arrived—'

'Is that all? How did he look? I hope he is not too downhearted—'

'No, that is, I did not notice.' Aunt Maude flapped her hands in excitement. 'Did you see the stranger he brought with him?'

'No, I was paying picquet with the major and had my back to the door.' Susannah looked around. 'Has Mr Barnabus brought another gentleman, then? That is good of him, and shows he has not taken umbrage at my refusal.'

'No, not a gentleman, Susannah. A *viscount*. There, I knew that would make you stare.'

'It does indeed. We have had nothing more prestigious than a baron here before, although I suppose General Sanstead is pretty high...'

Mrs Wilby tapped her niece's arm with her closed fan.

'Pray be serious, Susannah, his presence here adds distinction! You must let me make you known to him at once.'

'By all means, Aunt. Lead on.'

'No need, here he comes now,' Mrs Wilby responded in a shrill whisper, and Susannah looked around to see two gentlemen approaching. The first, a stocky young man with an open, boyish countenance beneath a thatch of fair hair, was Gerald Barnabus, and after a brief smile of welcome she turned her attention to his companion. The contrast with Mr Barnabus was striking. Gerald looked neat—even smart— in his evening dress, but the viscount's black coat bore all the hallmarks of a London tailor. It fitted perfectly across his shoulders and followed the tapering line of the body to his waist. Satin knee-breeches stretched over muscled thighs that hinted at the athlete, while the startling white of his quilted waistcoat and impeccable linen of his shirt and neckcloth proclaimed a level of sartorial elegance not often seen in Bath.

The man himself was tall and lean, with hair as dark as midnight. The golden, flickering candlelight accentuated the strong lines of his handsome face. When she met his eyes a little tremor ran down her spine. She was used to seeing admiration in a man's look, but the viscount's gaze was coolly appraising.

'Ah, there you are, Miss Prentess,' Gerald greeted her cheerfully. 'I have brought a friend with me; I made sure you would not object to it.

Well, I say friend, but he is some sort of cousin, actually…'

'Come, Gerald, you are taking far too long about this.'

The viscount's voice was low and pleasant, with just a hint of laughter. He turned to Susannah, the cool look in his eyes replaced by a glinting smile.

'I am Markham.' He gave a little bow. 'How do you do?'

'I am very well, my lord, thank you. And of course there can be no objection to your coming here with Mr Barnabus.'

'Aye, I knew you would be pleased,' said Gerald, grinning.

Susannah barely heard Gerald's words for the viscount had reached for her hand and lifted it to his lips.

'Are you making a long stay in Bath, my lord?' She struggled to ignore the fluttering inside, like the soft beating of birds' wings against her ribcage. The pad of his thumb had rubbed gently over her knuckles before he gave up her hand and her skin still tingled with the memory.

'I am on my way to town. I merely stopped off to look in on my cousin.'

'Aye, which is why I persuaded him to take pot luck here with me tonight,' added Gerald.

'And we are delighted to have you join us.' Mrs Wilby spread her fan and looked about her while Susannah stood mute at her side, trying to make sense of her reaction to this stranger. 'What would you care to play, my lord? There is macao, or loo, or euchre…or if you care to wait a little I am sure we can set you up with a rubber of whist—'

'You are too kind, ma'am, but if you have no objection I shall walk about a little.' He bestowed such a charming smile upon Aunt Maude that Susannah was not at all surprised to see her simpering like a schoolroom miss. 'I like to gauge the opposition before I commit myself to the game.'

'You will find no deep play here, my lord,' Susannah responded. 'And no hardened gamesters.'

'No?' His brows lifted. 'Not even yourself, Miss Prentess?'

Again that flutter down her spine. She was close enough to see his eyes now. Blue-grey, and hard as slate.

She shook her head. 'I am no gamester, my lord.'

'But she *is* good,' said Gerald. 'I'd wager she could match you, Cousin.'

'Indeed? Perhaps we should put it to the test.'

His voice was silky, but she heard the note of contempt in his tone. To her dismay she felt the blush rising to her cheeks. She could do nothing to hide it, so she put up her chin and replied to Gerald with a smile.

'You are too kind, Mr Barnabus. I have no wish to pit myself against one who is no doubt a master.'

She excused herself and walked away. As she passed the table where Mrs Logan was presiding at a noisy game of *vingt-et-un,* Kate stretched out her hand to detain her.

'You seem to have netted a big fish there, Susannah,' she murmured. 'Who is he?'

'Viscount Markham, Gerald's cousin.'

'Indeed? A very big fish then.' Kate's eyes flickered over the viscount, then came back to her friend. 'He does not please you?'

'He seems inclined to sneer at our little party.' Susannah shrugged. 'Let my aunt deal with him. If we are not to his taste I hope he will not stay long.'

A shout recalled Kate's attention to the game and Susannah moved on. She sat down with a large group who were playing loo and tried to give her attention to the cards, but all the time she was aware of the viscount's tall figure wandering around the room. Then, suddenly, she could not see him and wondered if he had been persuaded to sit down at one of the other tables, or if he had taken his leave. The unease she had felt in his presence made her hope it was the latter.

* * *

As the evening wore on and the crowd in the room thinned, Susannah noticed the familiar, subtle change in the card party. The chatter and laughter died away as those who were left concentrated on their game. Two young gentlemen challenged her to take them on at ombre and she was busily engaged with them until the supper gong sounded at midnight.

'*Sacardo* again, Miss Prentess,' laughed one of the young men, throwing down his cards in mock disgust. 'You are unbeatable tonight.'

'Aye, she has won almost every trick,' declared the other, watching as Susannah swept the small pile of coins from the table into her reticule. 'I hope you will allow Warwick and me the chance to take our revenge later?'

'More to the point, Farthing, I hope Miss Prentess will allow me to escort her down to supper,' added Mr Warwick, looking hopefully across at Susannah.

'Nay, as to that, surely the honour should fall to me?' said Mr Farthing. 'I at least won *codille*, sir, so it can be said I bested you!'

Susannah threw up her hands, laughing.

'Gentlemen, pray, do not fight over such a trifle.'

'Especially when the trick is already won,' said a deep, amused voice. 'I have come to escort you down to supper, Miss Prentess.'

Susannah looked round to find Lord Markham standing behind her, his hand on the back of her chair.

'Indeed, my lord?' His self-assurance rattled her. 'I rather think these gentlemen might oppose you.'

A glance back showed Susannah that the two young men might have been prepared to fight each other for the pleasure of taking her to supper, but they were far too in awe of a viscount to raise an objection. She was disappointed when they scrambled to their feet, uttering disjointed phrases.

'L-Lord Markham! N-no, no objections at all, my lord.'

'Only too happy...'

'There, you see? No opposition at all.' The humour glinting in Lord Markham's eyes did nothing to appease Susannah, but it would not do to show her displeasure, so with a smile of acquiescence she took his hand and allowed him to lead her off. As they moved through the room she looked around her.

'Ah, my aunt is setting up another game of loo. Perhaps she would like me to help her—'

'No, it was she who suggested I should take you downstairs.' When Susannah hesitated he added, 'You can see, Miss Prentess, that everyone is perfectly content. You may take a little time now to enjoy yourself. These parties are designed to be enjoyed. After all, it is not as if you are running a gaming hell here.'

She looked at him sharply, but could read nothing from his smile. His manners were perfectly polite, but she had the distinct feeling he was on his guard, that he was assessing her. Susannah gave an inward shrug. What did it matter? He was not staying in Bath.

She accompanied him to the supper room, where a selection of cold meats, fruits and sweets was laid out on the table. Susannah chose sparingly from the selection before her, but she was surprised when her escort showed no interest in the food.

'I am sorry I cannot offer you soup or ramekins, Lord Markham. Our guests make do with a cold collation, even in winter, although there is warm wine for anyone who wishes it.'

'I require nothing, thank you.'

They found an empty table and sat down. Susannah took a little minced chicken, but found she had no appetite with the viscount sitting opposite her.

'You work very hard at your…entertainments, Miss Prentess.'

'I help my aunt as best I can, sir.'

'And how often do you hold these little parties?'

'Every Tuesday.'

'Indeed? You must be prodigious fond of cards, ma'am.'

'My aunt enjoys them, yes.'

'I stand corrected.'

She looked up at him, understanding dawning.

'Ah, I see what it is,' she said, smiling. 'You are concerned for your cousin.'

'Should I not be?'

'Mr Barnabus will come to no harm here.'

'But you have already taken two hundred guineas from him in one night.'

She stared at him. 'How do you know that? Did Mr Barnabus tell you?'

'He did not need to. Such deep play excites comment.'

'Deep play?' She laughed. 'I am sure in your London club such a sum would be considered insignificant.'

He leaned forwards.

'But we are not in my London club, Miss Prentess.'

The unease she had been feeling all evening intensified. She put down her fork.

'It was unfortunate. I have not allowed it to happen again.' She met his eyes, returning his gaze steadily. 'I am not trying to entrap your cousin.'

'No?'

'Of course not.' She hesitated. 'You may not

know it, but he made me an offer of marriage and I refused him. Does that not tell you I have no designs upon him?'

'Perhaps you are hoping to catch a bigger prize.'

Some of the tension eased and she laughed at the absurdity of his claim.

'My lord, you have seen the guests my aunt invites. Couples, mainly, like General Sanstead and his wife, intent upon an evening's sport. And as for the single gentlemen, they are either too old to be looking for a wife or they have yet to make their way in the world.'

'And such men are very susceptible to the, ah, blandishments of a pretty woman.'

Susannah's brows snapped together.

'I find the implication insulting, sir.' She pushed her plate away. 'I must go back upstairs.'

'As you wish.'

What she *wished* was to order him from the house, but she could hardly eject a viscount from her aunt's card party without good reason, and it would not do to stir up gossip. Instead she contented herself with returning to the drawing room and quitting his company with no more than a nod of her head.

A rubber of whist with Kate as her partner did much to restore her spirits and later she took her turn at playing *vingt-et-un*, drawing a crowd of gentlemen, as usual. She concentrated hard on the game. This was her aunt's party, after all, so it was not for her to keep an eye on who was leaving. However, the game was over and the players dispersing when Gerald approached her, so she could not avoid him.

'Are you leaving us, Mr Barnabus?' She put aside her cards and rose to meet him.

'Aye, my cousin has invited me to take my brandy with him tonight, if you will give me leave?'

From the corner of her eye Susannah saw Lord Markham standing a little way behind his cousin. It would have given her great pleasure to tell Gerald that she would not release him. He would stay, she was sure of it from his look and the warm note in his voice. But that might raise his hopes that she felt something stronger for him than friendship, and she would not serve him such a trick. Instead she contented herself with giving him her warmest smile as he bowed over her fingers, and a murmur—loud enough for the viscount to hear—that she hoped to see him again *very* soon.

'I saw the viscount take you off to supper.' Mrs Logan came up as Susannah watched the two men leave the room. 'Another conquest, do you think?'

'Hardly.' She chuckled. 'The viscount is more

inclined to think me a gold-digger. I have no doubt that he will warn his cousin off.'

'Pity. He would have been a rich pigeon for the plucking.'

'I wish you wouldn't use such cant terms, Kate.'

'I am a soldier's widow, love. I know a lot worse than that.'

'I am sure you do, and I am pleased you have left that life behind.'

'Aye, and with it the need for a husband.'

'Come, Kate. You are still young, and I have seen how the men flock to you—are you sure you do not wish to marry again?'

'Put myself in the power of one man, when as a widow I can flirt and enjoy myself with anyone I wish?' Kate shook her head. 'Never. Never again. You know as well as I what monsters men can be, if one allows them dominance.'

Susannah shivered.

'Let us not think of that, Kate. It is all in the past.' She gave her friend a quick hug. 'Now, let us see what we can do to hurry these few remaining guests on their way. I need to get to bed since I have to be up early in the morning.' She lowered her voice. 'Odesse sent me a note. We have another client.'

Kate's eyes widened. 'Word is spreading,' she murmured.

Susannah nodded. 'As we knew it would. I

shall drive out tomorrow to make sure she is settled in.'

'That is not necessary,' said Kate. 'Mrs Gifford—'

'Is a dear soul, but I like to talk to each of our—er—clients myself, it reassures them.' She laughed. 'Pray do not look so disapproving, Kate. This was as much your idea as mine.'

'I know, but it was never my intention that you should be so personally involved.'

Susannah's laughter deserted her.

'Why not? It is my reason for living, Kate.'

The walk back to George Street was not a long one, but the icy blast that hit them as they stepped out on to the Crescent prompted Gerald to ask Jasper if they would not be better to go back indoors and send a servant for a cab.

'By no means,' he replied. 'The fresh air will do us good. Unless you mean to imply I am too old for such a journey…'

Gerald laughed.

'I would not dare. Let us walk, by all means.' He tucked his hand into Jasper's arm as they set off at a good pace towards the Circus. 'Tell me what you thought of Susannah.'

'Miss Prentess? At first glance, a beauty.'

'She *is* beautiful, isn't she? A golden goddess! But it is not just her looks, Jasper, it is her spirit, too. She is so good, so charitable.'

'Not so charitable that she won't take your money at the card table.'

'No, no, a mere trifle. She will not countenance anyone losing more than fifty guineas at a sitting.'

'That is not what I have heard.'

'Ah.' Gerald gave a self-conscious laugh. 'You said you had called upon my mother. I suppose she told you I had lost more, and asked you to come and rescue me.'

'Not in so many words.'

Gerald swore under his breath.

'Damn the Bath tabbies that report my every move! That was a single occurrence, and entirely my own doing. Susannah did not wish to take my money, I assure you—I had to almost beg her to do so. And I had thought hard beforehand. It was money I could afford to lose.'

'That is what all gamesters will tell you.'

Gerald stopped and pulled away.

'I am no gambler, Jasper. If I was I would be sporting my blunt in some hell, rather than in Mrs Wilby's drawing room!'

The flare of a nearby street lamp showed the boy's face to be serious. Jasper put a hand on his shoulder.

'No, I had not thought it of you, until now. I take it that Miss Prentess is the attraction, rather than the cards?'

'Of course. You must have noticed how many young bucks were there tonight.'

'And old roués,' added Jasper.

'It is all the rage to be in love with her.' Gerald began to walk on, his good humour quite restored. 'She is beautiful, and an heiress.'

'Indeed?'

'Aye. She is old Middlemass's heir, don't you know.'

'What, the nabob?'

'That's right.'

'Well, that explains the house in Royal Crescent.'

'Aye, the old man bought it when he returned from India, but rarely used it. Susannah was his only relative. She was living with him at his place in Westbury when he died, and he left everything to her in trust until she is five-and-twenty.'

'Then I am no longer surprised all Bath is at her feet. Yet why should Gloriana call it a disastrous attachment?'

'Not everyone in Bath is enamoured of Miss Prentess.'

'I would have thought her fortune would make her universally admired.'

'Yes, well, Bath is not London, Jasper. Respectability is everything here, don't you know. And there are some high sticklers in Bath, including those who write to my mother. And

Miss Prentess does not go out of her way to flatter them.'

'So what do they have against the lady?'

'For one thing they do not approve of her setting herself up in Royal Crescent with her aunt—if the truth were told I suspect they are jealous that she can afford to do so. Then there is her birth. Her father was a soldier and her mother an officer's daughter. Perfectly respectable,' he added quickly. 'I ascertained as much before I—'

'Yes?' Jasper prompted him.

'I offered her my hand.'

There was no mistaking the rather belligerent note in Gerald's voice. He clearly expected Jasper to be outraged. Instead Jasper said merely, 'I am glad you had so much presence of mind. When one is…head over heels, one is inclined to forget such things.'

Gerald relaxed again and aimed a playful punch at his ribs.

'Well, I didn't! I am not such a looby.' He sighed. 'I made sure the fortune would reconcile Mama to her, and I am sure it would have done, if Susannah had accepted me.'

'Does that matter now? Since the lady has refused you…'

'I hope she will be persuaded to change her mind.' They had reached George Street and the entrance to York House. Jasper stood back for Gerald to precede him but the young man turned to him, saying earnestly, 'You have met her, Jasper. You could speak to Mama for me. Susannah—Miss Prentess—is infinitely superior to every other woman I have ever met, you must see that.'

'Ah…' Jasper gave him a rueful smile '…but I have met rather more women than you, Cousin. Now, shall we go in out of the cold?'

Gerald took his leave a couple of hours later, but instead of retiring immediately, Jasper poured himself another brandy and settled himself into the chair beside the fire. He had done his duty by his cousin and warned him against proposing marriage again without careful thought, but Gerald had merely laughed at his concerns and asked him what fault he could find with Susannah Prentess. And indeed, Jasper could not find any, but something nagged at him.

He had spent the evening in Royal Crescent, watching and listening. The card party appeared to be quite innocuous and everyone enjoyed themselves, especially the numerous gentlemen who vied with each other for the opportunity to play cards with Miss Prentess, but he would be surprised if many of them left the house richer than they entered it. Both his hostess and her niece were excellent card players. He had observed them closely during the evening—their assessment of their opponents' hands was shrewd and the play was as clever as anything he had seen in town. Then there was the widow, Mrs Logan. She appeared to be very thick with Miss Prentess, and when the two ladies sat down together at the whist table they were unbeatable.

Jasper frowned, cupping his brandy glass between his hands. He had seen no evidence of sharp practice, and he noted that Miss Prentess kept the stakes deliberately low and gently turned away any gentleman who was losing too much. She was very clever, winning small amounts, not enough to cause the loser distress, or to arouse suspicion. And as Gerald said, they were safer playing there than in some gambling hell. But there were at least a dozen gentlemen present, and fifty guineas from each....

'Hell and confound it, she is an heiress,' he muttered. 'She cannot want the money!'

Perhaps they needed the extra funds for their lifestyle. But there had been nothing too lavish about the supper provided for the guests and Miss Prentess's gown of figured muslin showed quality rather than ostentation.

He finished his brandy in one gulp and set down the glass. He had fulfilled his promise. He could write to Gloriana and tell her that Miss Prentess was no harpy, but something still rankled. Gerald had laughed off his words of caution and was obviously too infatuated with the lady to make a rational judgement, so it behooved his older and more worldly-wise cousin to do it for him.

He would remain in Bath.

Chapter Three

'My dear, are you sure you want to go to the ball tonight? You are almost asleep there.'

Susannah looked up with a start. She and her aunt were sitting in the morning room, where the welcome heat from the fire had made her quite drowsy.

'Of course, ma'am. I shall be very well, once I have had dinner.' Susannah brushed aside her aunt's concerns with a smile.

'But you have been sitting there this past half-hour without saying a word.'

'Then I beg your pardon, I am a little tired after my travelling today.'

'You were gone for so long I was beginning to worry.'

'There was no need, Aunt. You know I had Dorcas with me.'

'But I *do* worry, my love. I can never be easy
when you are…visiting. One never knows what
you might pick up.'

Susannah smiled. 'My dear aunt, I assure you
there is no danger of contamination.'

'Not of the *body*, perhaps, but—'

'Please, Aunt, you know we have discussed
this often and often. There is no danger at all
in what I do, so let us not pursue it.' She looked
across as the door opened. 'Ah, here is Gatley
to tell us dinner is ready. Shall we go down?'

Susannah did her best to entertain her aunt at
dinner and to hide all signs of fatigue, but she
had to admit to herself that she *was* tired. It had
been three o'clock before the last of the guests
had left and she could fall into bed that morning.
She should not complain, for it proved how successful their little card parties had become. But
she had been up and out of the house before ten
o'clock, not returning to the Crescent until late
in the afternoon. Her aunt would argue that there
was no need for her to go out, that she could en-
trust such errands to a servant, but Susannah's
independent spirit baulked at that. She had set
herself a task and she would see it through. And
that included going to the ball tonight.

The Upper Rooms were already crowded
when Susannah and her aunt arrived. Their

chairmen weaved through the press of carriages and deposited them under the entrance portico, where the music from the ballroom could be faintly heard. It was ten o'clock, the hour when the fashionable would leave their private parties and proceed to the ball, so the entrance was buzzing with activity. There were many acquaintances to be greeted once the ladies had removed their cloaks and straightened their shawls.

Susannah waved to Mrs Logan, who had just arrived, then turned back to greet a turbaned matron who sailed up to her with two marriageable daughters in her wake.

'Oh, Miss Prentess—another new gown? You are always so beautifully turned out.' The matron sighed ecstatically as she regarded Susannah's flowered muslin. 'So fine, my dear. And the lace edging, quite, quite exquisite. Is it Brussels?'

Susannah smiled and shook her head. 'No, ma'am, it is made locally, and it is exclusive to Odesse, the new modiste in Henrietta Street.'

'Indeed? I thought you had ordered it from London, so fine as it is.'

'Thank you, Mrs Bulstrode. I find Odesse excellent. And she has excelled herself; I did not expect to have this gown for another week at least.'

The matron's eyes brightened. 'And in Henrietta Street, you say?'

'Yes, her prices are very reasonable.' Susanna dropped her voice a little. 'Especially when one considers what one has to pay for gowns in Milsom Street. Not that one objects to the price, of course, but Odesse does seem to have a certain style...'

'Indeed she does, Miss Prentess. That gown is quite superb. Well, well, I shall look her up.' With a smile Mrs Bulstrode gathered her daughters and went off, leaving Susannah to smile after her.

'Excellent,' murmured Kate, coming up. 'That could not have been better timed. Amelia Bulstrode is such a gabble-monger that our new modiste's name will be on every woman's lips by the end of the evening.'

'And her gowns will be on a good many ladies' backs by the end of the month,' added Susannah. 'I have achieved what I wanted to do without even entering the ballroom.' She noted the startled look in Mrs Wilby's eye and shook her head, laughing. 'You need not fear, Aunt, I do not intend to go home yet. I hope to drum up even more business for the new modiste before the evening is out.'

'Don't!' hissed Mrs Wilby in an urgent whisper. 'Pray, Susannah, do *not* mention the word business. It is not at all becoming.'

'Quite right,' agreed Kate, her lips twitching. 'Susannah is a lady and should know nothing about such matters. She is here merely to look beautiful and to stir up such envy that the other ladies will all want to know where she buys her gowns.'

'Kate!'

Susannah's protest evoked nothing more than a shake of the head from her friend.

'It is true, Susannah, and you know it. And I like the new way you have put up your hair,' she added. 'Quite in the classical style. What is it Mr Barnabus christened you? The golden goddess. Well tonight you could as well be called a Greek goddess.'

'Thank you, but enough of your nonsense,' said Susannah, trying to ignore the heat that burned her cheeks. 'Let us go in, shall we?'

They moved on to the ballroom. Heads turned as Susannah entered, but she was used to that. As Bath's richest heiress it was only to be expected that she would be pointed out wherever she went, and tonight it suited her purpose to be noticed.

The dancing was already in progress and the floor was a mass of bodies, swirling and skipping in time to the music. There were a good number of acquaintances present, including many of the gentlemen who had attended the card party the previous evening. As soon as she entered she was surrounded by hopeful suitors, all begging for the honour of a dance. Laughing, Kate carried Mrs Wilby off to the benches at the side of the room, leaving Susannah with her admirers.

The country dances were lively and in such a crowd it was necessary to concentrate to avoid jostling the other dancers. Nevertheless, Susannah enjoyed herself, and was happy to join a second and even a third set as the gentlemen lined up to partner her. She was hot and not a little dizzy by the time Mr Edmonds swung her through the final steps of a particularly lively country dance. He invited her to stand up again even as the last notes were fading.

'You are very kind, sir, but I am going to sit down now,' she said, half-gasping, half-laughing as she rose from her curtsy. 'I really do not think I could dance another reel for quite a while, but thank you—oh!'

As she turned to leave the dance floor she found her way blocked by a wall of black. A second glance showed her it was not a wall, but a gentleman's evening coat, and when she allowed her eyes to travel up from the broad chest they were dazzled by the snowy white linen of an intricately tied neckcloth.

'I am very pleased to hear it, Miss Prentess, for I have brought you a glass of wine.'

She stepped back and lifted her gaze even further, to the smiling face of Lord Markham.

Jasper noted with satisfaction Susannah's start of surprise. There was no denying she looked quite beautiful with her golden hair piled up on her head and a soft flush of exertion mantling her cheeks. And she used her looks to good effect, for most of the men he had seen at the Crescent last night were in the ballroom. He had watched the young pups—and some of the older ones—flock around her as she entered and he had no doubt that they had engaged her for every dance, which was why he had decided upon more subtle tactics.

'Oh,' she said again, the blush on her cheek deepening. He held out a wineglass and she took it. As she sipped gratefully at her wine he cast a swift, appraising glance over her.

'Madras muslin,' he said, displaying his knowledge of ladies' fashion. 'Is that in deference to your late uncle, the nabob?'

Immediately she was on the defensive.

'No, but I am not ashamed of the source of my fortune, Lord Markham.'

'I am glad to hear it.'

They stood in silence, watching the dancers, but Susannah was very much aware of the man beside her. His evening clothes were simple, a plain coat of black superfine with black knee-breeches of Florentine silk, but they were superbly cut and he wore them with an air of assurance. He was a man used to commanding attention, and she could not deny that he had hers. They were standing side by side, inches apart, and the skin on her arm tingled at his proximity. Her whole body was aware of him, of the power in that long, lean frame. No man had ever affected her like this before. Swallowing nervously, she sought for something to say.

'I thought you had left Bath, my lord.'

'Not yet. My cousin appears very happy with the attractions here and I decided to stay and— er—sample them for myself.'

A wary look appeared in her hazel eyes.

'For one used to the delights of London, I fear you will find it sadly flat.'

'Are you trying to discourage me, Miss Prentess?'

'Not at all. But I believe our entertainment is nothing to London.'

'And how long have you lived here?'

'We moved into Bath about a year ago.'

'Then you shall advise me on the entertainments available.'

'I am sure your cousin can do that, sir.'

'But I would value a different perspective.'

'I would be only too happy to help you, sir, if I had the time, but I regret I am too busy at present.'

'Busy? With what?'

She ignored his question.

'But here is someone who may be able to help you.' She looked past him. 'You know Mrs Logan, I think?'

'We met last night.' Jasper bowed. 'Madam.'

'Ah, yes, Viscount Markham.' The widow held out her hand to him. 'We played at euchre together. How could I forget?'

'The viscount is planning to remain in Bath for a while, Kate.'

Jasper's keen eye did not miss the look of appeal Susannah gave her friend.

'Indeed? How delightful.'

'Yes, and he is anxious to know what entertainments the city offers. Perhaps, Kate, you can assist the viscount? You must excuse me, but I see my next dance partner is looking for me...'

With a gracious smile she hastened away. Jasper watched her go, his eyes narrowing. Outmanoeuvred, by gad, and by a slip of a girl. He told himself he was amused by her antics, but to one more accustomed to being toadied to and courted wherever he went, Jasper could not deny a small element of annoyance.

'Well, my lord?' Mrs Logan's voice cut through his thoughts and he turned back to her, his urbane smile firmly in place.

'Yes, madam, pray tell me the delights I might expect to find in Bath...'

* * *

Susannah hurried away to join her partner for the next dance set. She found her encounters with the viscount strangely unsettling. He was undoubtedly handsome and charming, but her impression upon meeting him for the first time was that he was suspicious of her. He had as good as accused her of having designs upon his cousin, but she hoped she had reassured him on that point. He did not like her, she was sure of that. There was no warmth in his eyes when he looked at her. Why, then, was he singling her out?

'Wrong way, Miss Prentess!'

Her partner's urgent whisper brought Susannah back to the dance and she tried to concentrate upon her steps, but even as she twirled and passed and skipped she was aware that the viscount was watching her from the side of the room. Perhaps he was looking out for a rich wife. Another pass, another skip and she gave her hands to her partner to swing her around. She also gave the young gentleman her warmest smile. If Lord Markham thought he only had to parade his title before her and she would fall at his feet, then he was very much in error.

Susannah danced and laughed until her feet and her cheeks ached. Her partners had never known her so vivacious, nor so encouraging.

She never once looked for the viscount, but when the ball ended she was disappointed to learn from Mrs Logan that he had left soon after speaking to her.

'He was less interested in knowing about Bath than learning about you,' Kate told her as they waited for their cloaks.

'Oh?' Susannah tried not to be intrigued and failed miserably. 'What did he say?'

'He asked about your parents.' Kate's cynical smile dawned. 'If he is looking for a rich bride he could do worse.'

'No, he could not.' Susannah shivered. 'He is wasting his time with me. I do not want a husband, and certainly not one who looks down his aristocratic nose at me.'

'But you must admit he is devilishly handsome,' murmured Kate.

Susannah thought of those hard eyes boring into her. Something inside fluttered again when she thought of Viscount Markham, but she would not admit it to be attraction.

'Devilish, yes, I'll agree to that.'

'Well, for my part I like him,' declared Mrs Wilby, coming up. She cast an anxious look at her niece. 'That is, he has never been anything but charming to me.'

'Hah!' Susannah found two pairs of eyes upon her. Her aunt's held merely a question at her vehement exclamation, but Kate Logan's glance was brimful of merriment and a knowing look that brought an angry flush to Susannah's cheek. She said haughtily, 'Charm is the viscount's second nature, but it will not work with me!'

Thus, when she spied Lord Markham approaching in Milsom Street the following morning she determined to give him no more than a distant nod. She said as much to her companion, Mrs Logan, who gave a tiny shake of her head.

'I fear you will catch cold at that, Susannah. You see he has Mr Barnabus with him, and *he* will hardly be fobbed off with so slight a greeting.'

She was right. Gerald hailed them cheerfully and immediately enquired their direction. Kate responded even while Susannah was trying to frame an answer that would send the gentlemen in the opposite direction.

'We are going to the Pump Room to meet up with Mrs Wilby.'

'Then we will accompany you, will we not, Jasper?'

'Oh, but we do not want to take you out of your way.'

Susannah's protest was overruled.

'It is no trouble,' replied Gerald. 'I dragged my cousin from his bed for an early walk before breakfast, and we may as well go to the Pump Room as anywhere. Come, now, let us be moving!'

* * *

She was not sure how it happened, but moments later Susannah found the viscount beside her. He had said very little, but such was his address that somehow he had inveigled Gerald into escorting Kate and Susannah was left with no option but to accept his arm. She placed her fingers carefully on his sleeve, as if afraid the contact might burn.

'I remember you telling me how busy you are, Miss Prentess.'

'I am.'

Nerves made her respond more curtly than she intended.

'And is this the nature of your busyness, to be shopping all day?'

Her sense of the ridiculous put flight to her tension and a laugh escaped her.

'Not *all* day, my lord.' She held up her free hand, displaying the tight-fitting covering of fine kid leather. 'Besides, a lady always needs new gloves.'

'Undoubtedly. How did you enjoy the ball last night?'

'Very much. I suspect the company was a little provincial for you, sir, since you did not dance.'

'You noticed.'

The laughter in his voice brought a tell-tale flush to her cheeks, but she recovered quickly.

'No, my aunt told me as much. I take no interest in you at all.'

Too late she realised she should not have added those final words. She waited for him to tease her and could only be grateful that he changed the subject.

'Mrs Logan tells me you spent your early years following the drum.'

'Yes, my father was a captain in an infantry regiment.'

'You lived in Gibraltar, I believe.'

'Yes. That is where I met Mrs Logan.'

'And did she accompany you home to England?'

'No. I returned here when my father died nine years ago. Mama brought us back to live with her sister. Mrs Logan and I met again when I came to Bath last year. I was fortunate to find her here. She has been a good friend to me.' She added, in response to the question in his eyes, 'She is a soldier's widow, I am a soldier's daughter. We have similar interests.'

'And why did you come to Bath, Miss Prentess?'

'Why not?' she countered.

'It seems an odd choice for a young lady of means.'

'My Uncle Middlemass left me the house in the Crescent. It is not within my power to sell it.'

'But it is such a choice property, you could let it out and go where you will. Why not London?'

There was a heartbeat's hesitation before she replied.

'Bath suits me very well. And my aunt, too. She likes to take the waters. Ah, we are here.'

Susannah was never more glad to reach her destination. She was finding it far too easy to talk to the viscount, but it did not suit her to share her history with him. She released his arm as they entered the Pump Room and led the way towards Mrs Wilby. Her aunt was part of a lively group standing in the curved recess at one end of the room but as Susannah approached the crowd dispersed, leaving Aunt Maude alone to receive them.

'There you are, Aunt. I hope we have not kept you waiting.'

'In no wise.' Mrs Wilby's smile encompassed them all 'I have had a delightful time with my friends.'

'And drinking the waters, ma'am?' suggested the viscount.

Mrs Wilby made a face.

'Ugh, nasty stuff. I never touch it. Tea is my favoured drink here, my lord.'

'Indeed?' Lord Markham raised his brows as his glance flickered over Susannah. 'I thought—'

'Oh heavens, is that the time?' Susannah interrupted him hurriedly, looking at the long-case clock by the wall. 'I hope I do not rush you, Aunt, but Kate and I have an appointment in Henrietta Street later, so we should be on our way back to the Crescent to take breakfast. It is quite a long walk.'

'We will accompany you!' declared Gerald promptly.

'No, no, I will not hear of it,' replied Susannah firmly. 'There can be no need of a gentleman's escort when there are three of us and besides,' she added with an arch look, 'how are we to discuss our little secrets if you come with us?' She held out her hand. 'We will say good-bye here, if you please.'

'But I have barely had time to exchange a word with you,' objected Gerald.

'Nor have you,' agreed Mrs Wilby, her kind heart touched by the young man's despondent look. 'Perhaps you would like to join us for tea tomorrow afternoon? It is nothing special, of course. We stand on no ceremony, just a few close friends who drop by for a comfortable coze, but you are very welcome to come. And Lord Markham, too, if he would like.'

'Lord Markham would like, very much,' said Jasper, amused by Susannah's obvious disapproval. Those hazel eyes of hers darkened to brown and he read objection in every line of her body, although of course she could not contradict her aunt. He took her hand. '*Adieu*, Miss Prentess. I shall look forward to taking tea with you tomorrow.'

'Not if you are going to cut me out,' declared Gerald, half-laughing, half-serious.

'He will not do that, you may be sure, Ger... Mr Barnabus.' Susannah's soft words and warm look killed Jasper's amusement in an instant. He was still holding her hand and his fingers tightened angrily. She looked up at him, her eyes wide and innocent. 'My lord?'

Jasper caught his breath. That remark was not for Gerald's benefit but for *his*. So the minx wanted to cross swords, did she? A touch of uncertainty entered her gaze. Jasper bowed over her hand in his most courtly style. As his lips brushed her fingers they trembled in his grasp. The lady was not as confident as she would have him believe.

Jasper waited for the spurt of triumph to accompany the thought. It did not come. Instead he was aware of a sudden tenderness, a desire to press that little hand against his heart and assure her of his protection. Shaken, he straightened and released her.

'That worked out very well,' commented Gerald, as they watched the ladies walk away. 'This must be down to you, Jasper. Mrs Wilby has never invited me to take tea before.'

'Then I hope you are satisfied.'

'Very. Only, it makes it pretty clear that Mrs Wilby would prefer you as a match for Susannah.'

'Would that matter to you?' Jasper asked him. 'Have you set your heart on marrying her?'

'Oh, well, you know, she has already told me that she can never think of me as anything other than a friend, but I hope that when she comes to know me better—but she is so good, she is not one to raise false hopes in a fellow.'

'You know, Gerald, I wonder if Miss Prentess is quite the paragon you make her out to be.'

His cousin laughed at that.

'Oh but she is, Jasper. Good, kind—a veritable angel. She is quite, quite perfect.'

Jasper shook his head.

'My poor deluded boy, when you know as much about women as I do you will know there is no such thing!'

'My mother is convinced of that, certainly. Which reminds me, I had a note from her, asking me to visit. It is still early, I could go today, riding cross country would be a pleasure.' He put his hand on Jasper's shoulder. 'And you can come with me. You will be able to support me when I tell her about Susannah.'

'Why not, if we can hire a hack for me?' Jasper swallowed his misgivings. 'When I left Rooks Tower I sent my horses on to Markham, not expecting to need them in Bath. However—

and forgive me if this pains you, Gerald—your mother is not famed for her hospitality, so let us have breakfast first!'

After they had eaten, Jasper and Gerald rode over to Hotwells. Gloriana received them joyfully enough, but when Gerald happily disclosed that he was to take tea in Royal Crescent the following day, the look she threw at Jasper left him in no doubt that she was seriously disappointed in him. She despatched Gerald on an errand to fetch a further supply of tonic from her doctor and as soon as he was out of the door she turned on Jasper.

'I thought you were going to Bath to save my poor son from this woman?'

'I was going to look into the matter,' he corrected her. 'Having done so, I have given up all plans of returning to Markham for the time being.'

'Aha. Then you admit my son is ensnared.'

'Miss Prentess is an heiress, Gloriana. Does that not please you?'

'If that is the case why did she take his money from him? Besides, she is a nobody, and she is too old for him.' Gloriana was determined not to be appeased. 'She is three-and-twenty if she is a day. And her birth—who knows anything about the girl, save that she is heir to the Middlemass fortune?'

He smiled slightly.

'That would be enough for most mothers.'

Gloriana looked at him and for a moment her guard dropped.

'I only want his happiness, Markham. If you could assure me of that I could be reconciled.'

'I wish that were possible, but I cannot believe it.' He frowned. 'You know he has offered her marriage, and she refused him?'

'He wrote to tell me. I hoped that would be the end of it, but today he seems as beguiled as ever.'

'I know, ma'am. I have failed to find anything against the lady. However, my enquiries about her friend Mrs Logan have proved far more interesting. She is the widow of a soldier and the story goes that he quit the army to open a gambling house in Portsmouth. When Logan died, his widow sold up and came to Bath, where she now lives in respectable retirement. I am not in the habit of listening to the gossip-mongers, but having watched the lady at work at one of Mrs Wilby's little parties I know that she is very good with the cards. Good enough to be a professional.' He strode to the window and stood for a moment, looking out. 'Add that to the skill shown by both Miss Prentess and her aunt and I cannot help thinking that there is more to their little card parties than mere social entertainment. I would wager that at the end of the evening the three ladies come away from the tables considerably richer than they started.'

'A gaming hell. Oh my heavens.' Gloriana resorted to her handkerchief. 'To think my poor boy should be caught in the tangles of such women.'

Jasper shook his head.

'By London standards the stakes are trivial, and the play is certainly not deep enough to cause concern. There is no faro bank, something which attracted a great deal of criticism when employed by several high-born ladies in London twenty years ago. But the suspicion persists that they run their little parties at the Crescent for profit. Not that there is anything wrong with that, if they would but own it.'

'In Royal Crescent? It would never be permitted!'

'No, ma'am, I suppose you are right.'

'And you have spoken to Gerald about this? You have told him the sort of woman he has given his heart to?'

'I have tried, but he is deaf to any criticism of Miss Prentess.' He turned away from the window, his jaw set. 'My cousin is seriously besotted with the woman. I think he would have to witness the lady's fall from grace for himself before he would see her for what she really is.'

'Then that is what must happen.'

There was such an air of grim determination

behind the words that the corners of Jasper's mouth lifted a trifle.

'I'm afraid wishing won't make it happen, ma'am.'

'No, but *you* could,' came the confident reply. 'You have a reputation with the ladies, Markham, your flirtations are forever gracing the society pages. *You* must seduce Susannah Prentess!'

Chapter Four

Whatever startled response Jasper would have made was silenced by Gerald's coming back into the room at that moment. Nor was there opportunity to discuss the matter again, for very soon afterwards the gentlemen took their leave. Gloriana squeezed Jasper's fingers as he bowed over her hand, and the speaking look in her eyes told him that she relied upon him to comply with her outrageous suggestion.

But was it so outrageous? Jasper pondered the matter as he rode back to Bath beside Gerald, the setting sun casting long shadows before them and the chill wind cutting through their coats. If he succeeded in turning the lady's head then it would destroy his young cousin's infatuation at a stroke. Many men would not hesitate, but for all his reputation Jasper had never yet set out to make any woman fall in love with him. He might have done so with Zelah, if it had not become plain to him that she was head over heels in love with his brother. She was the only woman he had ever loved, the only woman he had ever considered taking as his wife, so there was no danger that he would succumb to Miss Prentess's charms. He could flirt with her, court her, even seduce her without risk to himself.

He shifted in the saddle. What of the risk to the lady? If he went that far it would ruin her reputation and she would lose her good name. He hardened his heart. She had every young man in Bath at her feet and from what he had seen at her aunt's card party she was fleecing them quite ruthlessly. The amounts might be small, but over the weeks they would mount up to a considerable sum. Enough to live quite comfortably. Dammit, the woman was running a gaming hell, she deserved no good name!

'Eh, what's that?' Gerald looked round. 'Did you say something?'

Jasper glanced at the young man riding beside him.

'Aye. I was wondering about those little card parties of Mrs Wilby's. Do you think they profit from them?'

Gerald shrugged.

'A hundred or two, perhaps. I doubt it is ever more than a monkey.'

'I should hope not.' He paused. 'Does it not concern you that they are making money out of these parties?'

Gerald looked at him.

'No, why? The sums are negligible.' He laughed. 'Mother told me that when she was young the London hostesses made thousands in an evening, especially those who ran a faro bank. *And* they charged their guests card money, to cover the cost of the new packs. Mrs Wilby does nothing like that. Her parties are for friends to gather together and enjoy themselves.'

'And lose money.'

'Not everyone loses.'

'But enough to make it a worthwhile evening for the hostess.'

'And why not?' countered Gerald. 'We might all go elsewhere and lose a great deal more.' He shook his head. 'Let be, Jasper. Those of us who go there choose to do so, and if we lose a few guineas, well, what does it matter? I would lose twice as much to Miss Prentess and think it money well spent.'

Jasper said no more and the subject was not mentioned again during their ride back to Bath. It irked him that Susannah Prentess, with her charming smile and beautiful face, had quite beguiled his cousin, and if he had to make her fall in love with him to free Gerald from her clutches he would do it. He would even risk ruining her good name, if that was the only option, though his innate sense of honour balked at such a course. But it would be a cruel trick to play upon his young cousin. If it was at all possible he would find another way to prove to Gerald that the lady was not the angel he thought her to be.

As soon as they had left the Pump Room, Mrs Wilby made clear her disapproval at being dragged away so precipitately.

'What will everyone think of you, Susannah? To dash away so suddenly, with Mr Barnabus and the viscount only just arrived.'

'They will think nothing of it, Aunt. And besides, I am quite out of sympathy with you for inviting them to join us tomorrow.'

'But why? What possible objection can there be?'

'None, to Mr Barnabus, but the viscount...' She bit her lip, wondering how to explain her reluctance to see more of Lord Markham. 'I think he suspects something.'

Mrs Wilby stopped.

'Oh heavens, never say so! Oh, Susannah—'

'No, no, he can have no inkling of the truth, and Gerald would never tell him, I am sure.' She took Aunt Maude's arm and gently urged her on. 'It is just the comments he made to me, as if he thinks we run some sort of gambling den.'

'All the more reason, then, for him to take tea with us and see that it is not the case,' declared Mrs Wilby. 'A gambling den! How perfectly ridiculous.'

Her aunt's outraged dignity made Susannah chuckle.

'But if he *is* suspicious of you,' continued Mrs Wilby, 'perhaps it would be best if you curtailed your visits to...'

'My dear aunt, I will do nothing of the sort. In fact, I am going there tomorrow morning. Really, I did not realise, when I started this, this *project*, that there would be so much to do, or that it would cost so much.'

'If people knew of it, Susannah, they would be quite scandalised.'

'I am an heiress, Aunt,' she said drily. 'They would merely think me eccentric. If only I had control of my fortune now there would be no problem over money, but my uncle has bound it all up so tight I cannot even borrow upon the expectation, unless I go to a money-lender.'

'Oh heavens, child, pray do not even think of it!'

'I don't. But we will need to find extra money soon.' She sighed. 'My dependence is upon you and Kate to win a little more at our next card party.'

'Which will make Lord Markham even more suspicious,' said Mrs Wilby bitterly. 'I have a mind not to take tea with anyone tomorrow. I shall write and tell them all I have been laid low with a fever.'

'No, no, dear Aunt, let them all come. 'Pon reflection, I think you are quite right. Nothing could be more respectable than the guests you have invited. Lord Markham is most likely to be bored to death and will beat a speedy retreat!'

It was a cold, clear afternoon, but a biting wind made Susannah glad she had ordered her carriage to take her and Kate to Henrietta Street. They drew up on the gentle curve of the street outside one of the elegant three-storey houses, where only the array of fabrics displayed in the window gave an indication that this was not a private residence. A young woman in a plain dark gown opened the door to them.

'Good day to you, Mabel. Is Odesse upstairs?'

'Good day, Miss Prentess, Mrs Logan. Yes, Madame Odesse is in the showroom with Mrs Anstruther.'

'And how is little James?' murmured Susannah as she followed the girl up the stairs.

'Oh, he is doing very well, miss, putting on weight just as he should, and sleeping through the night now.' Mabel cast her a quick, shy smile. 'It is so good to have him close, where I can keep an eye on him.'

They had reached the landing and Mabel showed them into the large reception room, where a dark-haired woman wearing a plain but exquisitely sewn round gown was talking with a formidable matron in a Pomona-green redingote and matching turban, assuring *madame* in a lilting foreign accent that her new gown would be completed *tout de suite*.

She looked up as her new visitors came in, but Susannah waved her hand.

'No, no, *madame*, please continue serving Mrs Anstruther. We are happy to browse amongst these new fabrics.' Her smile included the matron, who quickly looked away.

'Thank you, I have finished here.' Mrs Anstruther hastily pulled on her gloves and headed for the door. 'If you will have the new gown delivered to me this afternoon, *madame*…'

She hurried out and Madame Odesse shut the door carefully behind her.

'Miss Prentess, Mrs Logan, how good of you to call. Will you not be seated?'

Susannah noted with a smile that all trace of the vague European accent had disappeared from the modiste's tone.

'This continuing cold weather has made it necessary for me to order a new redingote, and I have persuaded Mrs Logan it is time she bought a new gown. We have brought with us a length of silk especially for the purpose.' Susannah smiled. 'I trust everything goes well here?'

'Very well, thank you, we have made some changes.' Odesse paused. 'Would you like to come and see?'

'We would indeed!'

She took them back down the stairs and through a door on the ground floor. The room was alive with quiet chatter, which stopped as they went in. Four young women were present, sitting near the large window. Each one was engaged in sewing the swathe of material spread over her knees, while a nearby table was covered in a confusion of brightly coloured material and threads. Madame Odesse waved an expressive hand

'This is now our sewing room.'

Susannah smiled at the young ladies but hastily begged them not to get up or stop their work. She was acquainted with them all and knew that each one had a baby to look after. The absence of cribs and crying was noticeable.

'Where are the children?' she asked.

'We take it in turns now to stay in the nursery with the babes,' offered one of the girls in a shy voice. She added, indicating the cloud of pale-blue woollen fabric on her lap, 'I am sewing the final seam of your walking dress now, Miss Prentess.'

'My girls find they prefer to work away from

the babies,' added the modiste. 'We have six seamstresses living here now, and Mabel, of course, who is proving herself a valuable assistant to me. Two of my girls stay in the nursery while the others get on with the sewing.'

'And the lace-makers?' asked Kate. 'How do they go on?'

'Very well.' Madame Odesse's dark eyes twinkled. 'The fashion for extensive trimming on gowns could not have come at a better time. Demand is growing for our exclusive lace, and I hope they will be able to train up a few more girls soon.'

'And have you room for more seamstresses?'

'Certainly,' agreed Odesse. 'If we keep getting new customers then I shall have work for them, too.'

She led them down another flight of stairs to the nursery, where two young women were looking after the babies in a large, comfortably warm room. Susannah and Kate spent some time in the nursery before making their way back upstairs, Susannah declaring herself very satisfied with the arrangements.

'It appears to be working out very well,' she remarked, when they were once again in the reception room. 'The children are content and their mothers seem happy.'

The modiste took her hands and pressed them, saying earnestly, 'We all appreciate your giving us this chance to keep our babies *and* earn a living, Miss Prentess.'

'I am glad to do it, and the gowns you have made for me are very much admired, Olive—I mean Odesse,' Susannah corrected herself hastily. 'I beg your pardon!'

The seamstress laughed and shook her head. 'I would not have you beg my pardon for anything. When I consider what might have happened, to all of us....' There was a moment's uneasy silence before she shook off her reflective mood and said brightly, 'The new apricot silk you ordered arrived this morning, and I know just the design I would like to make for you...'

An hour later the ladies were on their way back to Royal Crescent, a number of packages on the seat beside them and the prospect of more new gowns to follow.

'I must say, I never thought charity would be so pleasurable,' declared Kate, smiling. 'Your idea of setting the girls up in their own establishment was a very good one, Susannah.'

'I merely made use of Olive's talent for sewing. She has such a shrewd eye for design, too.'

'But it is unlikely she would have succeeded alone, and with a young baby to support.' Kate reached out and squeezed her arm. 'You should be very proud of yourself, my dear.'

'I am very proud of my ladies,' replied Susannah. 'I have merely provided the means. It is their hard work that is making it such a success.'

'If only the starched matrons of Bath knew that their gowns were being made by unmarried mothers they might not be so keen to patronise Odesse.'

'I do not think they care who makes their clothes as long as they are fashionable and a good price,' retorted Susannah. 'Florence House, however, is a different matter. News of that establishment will scandalise the sober matrons, so I hope we can keep it a secret, at least until I have control of my fortune and can support it without the aid of Aunt Maude's card parties.'

Winter would not release its grip and when Jasper rose at his usual early hour the following morning, there was a hint of frost glistening on the Bath rooftops. He decided to take a long walk before breakfast. Enquiries of the waiter in the near-empty coffee room elicited the information that the view from Beechen Cliff was well worth the effort, so he set out, heading south through streets where only the tradespeople were yet in evidence. Striding out, he soon came to the quay and the bridge that took him across the river, and he could begin the climb to Beechen Cliff.

When he reached the heights he considered himself well rewarded. Looking north, Bath was spread out in all its glory below him. Smoke was beginning to rise from the chimneys of the honey-coloured terraces but it was not yet sufficient to cloud his view and his gaze moved past the Abbey until it reached the sweeping curve of the Royal Crescent. Immediately his thoughts turned to Miss Prentess and Gerald. If it wasn't for those damned card parties he would be inclined to tell Gloriana to give Gerald her blessing and let nature take its course. After all, the lady had refused him once. He would wager that if he was left alone, Gerald would recover from his infatuation and settle down with a suitable young bride in a year or so.

But it was Susannah Prentess who set the alarm bells ringing in his head. Why did a rich young woman need to engage in card parties to raise money? If she was looking for a brilliant match then why was she not in London? With her good looks and her fortune there were plenty of eligible bachelors who would be eager to win her hand. Clearly there was something more to the lady than met the eye, and he was determined to discover it.

The icy wind cut his cheeks, reminding him of his exposed position and a sudden hunger made him eager for his breakfast. Jasper set off on the return journey at a good pace. The streets were busier now with a constant stream of carts and wagons making their way across the bridge. He heard the jingle of harness behind him and looked round. The equipage was quite the smartest to pass him that morning and clearly a private carriage, although there was no liveried footman standing on the back. The sun's reflection from the river shone through the carriage window and illuminated the interior so that Jasper could see its occupant quite clearly. There could be no mistaking Susannah Prentess's perfect profile, nor the guinea-gold curls peeping out beneath her silk bonnet. Jasper raised his hat but even as he did so he knew she had not seen him. The lady appeared to be deep in thought. However, Jasper had to own that to see her out and about so early in the day, when most of her kind would be still at their dressing table, did her no disservice in his eyes. His spirits, lifted by the exercise, rose a little higher, and he found himself looking forward to the forthcoming visit to Royal Crescent.

'Ah, my lord, Mr Barnabus, I am so pleased you could join us.'

Mrs Wilby came forwards as the butler ushered them into the drawing room. There were already a dozen or so people present, grouped around little tables, the same ones that had been used for cards, but they now held noth-

ing more exciting than teacups. Gerald immediately headed for Susannah, who was sitting
near the fireplace, dispensing tea. Jasper would
have followed, but Mrs Wilby, conscious of her
duties as a hostess, gently drew him aside, intent upon introductions. The stares and whis-
pers that had greeted his entrance made it clear
that the appearance of a viscount was an occurrence of rare importance. It was therefore some
time before he was free to approach Susannah.

Gerald was beside her, and hailed him cheerfully.

'Come and join us, Markham. I was just telling Miss Prentess how we rode over to Bristol
yesterday.'

'I suspect you wish you were out riding now,
my lord.' There was laughter in her eyes as she
regarded him, as well as a hint of an apology.
'Some of my aunt's friends appeared to be fawn-
ing over you quite disgracefully. And Mr Barnabus assures me that is *not* something you enjoy.'

'Aye, I've told Miss Prentess that even if you
are a viscount you are not at all high in the instep,' added Gerald, grinning.

'Very good of you,' retorted Jasper.

'Bath is now the home of a great many retired people,' said Susannah, keeping her voice
low. 'Perfectly genteel, but not the highest ranks
of society. I'm afraid some of those present are

rather overwhelmed to have a viscount in their midst.'

'Not overwhelmed enough to be tongue-tied, unfortunately,' murmured Jasper. 'The lady in green was particularly garrulous.'

'Amelia Bulstrode.' She gave a gurgle of laughter. 'And her friend, Mrs Farthing. When my aunt told them you were expected they were exceedingly put out. They have sent their girls to dancing class today, you see. But it is no matter. Now they can claim acquaintance they will make their daughters known to you at the first opportunity. But you need not be alarmed,' she added kindly. 'They are very well-mannered girls, albeit inclined to giggle.'

'Nothing wrong with that,' remarked Gerald nobly. 'They are very pleasant, cheerful young ladies.'

'And one of their pleasant, cheerful mothers is approaching,' muttered Jasper. 'I shall retreat to that corner, where I see my old friend General Sanstead and his wife. I must pay my respects, you know.'

Susannah's eyes were brim full of mirth and she mouthed the word 'coward' at him before turning to greet Mrs Bulstrode. Jasper made good his escape, but behind him he heard the matron's carrying voice.

'If there is more tea, Miss Prentess, I would be happy to refill my cup. So refreshing, is it

not? I do not believe those who say it does you
no good. Why, they have only to look at you. A
picture of health, if I may say so.'

'Thank you, Mrs Bulstrode. This is a particularly pleasant blend…'

He smiled to himself, appreciating the way
she dealt with the overpowering matron. Enjoying, too, that warm, laughing note in her voice.

'And you are a wonderful advocate for the
benefits of tea drinking,' continued Mrs Bulstrode. 'You have so much *energy*, always out
and about, like this morning, for example. I saw
your carriage at the Borough Walls—'

Jasper halted, under the pretence of remov-
ing a speck of dirt from his coat. Perhaps now
he might find out what she was doing so early
in the day.

'No, no, ma'am, you are mistaken. I have not
been abroad today.'

He turned. Susannah was smiling serenely as
she poured more tea for the matron.

'No? But I made sure it was your carriage…'

'Very likely,' returned Susannah, handing
her the cup. 'I believe my aunt sent Edwards
to collect some purchases for her. Is that not
right, Aunt?'

'What's that, dear? Oh, oh, yes—yes, that's
it.'

Mrs Wilby's flustered response was in itself
suspicious, yet if he had not seen Susannah in

the carriage with his own eyes Jasper would be as ready as Mrs Bulstrode to believe her story.

Schooling himself, he continued towards General Sanstead. It was clearly not the time to question Miss Prentess, but he would get to the bottom of this. Later.

The General, an old friend, was delighted to see Jasper and kept him talking for some time, asking after the family. The viscount responded suitably and once he had fetched more tea for Mrs Sanstead, he sat down and engaged them in conversation for the next half-hour while he observed the company.

Jasper realised this was a very different gathering from the discreet little card party he had attended. Gerald was staying close to Susannah and Jasper couldn't blame him, they were by far the youngest people in the room. Apart from Gerald, Jasper could see he was the only unmarried man present and for the most part the visitors were older matrons, who moved about the room, forming groups to gossip and disperse again.

Jasper played his part and was much sought out by the other guests, who were all eager to claim acquaintance with a viscount. No one could have faulted his manners, but he was all the time watching Susannah, and when at last he found her alone beside the tea-table he moved across to join her.

'No, thank you.' He put up his hand as she offered him tea. 'Are your rooms never empty, Miss Prentess?'

'My aunt enjoys entertaining.'

'And you?

'Of course.'

He looked about the room.

'But this company is not worthy of you, madam.' She looked at him, her hazel eyes puzzled and he continued. 'Apart from Barnabus and myself it is all matrons and married couples'

'This is my aunt's party, sir.'

'Perhaps your milieu is the cardroom.'

She looked down, smiling.

'No, I do not think so.'

Jasper hesitated, wondering if he should mention seeing her on the bridge that morning and into the lull came Mrs Sanstead's voice as she moved across to join the other married ladies.

'We are missing Mrs Anstruther today, Mrs Wilby. Is she not well?'

Immediately Miss Prentess was on the alert. Jasper could not fail to notice the way she grew still, nor the wary look in her eye. There was some coughing and shuffling and from the furtive looks in his direction it was clear this was not a subject for his hearing. He turned away, pretending to interest himself in a pleasant landscape on the wall, but not before he had seen Mrs Bulstrode turn quickly in her seat, setting the tassels on her green turban swinging wildly.

'Lord, Mrs Sanstead, have you not heard? The Anstruthers have retired to Shropshire. They left Bath this morning.'

'Heavens, that was sudden. When do they mean to return?'

'Who can tell? Their daughter…'

He could not make out the next words, but he heard Mrs Sanstead sigh.

'Oh, you mean she is with child? Poor gel.'

'Yes. I understand she refused to say who the father might be and Anstruther has banished her.' Mrs Bulstrode's whisper was easily audible to Jasper's keen ears. 'Thrown her out of the house in disgrace.'

'Flighty piece, I always said so,' muttered Mrs Farthing with a disdainful sniff. 'My son William showed a preference for her at one time, but I am glad it came to nought. She has obviously been far too free with her favours.'

'Whatever she has done she does not deserve to be cast off,' murmured Mrs Wilby. 'And what of the father? Do we have any idea who he might be?'

'No one will say, although there are rumours.' Mrs Farthing dropped her voice a little and ended in a conspiratorial whisper that somehow managed to carry around the whole room. 'Mr Warwick.'

'What? Not the young man we met here the other night?' exclaimed Mrs Sanstead. 'Why, he made a fourth at whist, and seemed so charming.'

'The very same.' Mrs Farthing nodded. 'He denies it of course.'

'Naturally,' muttered Susannah.

She had not joined the matrons, but she was listening as intently as Jasper. Now he heard her utterance, and saw the angry frown that passed across her brow.

'But what of Anstruther?' barked the General, with a total disregard for the fact that the ladies considered their gossip confidential. 'If it was my gel I'd have it out with the rascal, and if 'tis true I would make him marry her.'

'That certainly would be preferable to her being cast out and having to fend for herself,' sighed Mrs Wilby.

Susannah's lip curled. 'An unenviable choice,' she said, *sotto voce*. 'Marriage to a scoundrel, or destitution.'

'You do not agree, Miss Prentess?' Jasper kept his voice low, so that only she could hear him. 'You would rather he did *not* marry her?'

'If there is resentment on either side, the match is doomed to failure. But having said that, he should know the damage he has caused.

Too many men think that women are put on earth purely for their pleasure.' She looked up, a challenge in her eyes. 'I would have the father face up to the consequences of his actions. But whoever he may be he will not do so, and the poor girl is cast off to make her own way as best she can.'

'She will no doubt find her way to Walcot Street,' said Mrs Farthing, overhearing. 'It is a Magdalen Hospital, after all, and the right place for such women, though heaven knows there are more entrants than we can accommodate at the present.'

Mrs Bulstrode fluttered her hands in agitation.

'My dear Mrs Farthing, I am not sure we should be discussing this here, now…'

Her eyes darted about the room, and Jasper quickly moved to the mirror to adjust his neckcloth. He saw her glance flit over Gerald, who was studiously brushing a fleck of dust from his sleeve and avoiding everyone's eyes. Susannah was not so reticent. She stepped into the group.

'If you fear for my sensibilities then pray do not be anxious,' she replied, her head up. 'I am no innocent miss fresh from the schoolroom and I think this is a subject that should be discussed in *every* lady's drawing room.' She turned her challenging eyes upon Mrs Farthing. 'I believe you are on the committee for Walcot Street Penitentiary, are you not, ma'am?'

'I am. We do our best to teach the inmates the folly of their ways…'

'Inmates. Yes, I believe the young women there are more prisoners than patients.'

Mrs Farthing's thin lips curved into a patronising smile.

'My dear Miss Prentess, these young women come to us in desperation and we look after them. In return, of course we demand their compliance. They arrive sick, often with child. We look after them, train them in an occupation and put them out to service where we can.'

'We?' Susannah's voice was deceptively sweet. 'You take an active interest in these poor women, do you, ma'am? Perhaps you take your daughters to visit them.'

'Heavens, my dear, what can you be thinking of?' declared Mrs Bulstrode with a nervous laugh. 'Mrs Farthing didn't mean *that*, I am sure.'

'Of course not. Why, Mr Farthing would never allow me to set foot in such a place, let alone our daughters. It would be to risk physical and moral contagion.'

Jasper saw the light of battle in Susannah's eyes, but before she could reply Mrs Wilby swept forwards.

'Dear me, where is that girl with the water?

Mrs Sanstead, I am sure you would like more tea, and the General, too. This cold weather we are having is very drying on the throat, don't you find?' She bustled towards the tea-table. 'Susannah, dearest, ring the bell again, if you please. We cannot have our guests go thirsty...'

Jasper sauntered over to Gerald.

'A skilful interruption,' he murmured appreciatively. 'Pity. The conversation was becoming interesting. Far better than the usual dull inanities.'

Gerald gave him a distracted smile.

'Indeed, but some of the guests are uncomfortable with the subject in mixed company.'

'But not all.' Jasper fixed his eyes on Susannah, who had approached with a cup of tea for Gerald. 'Miss Prentess advocates more discussion about the Magdalen Hospital, do you not, madam?'

She handed the cup to Gerald, saying as she did so, 'It would do no harm for young women to be a little more informed on these matters. If they knew the risks of flirting with gentlemen they would be more cautious.'

'You disapprove of flirting?'

'It can be very dangerous.'

'It can also be very enjoyable.'

Susannah turned her head to find him regarding her, that familiar, disturbing glint in his eye. She discovered that her breathing was restricted,

as if Dorcas had laced her corsets too tightly.
Yet the sensation was not unpleasant. Enjoyable.

He is flirting with me.

Sudden panic filled her, turning her bones
to water so that she was unable to move. Those
intense, blue-grey eyes held her gaze. She felt
like a small animal in thrall to some predator.
She swallowed, desperately trying to regain her
composure. The glint in his eyes deepened to
pure amusement and a sudden spurt of anger
released her.

She stepped back, distancing herself. She
could excuse herself and move away, but such
was her perverse nature that she preferred to
make a retort.

'Enjoyable? Yes, if both parties know it is
nothing more than a game.'

'So you do not disapprove.'

She forced herself to hold his gaze.

Walk away, Susannah. Walk away now. Instead, she lifted her chin.

'I disapprove of gentlemen who take advantage of innocent young women.'

He moved closer, filling the space she had
made between them and setting her skin tingling with anticipation.

'But you are no innocent miss,' he murmured
provocatively. 'You said so yourself.'

'Jasper, do not tease her so!' Gerald's laughing protest hardly registered.

Susannah's brows lifted. She continued to give Jasper look for look.

'Then you will not be able to take advantage of me, my lord.'

'No?' The gleam in his eyes became even more pronounced. If she was fanciful she could imagine twin devils dancing there.

Devilishly handsome, Kate had called him. The faint, upward curve to his mouth brought the words rushing back to her.

'Is that a challenge, Miss Prentess?' His voice was low, sliding over her skin like cool silk and raising the hairs at the back of her neck.

Gerald was watching them, his smile uncertain and a faint crease in his brow. Common sense reasserted itself, yet Susannah's stubborn pride would not let her bow her head and move away. Instead she gave the viscount a haughty smile.

'Of course not. I would not have you waste your time.'

She excused herself and walked off, head high, hoping her knees would not buckle beneath her. What was she doing, responding to him in that way? As well tease a wild animal! The last thing she needed was to have him paying attention to her.

Jasper watched her walk away and realised he was smiling. The blood thrummed through his body, a sure sign that he had enjoyed the interchange.

'Jasper?'

He looked up to find Gerald regarding him.

'Jasper, I won't have you pursuing Miss Prentess if you mean nothing but mischief. She is too good, too honourable, to deserve that.'

He observed the slightly anxious look in Gerald's eyes. Good? Honourable? Perhaps she was, but why then should she lie about being abroad in her carriage that morning? He still wanted an answer to that one, but he was experienced enough to know that he would not get it today. He shrugged.

'Believe me, Gerald, I have never intended mischief towards any young lady. Let us take our leave. I have had enough tea for one day.'

'Oh heavens, I have never been so uncomfortable in all my life.'

Mrs Wilby sank back in her chair and fanned herself vigorously once the last of their visitors was shown out. Susannah was standing by the window but she turned at this.

'No, ma'am, and why should that be?'

'My dear, I never thought to hear such things in our drawing room. The talk of, of fallen women and by-blows—and with gentlemen present, too! I am sure General Sanstead did not know where to look.'

'I thought the General took it rather well,' mused Susannah.

'But what of Mr Barnabus, and Lord Markham? I am sure they must have overheard the conversation.'

Susannah frowned.

'If it were not for *gentlemen* such as they, many of these girls would not be in such dire straits, and girls like Miss Anstruther would not be thrown on to the streets.'

'Ah, yes.' Mrs Wilby sighed. 'That poor child. I do hope she is safe.'

'There at least I can put your mind at rest.' Susannah came away from the window, smiling slightly as Mrs Wilby's mouth dropped open.

'What! Never say she is…'

'Yes, she is our newest client. I took her to Florence House this morning.'

Chapter Five

Jasper spent the following week doing everything he could to distract his cousin's thoughts from Susannah. It seemed to work—he even persuaded Gerald to accompany him to the theatre rather than attend the card party in Royal Crescent. Gerald was happy enough to go with him and he never once mentioned Miss Prentess. Perversely, she was rarely out of Jasper's thoughts. He told himself it was the unanswered questions he had about the woman and nothing to do with their last exchange, the way she had boldly returned his gaze, challenged him to flirt with her. That merely showed how dangerous she was to innocents like Gerald.

He sent his valet off to make discreet enquiries about Miss Prentess. Peters was a loyal, intelligent employee who had proved his worth over the years in ferreting out secrets others would prefer to keep hidden. But on this occasion he was unsuccessful.

'No one will say a word against the lady,' he reported back. 'The men know nothing, and the women—the maidservants I have spoken with—they have nothing but praise for her.' The valet shook his head. 'Odd, very odd, if you asks me, m'lord. There's usually some juicy gossip to be had.' He coughed. 'There was one thing, though.'

'Yes?'

'Friday morning, my lord. You asked me to lay out your riding dress because you was going riding with Mr Barnabus, but then you had a message from the young gentleman, sir, saying as how he was indisposed.'

'Yes, I remember that,' said Jasper, a touch impatiently. 'What of it?'

Peters fixed his eyes on some spot on the wall and said woodenly, 'I saw him walking with Miss Prentess that self-same morning. They was in Henrietta Street. I didn't think anything of it at the time, and wouldn't have mentioned it, only you wanted to know about the young lady, and I thought that mighty odd...'

Yes, very odd indeed, thought Jasper, and when he had tackled Gerald, his cousin looked sheepish and laughed it off.

'Oh, well, you know how it is, cos,' he said.

'I thought you'd be a trifle vexed if you knew why I had cried off, but Miss Prentess asked me particularly to come with her.'

Gerald apologised and they left it at that, but Jasper didn't like to think his cousin was keeping secrets from him, and even less did he like the thought that Susannah was encouraging him to do so.

Jasper had even taken to walking out every morning and keeping a watch for Miss Prentess's carriage. He had been rewarded just once, on a misty morning when he saw the vehicle bowling along Horse Street. He had quickened his pace and was just in time to see it sweep across the bridge and turn on to the Wells Road. He did not know if Miss Prentess was inside on that occasion, nor did he have any idea of its destination. All he knew was that both Miss Prentess and her aunt were in Bath for the concert the same evening.

He had seen her almost as soon as he entered the Assembly Rooms. Her gown of kingfisher-blue satin was an unusual choice for an unmarried lady, but he had to admit it suited her, contrasting with the gleaming golden curls piled around her head. He tried to approach her at the interval, but she was at the centre of a crowd and not all Jasper's considerable address could separate Miss Prentess from her friends and admirers. Instead he escorted Mrs Wilby out of the concert room in search of refreshment.

'We have not seen you since the afternoon at Royal Crescent,' she remarked, encouraged to speak by his silence.

'No, I have been rather busy,' he handed her a glass of wine. 'I thought I saw Miss Prentess, however. Early this morning, heading out of Bath.'

If he had not been watching closely he would have missed the slight tremor of the widow's hand as she held the wine to her lips. Her answer, when it came, was composed.

'You are mistaken, my lord. That was merely our carriage, going off to collect provisions.'

'You send your servants in your own carriage, ma'am? Is that not rather extravagant? How far do they have to travel?' He added helpfully, 'I saw it heading off on the Wells Road.'

The hunted look in the widow's eyes convinced him he was on to something.

'N-not far, but the vegetables are so much better, you know, from out of town.' Her fan fluttered nervously. 'We should be going back, my lord. The concert will be starting again soon and I do so dislike latecomers...'

He escorted her back to her seat and as soon as he moved away she had her head close to her niece and was talking animatedly. Jasper stood watching, until Susannah looked up and met his eyes. Her face was impassive but he was close enough to read a frown in her clear gaze. He smiled and inclined his head, but she immediately looked away, and when the concert ended she whisked her aunt out of the building before he could approach them.

'If mine was a suspicious nature I should say Miss Prentess was avoiding me,' he murmured, thinking back to that concert as he strode along High Street a few days later. It was Tuesday. Gerald was intent upon going to Royal Crescent that evening and Jasper could offer no good reason why he should not do so. 'Well, I shall accompany Gerald this evening. She can hardly avoid me in her own drawing room.'

A familiar figure on the other side of the road caught his eye.

'Charles!' As the man stopped, Jasper crossed the road to greet him. 'What the devil are you doing in Bath?'

'I might ask you the same thing,' retorted Charles Camerton, taking Jasper's hand in a friendly grip.

'Family matters,' said Jasper vaguely. 'Are you staying at the York or the Christopher?'

'Devil a bit, they are too far above my touch,' replied Charles. 'I am at the White Hart. I have been visiting my godmother in Radstock. Doing the pretty, you know, in the hopes that she will die soon and leave me her fortune.'

Since Jasper knew Charles to be very fond of his godmother, he grinned at this.

'Then what are you doing in Bath?' he asked again.

'She thinks that a treatment at the hot baths will do her good. I am here to seek out lodgings for her.' He glanced up at the lowering sky. 'Although I have persuaded her she should not attempt the journey for another month at least. We are barely out of February and it looks like snow is on the way.'

'So you are here for a few days?' Jasper said, an idea growing in his mind. 'Will you dine with me this evening?'

'With pleasure,' returned Charles, promptly. 'There is little else to do in a watering place populated by the old and the infirm.'

Jasper smiled. 'Oh, I think I can find you some entertainment. You are fond of cards, I believe…'

'Miss Prentess!'

Susannah gave her hand to Gerald and he raised it to his lips.

'Welcome, sir.' She looked behind him. 'You are alone?'

'Yes. I am sorry I missed your last party.'

She smiled at him as she gently withdrew her fingers from his grasp.

'I do not expect you to attend us every week.'

'But I like to come.' He glanced around the drawing room and lowered his voice. 'I like to help where I can, Susannah, which is why I was so pleased you allowed me to escort you to see Odesse the other day.'

'I hope your mama will like the lace you ordered for her.'

'I am sure she will, and if she tells her friends that may bring in more orders.'

Susannah smiled at him.

'It may indeed. You see, you have been a great help, Mr Barnabus—'

'Gerald,' he corrected her. 'Are we not friends enough now to dispense with formalities?'

'Gerald, then.' She shook off the twinge of guilt at allowing such familiarity. She had made it plain they could only ever be friends, after all. Then, hating herself for succumbing, she asked the question that had been in her mind ever since he arrived. 'Has Lord Markham left Bath?'

'No, he is still here and means to look in presently. But enough of this. Are you free? Will you play picquet with me?'

She shook her head.

'You know you always lose.'

'Tonight I feel lucky,' he declared. 'And I

have improved vastly since we last played. Mrs Logan said so.'

She laughed at that.

'Very well, then, but do not expect me to hold back. I shall show you no mercy!'

In the event, mercy was not necessary. Susannah had chosen a table where she could watch the door, and such was her distraction that Gerald won the first game. The second was closer, but the entrance of more visitors caused her to lose track of the discards and she was defeated again.

'I told you I had improved,' chortled Gerald, sweeping the coins from the table.

'You are very right,' agreed Susannah, getting up. 'But perhaps you will oblige me by taking your winnings to the loo table and giving my aunt a chance to recoup.'

With a smile she excused herself, glancing at the clock. It was gone ten, there would be very few visitors arriving now. Even as she thought this the door opened and Lord Markham walked in. His appearance made her spirits leap most shamefully. Susannah could not deny that she had been looking out for him, as she had done in vain the previous week. He might be suspicious of her, and cause her nerves to flutter alarmingly, but any party where he was not present was an insipid affair. When she had seen him at the concert she had wanted so much to speak to him, but Aunt Maude had warned her that he had asked awkward questions, and she knew it would be folly to linger and risk further interrogation. All such thoughts were bundled into the back of her mind now as she moved forwards to greet him, wondering why it was that he was not charmed by her smile like every other man in the room.

'Lord Markham.'

She held out her hand but, despite steeling herself, his touch still sent a tremor of excitement running up her arm, and when his lips brushed her fingers the excitement flooded through her before settling into an indescribable ache somewhere low in her body.

'Your servant, Miss Prentess. I have brought someone to meet you. May I present Mr Charles Camerton? He is an avid card player.'

'Indeed?' She subjected the newcomer to a swift appraisal. He looked genial enough, some years older than the viscount, she guessed. His figure was good, his clothes elegant and his curling brown hair was fashionably short. A man used to the London salons, perhaps. 'I hope we will not disappoint you, sir. This is merely a friendly little gathering.'

'Those are the best sort, Miss Prentess. I am here with every intention of enjoying myself.'

'Then what will you play, sir? I could find

two more players, if you and Lord Markham would like to play whist, or…'

Mr Camerton looked around the room until his eyes came to rest upon Kate, who was at that moment opening two fresh packs of cards.

'*Vingt-et-un*,' offered Susannah, following his gaze. 'It is very popular.'

'And it is my favourite game. If you will excuse me?'

With a practised smile and a bow he moved off towards Kate's table.

'Which leaves you with me.'

The viscount's low murmur was like a feather on her skin. She glanced at her arm to see if it was covered in tell-tale goose-bumps. Thankfully there were none.

'I am sure we can find something—'

'I thought we might play picquet. You and I,' he added, so there should be no misunderstanding.

'Thank you, sir, but I think not.'

'Afraid?'

She would not rise to his taunt. Instead she replied frankly, 'Your cousin tells me you are an expert at the game. I will not risk it.'

She looked about her, hoping to distract him. 'My aunt is playing macao and there is room at her table…'

'If you were a true gambler you would not be able to resist the challenge.'

Her chin went up.

'If you were a true gentleman you would not press me so.'

That only made him smile more.

'Is it the game that frightens you, or me?'

Her cheeks flamed at his quiet words. She could feel the heat flooding through her and her heart was beating wildly, making her breathless. Her senses were heightened, as if by a sudden danger. She was enveloped by his closeness. She wanted to flee, but was rooted to the spot. She must be rational. This was her drawing room, they were surrounded by people. What possible harm could come to her here? Yet everything around them was muted. It was as if they were alone, shut off from the world. She could smell the tangy scent of him, sandalwood and lemon and a faint, indefinable fragrance that she now recognised was his alone.

Her eyes were fixed on his chin, on that mobile mouth with its finely sculpted lips and the faint creases at each side that deepened when he smiled. She dare not look higher and instead dragged her eyes down and stared at the diamond winking from the folds of his neck cloth.

'Well, Miss Prentess?'

He was so close she felt his breath on her brow, soft as a caress.

This must stop. Now. Gathering all her

strength she drew herself up and forced herself to look him in the face.

Well, she fixed her eyes somewhere around his left temple.

'It is not fear, Lord Markham,' she said coolly. 'It is common sense. One should never take unnecessary risks.'

She turned to walk away and he touched her arm.

'One more thing. You were seen with Gerald on Friday morning.'

She spun back, quickly schooling her features into a look of haughty unconcern.

'What is so wrong about that, my lord?'

'He cried off from an appointment with me to accompany you.'

She had not known that, and regretted it, but she was determined the viscount should not know it. She summoned a glittering smile, as if it was her victory.

'That is unfortunate, of course, but it is no concern of mine.'

The tightening of his jaw told her he was angry. With a slight nod she turned and walked away from him, the knowledge that he was watching her sending a ripple of unease along the length of her spine.

'Well, Camerton, what did you think of Bath's latest hell?' asked Jasper.

They were walking away from Royal Crescent, keeping up a brisk pace to offset the icy wind that whipped around them, tugging at their coats. Charles Camerton laughed at Jasper's description.

'Mrs Wilby's soirée is no hell, my friend. The stakes are so low they would be ridiculed in town.'

'True, they are unlikely to arouse the interest of the magistrates,' agreed Jasper. 'You saw no instances of foul play?'

'None. Mrs Wilby and her niece are canny players, as sharp as any females I have ever encountered.'

'Aye, and they favour the games where skill and a good memory will aid them. What of Mrs Logan? I noticed you spent a great deal of time at her table.'

Camerton grinned.

'With such paltry sums at stake I had to find something to entertain me! She is different and I like that. I suspect she was a professional gamester at some time. She gave me a run for my money. However...' he patted his pocket '...I came away the richer, so I am not complaining.'

'Nor do the other men that play there, but I am convinced they rarely win.'

'Ah, but they are not there for the cards. They are there to worship at the feet of La Prentess.'

'You noticed that?'

'Of course. She is a diamond. Your cousin Barnabus is most definitely enamoured.' Jasper frowned. That was not what he wanted to hear. He dragged his thoughts back to Charles, who was still speaking. 'And you say she is an heiress? Interesting. With her looks she should be in town. She could make a brilliant alliance.'

'That is what I thought,' agreed Jasper, frowning. 'I believe her family come from London. Dammit, Charles, there is some mystery here.'

'And you have an interest in La Prentess so you want to know what it might be?'

Jasper was quick to disclaim.

'I am only interested in saving my cousin from a disastrous liaison.'

'Don't see that marriage to an heiress would be that much of a disaster.'

Jasper had said very much the same to Gloriana, but now it was important to him that Susannah Prentess should not marry Gerald.

'You know,' mused Charles, 'I might even have a touch at La Prentess myself.'

'I beg you won't!'

Charles laughed. 'No, I won't. Her friend Mrs Logan is much more to my taste. I shall leave La Prentess to you, Jasper.'

They had reached the top of Milsom Street and Jasper was relieved to part from his friend. Their conversation was becoming far too uncomfortable.

* * *

A week of chill winds and snow flurries kept all but the most hardy indoors. Servants scattered cinders over the footpaths to prevent pedestrians from slipping and Aunt Maude insisted they take chairs to the Assembly Rooms the following Monday, rather than risk the horses on the icy cobbles.

Susannah expected the rooms to be very thin of company, but the Dress Ball was incentive enough for Bath's residents to turn out in force. Susannah was wearing another new gown from Odesse, a cream silk with a finely frilled hem and short puff sleeves, the rose-coloured decoration set off by matching long gloves. She carried a silk shawl embroidered with tiny rosebuds to combat the icy air that she knew would penetrate even the building, at least until the ballroom filled up and everyone was dancing.

Gerald was looking out for her and immediately led her away to join a country dance. Susannah was surprised to find Kate was already on the floor, partnered by Charles Camerton.

'You, Kate, dancing?' she teased when the movement of the dance brought them together.

The widow's self-conscious look surprised Susannah even more and when there was a break in the dancing she sought out her friend.

'I do not think I have ever known you to

dance here,' she remarked. 'And with Mr Camerton, too.'

Kate shrugged one white shoulder and busied herself with her fan.

'He seems keen to dance with me. And after the way he fleeced me so unmercifully on Tuesday I thought it might help to find out what he is about.'

Susannah sighed, momentarily diverted.

'Our losses last week were very disappointing. Aunt Maude went down a couple of hundred pounds to Lord Markham and I even lost at picquet to Gerald Barnabus.'

'I am beginning to suspect it was a concerted effort by those three gentlemen.'

'By Mr Camerton and the viscount, perhaps, but not Gerald, that was entirely my own fault. I was…distracted.'

'Well, we must be on our guard,' said Kate. 'Such losses cannot be sustained for long.'

'Perhaps we should refuse to admit Mr Camerton and the viscount in future.'

Kate's response was swift.

'Oh, no, we must hope they keep coming.' She added airily, 'That is why I am going to dance again with Mr Camerton now. I hope to lull him into complacency, so that when we play again I will catch him off-guard.'

Kate sailed off in search of her prey. She was clearly enjoying herself and Susannah was not convinced by the reasons she had given for dancing with Mr Camerton.

'Something amuses you, Miss Prentess?'

The viscount's voice at her shoulder was warm and seductive, like being wrapped in sables. Susannah scolded herself for being fanciful.

'I have been talking to Mrs Logan. She always amuses me.'

He glanced across the room.

'She certainly seems to be on the best of terms with Charles Camerton. He is leading her out for another dance.' He held out his arm. 'Shall we join them?'

Susannah had already made up her mind that she would avoid the viscount whenever possible, but surely Kate's arguments had some merit. Perhaps instead of alienating Lord Markham she should try harder to charm him. In that case, it was clearly her duty to dance with him.

She placed her fingers on his arm and accompanied him on to the dance floor. It was a lively affair and Susannah enjoyed it immensely. She was surprised when the music ended—surely the orchestra had stopped too soon? Lord Markham invited her to remain on the floor for a second set and she thought it would be churlish to refuse him.

When he finally led her from the floor she was happy to stand with him at the side of the room, watching the dancing. Even when he mentioned seeing her carriage on the Wells Road again she was not discomposed.

'Surely it is no one's business if my servants use my carriage for their errands?'

'True.' He guided her to an empty bench and sat down beside her. 'It is, however, unusual. But in an heiress such extravagance will not be criticised.'

It was on the tip of her tongue to explain that for the next couple of years she had no access to anything more than an allowance, but that would undermine her explanation. She held her peace.

Sitting with the viscount was causing some comment. Brows were raised, Susannah saw one or two of the matrons whispering behind their fans, but when one particularly haughty lady smiled and inclined her head towards Susannah, a chuckle escaped her.

The viscount's brows went up.

'Being seen in your company is proving most useful for me,' she explained, her eyes twinkling. 'There are several very high sticklers here tonight and I have never known them to look upon me with such approval.'

'Why should they not approve of you?'

'Oh, well…' she waved her hand '…because my father was a mere captain. Because my uncle was a nabob.'

'A very rich nabob,' he corrected her.

'True.' She sipped at her wine. 'But birth is everything.'

'Is it?' He shifted his position to face her. 'You are a gentleman's daughter, and heir to a fortune. I should have thought that would open every door in Bath to you.'

'Perhaps it would, if I would conform and toady up to those matrons who think themselves so superior.'

'From what I know of you, I cannot imagine you doing that.'

His sudden smile flashed and for a moment she was dazzled by his charm, as if someone had knocked all the breath out of her body. She looked away quickly. She was meant to be charming *him*.

Jasper felt rather than saw her sudden withdrawal. She had been relaxed, prepared to confide in him and he was reluctant to let the moment go. He remembered something Gerald had said to him.

'Living in the Crescent, in such an elevated position, could be seen as having pretensions.'

'Perhaps.'

He smiled. 'But you don't really care for their good opinion, do you?'

He read the answer in her face.

'To have their approval could be very useful,' she said carefully.

'To enhance your little card parties?'

'Of course. Imagine how much I would like to have a dowager duchess in my drawing room.'

Her eyes twinkled wickedly. She was teasing him again and Jasper was surprised how much he enjoyed that.

'No doubt you would not refuse to play picquet with her.'

'Of course not.'

'But you will not play with a mere viscount.'

'Not with you, my lord.'

'Why not? You have played picquet with my cousin on more than one occasion.'

'That is different.'

'Why, because you are going to marry him?'

'No!'

He cursed inwardly as soon as he uttered the question, but the tone of her denial and the serious look in her eye reassured him. She was sincere.

She gave a sigh. 'Can you not content yourself with winning two hundred pounds from my aunt last week?'

'A mere trifle. Two games of picquet for pound points would recover that.'

'Or double the loss.'

'True.' He leaned forwards. 'What would it take, Miss Prentess, to make you play with me?'

He saw the shutters come down. He had

pressed her too hard. She laughed and shook her head at him.

'Fie, my lord, I have no doubt you are used to playing in the London clubs, to losing thousands at a sitting. Do you expect me to risk my pin-money against you?' She rose. 'You may come to Royal Crescent, my lord, and I will play with you at *vingt-et-un*, or loo, where there are others at the table.'

'You consider me too dangerous an opponent to play alone?'

Jasper was standing, too. The top of her head, crowned by those guinea-gold curls, was level with his eyes. She was the perfect height for kissing. He shrugged off the distracting thought as he held her gaze. She returned look for look, but there was no sign of laughter now in those hazel eyes. Suddenly all Jasper's senses were on the alert, aware that they were not speaking merely about playing cards.

'I think you could be extremely dangerous, my lord.' Her words fell softly between them before she turned and walked away.

'The lady seems displeased with you, Markham.' Charles Camerton came up to him. 'What did you say to her?'

'I asked her to play cards with me.' He did not take his eyes off the retreating figure. 'She refused me.'

Camerton chuckled.

'You must be losing your touch, old friend.'

The comment rankled, but Jasper tried to ignore it.

'Or perhaps,' mused Charles, 'she is playing with you, to excite your interest.'

'Perhaps.' Jasper kept his tone light, but in his heart he didn't want to think that Susannah was toying with him.

'Good morning, Miss. I've brought your hot chocolate.'

Susannah groaned. After tossing and turning all night, she had only just dropped into a deep slumber when Dorcas's cheerful voice disturbed her. The curtains were thrown back and the feeble light of a grey winter morning filled the room. Susannah groaned again and pulled the covers over her head. Her maid responded with a tut.

'Come on now, mistress. You ordered the carriage to be here in an hour. That doesn't give us long to get you ready...or shall I tell Edwards to go away again?'

'No, no, I will get up.'

Susannah sat up and rubbed her eyes. She stared at the flames blazing merrily in the hearth. She had not heard the maid come in to light the fire, so she must have had some sleep, even if it had been disturbed by dreams. She sipped at her cup of chocolate while Dorcas bustled about the room.

'It's a cold morning, miss, will you wear the high-collar spencer?'

She held out the short, rose-coloured jacket with its fur trim.

'Yes, yes, that will do.' Susannah cast an eye at the bleak, overcast sky outside the window. 'And you had better look out my old travelling cloak as well.'

The clock was just chiming the hour as Susannah descended the stairs. Gatley informed her that the carriage was ready, but instead of opening the front door for her, he accompanied his mistress to the lower floor and let her out of the door leading into the garden. Susannah was enveloped in her serviceable cloak and with the hood pulled over her curls she hoped she might pass for a servant as she sped through the garden and into the narrow alley that led between the stables fronting Crescent Lane, where her carriage was waiting. Before settling into her seat she drew down the blinds. If Lord Markham was abroad again this morning she would not risk being seen, even if she did have Lucas, her footman, standing at the back to give her countenance.

She stifled a yawn. It was thoughts of the viscount that had disturbed her sleep. She had gone to bed after the ball with her head spinning. When she closed her eyes she was once again dancing with Lord Markham, fingers tingling from his touch, heart singing from the caress of his smile. Yet no sooner did she relax in his company than he began to talk of the card parties and she would be on the defensive, suspicious of every remark. She rubbed her arms, suddenly chilled, despite the thick cloak and the warm brick her servants had placed in the carriage for her feet to rest upon. If Lord Markham would only leave Bath then she could be easy again.

But how dull life would be without him.

Susannah gave herself a mental shake. These megrims were unlike her, brought on by lack of sleep and travelling in this gloomy half-light. She pulled at the side of the blind and peeped out. They were well out of Bath now, and she thought she might safely put up the shades. The carriage rattled along through the country lanes, up hill and down dale until at last the carriage slowed and turned off the main road towards the village of Priston. Susannah sat forwards, knowing that very soon now she would have her first, clear view of her destination.

The carriage picked up speed as it followed the road that curled around the side of the valley and there, nestling against the hill on the far side of the valley, was a rambling Jacobean mansion built of the local Ham stone which glowed warmly, even in the pale wintry sunlight. It was not as grand as the other properties she had inherited from her Uncle Middlemass and it was in dire need of repair, as witnessed by the scaffolding surrounding the east wing, but she thought it by far the most charming. She was impatient to reach five-and-twenty, when she would have control of her fortune and would be able to fully renovate the building. Until then she must make do with what little money she could spare from her allowance, and the profits from the weekly card parties.

The carriage slowed again to negotiate the turning and her heart swelled with pride when she saw the newly painted sign fixed to the stone gatepost: Florence House. They bumped along the drive and on to the weed-strewn carriage circle in front of the house. They came to a stand before the canopied front door and Lucas jumped down and ran around to let down the steps.

As she descended, a motherly figure in a black stuff gown came hurrying out to meet her, the white lappets from her lace cap bouncing on her shoulders.

'Miss Prentess, welcome, my dear. Pray come you in and do not be standing out here in this cold wind.'

'Thank you, Mrs Gifford.'

The older lady ushered her indoors to a small parlour off the hall, where a welcome fire was burning.

'Has our builder arrived yet?'

'Not yet, ma'am, but you have made very good time—I do not expect him for another half-hour yet. You have time for a little refreshment. Jane is bringing a glass of mulled wine for you.'

'Thank you, that is very welcome.'

Susannah untied the strings of her cloak and looked about her. She had always thought this parlour a very comfortable room. With its low, plastered ceiling and panelled walls it was certainly one of the easiest to keep warm. A door on the far side led to a much larger dining room, but that needed refurbishment and was currently not in use, the occupants of the house finding the smaller apartment sufficient for their needs. A padded armchair and sofa were arranged before the fireplace while under the window a small table and chairs provided a surface for dining or working. At present the table was littered with writing materials and a large ledger, indicating that the housekeeper had been at work on the accounts. Susannah draped her cloak over one of the chairs and went to the fire to warm her hands. She turned as the door opened and a heavily pregnant young woman entered, carrying a tray. She walked slowly, holding the tray well out in front to avoid her extended belly. Susannah straightened immediately.

'Jane, let me take that, you should not be waiting upon me—'

'Thank you, but I can manage perfectly well. And it is a pleasure to bring your wine for you.'

Susannah sat down, recognising that to insist upon taking the tray would hurt the girl's pride. 'Thank you, Jane, that is very kind of you.' She watched her place the tray carefully on a side table. 'When is the baby due?'

'The midwife thinks it won't be for a week or two yet.' Jane smiled and rubbed her hands against her swollen stomach. 'It cannot come soon enough for me now, Miss Prentess.'

'Call me Susannah, please. There is small difference in our stations.'

Jane's smile disappeared.

'Perhaps there was not, at one time, but now—' She looked down at her body. 'I am a fallen woman.'

'I will not have that term used here,' Susannah replied fiercely. 'You have been unfortunate. 'Tis the same for all the ladies we bring in.'

'And if it was not for your kindness we would be even more unfortunate,' replied Jane. 'We would have to go to Walcot Street, and we would not be called ladies there,' she added drily.

'Will you not sit down?' Susannah indicated a chair, but Jane shook her head.

'If you will excuse me, I will go back to my room now and rest. The midwife might say this little one isn't ready to be born, but it seems pretty impatient to me.'

'She is a dear girl,' said Mrs Gifford, when Jane had gone. 'Her stitching is so neat that Odesse says she will be happy to take her on, once the babe is born.'

'Good.' Susannah sipped at her wine. 'Since we have a little time perhaps you would like to give me your report now, rather than wait until after I have spoken to Mr Tyler.'

Mrs Gifford sat down and folded her hands in her lap.

'I have had to move everything out of the east wing because the chimney is unsafe and we fear it might come crashing through the roof if we have a storm. Then there is the leak on the south gable, which is getting worse. But this section of the house is reasonably sound, and I have been able to find dry bedchambers for each of our guests. Miss Anstruther—Violet—is settling in well, although she is still very despondent and keeps to her room.'

'That is to be expected, having been cast off by her family,' replied Susannah. 'I will go up to her later, if she will see me.'

'If?' uttered Mrs Gifford. 'Of course she will

see you. 'Tis you who made it possible for her to be looked after. She has much cause to be grateful to you, as do all the others...'

Susannah shook her head.

'I will not trade on their gratitude,' she said quietly. 'Everyone here is a guest, and I want to treat them with the same respect I would like for myself. But enough of that. Do go on.'

'We have only three ladies here at present: Lizzie Burns, Jane and Miss Anstruther.'

'And how is Lizzie? When I was here last she was not well.'

'I think we have avoided the fever, but the doctor says she should keep to her bed for another week. However, her baby is now three weeks old and doing well.'

'That is some good news then. And what of you, Mrs Gifford? How is your sister?'

The older lady's face was grave.

'Very poorly, I'm afraid.'

'Then you must go to her as soon as maybe. The woman we interviewed to replace you— Mrs Jennings—how soon can she be here?'

'She is moving in this afternoon. I hope to get away this evening.'

'Good. And you have enough money for your journey?'

'Yes, thank you.' The old woman blinked rapidly. 'Bless you, Miss Prentess, you have been very good. I do not expect to be away for long, I fear my sister's end is very near.'

'You must take as long as you need,' Susannah told her softly. 'We shall manage here. Now—' she looked towards the window '—if I am not mistaken, the builder has arrived, and we will find out just what work is needed.'

Chapter Six

Susannah's cheerful, business-like manner did not desert her until she was alone in her carriage on the way back to Bath. Mr Tyler was a tradesman she had used before, and she trusted him not to mislead her, but his report on the house was not encouraging. He had already carried out some of the most urgent repairs but needed payment for the materials he had used before he could continue. He had pleaded his case with her. He was a family man, with debts of his own, and if she couldn't pay him something now he would have to remove his scaffolding and his men, and once he had left the site he would not be able to return until late summer. She had promised to send him something by the morning, but her concern now was where to find the money.

When she had first embarked upon this project she had approached her uncle's lawyer, now her own man of business. He had politely but firmly rejected her requests for an advance upon her inheritance. She was allowed sufficient funds to run the house in Bath and a sum that her uncle had considered enough for her personal use, but it would not run to the cost of repairing Florence House.

'If only we had not lost money at last week's card party,' she muttered, staring unseeing at the bleak winter landscape.

However, it was not her nature to be despondent and she put her mind to ways of raising the capital she needed. Her fingers crept up to the string of pearls about her neck. She had inherited her aunt's jewel box. It was overflowing with necklaces, brooches and rings, most of them quite unsuitable for a single lady. Susannah did not want to sell any of them. They were part of her inheritance and she owed it to her uncle's memory to keep them if she possibly could. But Florence House was important to her, and she had to do *something*, and urgently. By the time she reached Bath she had come up with a plan, and when she spotted Gerald Barnabus on the pavement she pulled the check-string and stopped the carriage.

'Gerald, good day to you! I wonder if I might have a word…'

* * *

March had arrived. The first flowers of spring were in evidence and Jasper was conscious of the fact that he had planned to be back at Markham by now. He was receiving regular reports from his steward, which assured him all was well, but he wanted to be back before Lady Day. The yearly rents were due then and he liked to discuss future agreements with his tenants. Honesty compelled him to admit that there was no real reason for him to stay in Bath, so what was keeping him here? He might argue that it was the mystery surrounding Susannah Prentess, but an uncomfortable honesty forced him to admit that it was the woman herself who fascinated him. It would not do. It would be best if he forgot all about Miss Prentess. When Tuesday dawned he found himself looking forward to going to Royal Crescent that evening. It would be the last time, he promised himself. He would bid goodbye to Mrs Wilby and her enchanting niece and return to Markham.

Jasper went out for his usual early walk, but this time turned his steps towards Sydney Gardens, determined that he would not even look to see if Miss Prentess's carriage left the city that morning.

He returned to York House for breakfast and spent the next few hours at the desk replying to his steward and writing various letters. The afternoon was well advanced by the time he applied his seal to the last letter, and when Jasper glanced at the clock he was surprised to find it was so late. It had become something of a habit for Gerald to call in York House each afternoon, if they had not met earlier in the day, to discuss plans for the evening. Jasper shrugged. He was not his cousin's keeper. Gerald was of age, after all, and had gone on very well in Bath before his arrival. Jasper finished his letters and called for Peters to bring his hat and cane: he would call upon Gerald at his lodgings in Westgate Buildings and invite him to dinner.

In the event Jasper never reached Gerald's abode, nor did he issue the invitation. He had stopped in Milsom Street. It was in his mind to buy a little gift to send down to his godson at Rooks Tower, but his attention was caught by a reflection in the toyshop window. The shop was on the shady side of the street, so the image from the far side of the road was particularly clear. Gerald had emerged from the jewellers and paused to pull on his gloves. Jasper turned and was about to hail his cousin when he noticed the veiled figure of a lady being ushered out of the shop with much bowing by a black-coated assistant. It was obvious to Jasper that Gerald was waiting for the lady. He held out his arm to her, but before setting off she put up her veil to display the lovely countenance of Susannah Prentess.

Jasper froze. Susannah slipped her hand through Gerald's arm and they set off down the street. There was such a warm smile on her face that Jasper felt winded. He stepped back, almost reeling from the sudden bolt of jealousy that shot through him.

The low sun was shining upon them and they did not notice him watching from the shadows. Had Gerald proposed again, had he been accepted? No. He could not believe it. He *would* not believe it until he had spoken to his cousin. With an effort he forced his unwilling feet to carry him onwards. His brain seethed with conjecture, but he refused to admit his worst fears. He wandered about the town, visiting the Pump Room and the circulating library, but nothing could satisfy his restless spirit. He called at the White Hart but discovered that Charles Camerton had gone out. No matter, Charles was joining him for dinner, so he would see him then. However, as he turned his steps once more towards his hotel he saw Gerald walking down High Street towards him. He was somewhat reassured by the way Gerald hailed him cheerfully, but after they had exchanged greetings, Jasper could not resist telling him that he had seen him earlier.

'You were outside the jewellers with Miss Prentess. Would you like to tell me what that was about?'

'Actually, I am not at liberty to say at the moment.' Gerald's boyish face flushed. 'I promised Susannah.'

'I see.' Jasper's jaw clenched at the familiar use of her name and there was a hollow ache in his stomach.

'It is nothing terrible,' Gerald hurried on, watching him anxiously.

Jasper forced a smile to his lips.

'If that is the case then why can you not tell me?'

Gerald looked uncomfortable.

'It is just that I know Mama would not approve. She might quiz you, and if you do not know, then you cannot tell her anything, can you?'

'Gerald—'

His cousin cut him short.

'Will you be at the Crescent this evening? I will ask Susannah. If she is willing, I will tell you then. I promise. For now you must excuse me, I am on an errand.'

'Come and dine with me tonight,' said Jasper. 'Charles Camerton will be there, we can go on to the Crescent together.'

Gerald shook his head.

'I am sorry, Jasper, I should like to join you, but I do not think I will be back in time.'

'Why, where are you going?'

'I told you, an errand,' was all the answer Gerald would give before he dashed off, leaving Jasper prey to such a fierce anger that for several minutes he remained rooted to the spot. An engagement. It had to be. It was the only thing that could account for Gerald's odd speech, and the happiness he had seen in both their faces earlier. Clutching his cane, Jasper strode angrily back to York House. She had tricked him. Why should he be surprised? She had told him her actions were no concern of his, but Gerald *was* his concern. Damnation, he was head of the family. How dare she make Gerald act in this underhand manner!

By the time Charles Camerton arrived for dinner Jasper's rage was contained. Outwardly he was smiling, urbane, but it still burned, a steady, simmering fury inside him. Years of training came to his aid, allowing him to converse with seeming normality during the meal, but he tasted nothing of the dishes set before him and allowed his glass to be refilled more than normal.

Only when the covers were removed and the servants had withdrawn did he allow himself to think back over his day.

'I looked for you at the White Hart today, Charles, and you were not in the Pump Room. Did you go out of town?'

'Yes. It was such a fine day I took Mrs Logan for a drive.'

'Really?'

Charles shrugged. 'Just being friendly, you know.'

'I hope you are not developing a *tendre* there, Charles. I shall require you to be on winning form again at the Crescent tonight.'

Charles refilled his brandy glass.

'I am more than happy to accompany you there, Markham, but I am not sure your plan is necessary. I have been watching your cousin. He does not seem in any danger of making a cake of himself over La Prentess. At least, no more than any of the other young bucks who are fashionably in love with her.'

'I wish I could agree with you.' Jasper pushed back his chair. 'I plan to leave Bath soon, but before I do I want to make sure Gerald is in no danger.'

'Very well then.' Charles rose and followed him to the door. 'Let us to the Crescent, by all means.'

Jasper escorted him out of the hotel. During the meal he had convinced himself that there was only one way to protect Gerald from that scheming woman: he would have to seduce her.

* * *

Susannah gazed about her with satisfaction. The drawing room looked very welcoming, the curtains were pulled against the darkness and the cheerful fire kept the icy weather at bay so effectively that she did not need to wear a shawl over the flowing creation Odesse had fashioned for her. The apricot silk was embroidered at the neck and sleeves with a pattern of vine leaves, the detail cleverly picked out in silver thread to catch the candlelight. She heard the distant rumble of voices. The first guests were arriving. Almost upon the thought Mrs Wilby hurried in.

'Is everything ready, my love? Tables set, new packs of cards... I have told Gatley to have plenty of mulled wine available for our guests as it is such a cold night.' She looked about her. 'Where is Mrs Logan?'

'She sent me word she might be a little late. She went out driving this afternoon.'

'Oh, with whom?'

'She did not say.' It was true, but Susannah suspected she had been in the company of Mr Camerton. She had seen them talking together after the Sunday service at the Abbey, and although Kate would tell her nothing, her smile had been very self-satisfied. She wondered if the widow had formed an attachment, then quickly dismissed the idea. Kate might smile and flirt with the men she encountered but Susannah knew it was a charade. Kate had often voiced her opinion of the male sex. They were at best deceivers, selfish brutes who cared for nothing but their own pleasure. It was much more likely that she was, to use Kate's own phrase, keeping Mr Camerton sweet in the hopes of winning his money from him this evening.

'Well, I hope she will not be too long,' muttered Mrs Wilby. 'We need her to run one of the tables.'

There was no time for more. General and Mrs Sanstead were announced and after that there was a steady stream of arrivals. Susannah organised four guests at a whist table, found a partner to play picquet with Major Crommelly, explaining to him that she was unable to do so as she had to help her aunt entertain all the guests. Later, she gave in to the pleas of a group of young gentlemen to sit down with them to play a noisy game of *vingt-et-un*. She laughed and joked and flirted gently with them all, making sure that not one of them lost more than fifty pounds. Of course she could not dictate to her guests when they played amongst themselves, but it was her strict rule, and she insisted that her aunt and Kate Logan kept to it, despite many of the younger men bragging how much they could lose in one sitting at other houses.

* * *

She was pleased when Kate arrived and she could leave the table and tour the room, making sure that every one of her guests was occupied. No one would guess from her smiles and serene countenance that her mind was elsewhere, that she was watching the clock, and wondering what time Gerald Barnabus might arrive.

There was the bustle of another arrival and Susannah looked up hopefully. It was with mixed feelings that she saw Lord Markham and Mr Camerton walk in. Aunt Maude was already near the door to welcome them so Susannah made no attempt to approach. She watched Mr Camerton seek out Mrs Logan and join her table, while the viscount was persuaded to sit down with his hostess for a game of loo. Susannah could relax a little, at least until the game broke up and she saw the viscount crossing the room towards her.

The tug of attraction was as strong as ever. He moved between the tables with lithe grace, his tall, athletic form clad in the uniform black evening coat and black knee-breeches. She was forcibly reminded of a hunting panther.

And she was the prey.

Shaking off such nonsensical notions Susannah greeted him coolly, which he did not seem to notice. Her hand went automatically into his grasp without her even realising it. As he bowed she gazed at his dark head, trying to calm the fierce tattoo that was beating within her breast as his lips skimmed her fingers. It was as much as she could do to stand still. She must talk to Kate about what these sensations might mean— some instinct told her that Aunt Wilby would not give her an honest answer.

'Miss Prentess.' He straightened, subjecting her to that glinting smile. There was something else in his eyes, a dangerous recklessness that did nothing to calm her pulse. She withdrew her fingers, resisting the urge to cradle them in her other hand. She must act naturally, to treat him as she would any other guest.

'Are you tired of Lanterloo, my lord?'

'For the moment. I came to see if you would play picquet with me.'

She managed a soft laugh.

'You know I will not, my lord.'

'Then for the moment I shall be an observer.'

'As you wish.' He made no attempt to move out of her way. 'How long do you intend to remain in Bath, my lord?'

'That depends.'

'Upon what?'

As soon as the words were uttered she knew she had fallen into his trap. He turned his dark eyes upon her again. She had no doubt that those handsome features and charming smile had undone many a young lady. Flirting with the other young gentlemen of Bath had always seemed an innocent, harmless pastime, but with Lord Markham no remark was ever innocent or harmless. Once again she found breathing difficult, she knew the colour was fluctuating in her cheeks. She wanted to move closer to that lean, muscular body and it was almost a physical effort to keep her distance.

'Mr Barnabus!'

The butler's sonorous announcement could not have been better timed.

She blinked, as if woken from a trance, and with a hurried 'excuse me!' she stepped past him and moved swiftly across the room.

'Mr Barnabus.' She held out her hands to him. 'You are very welcome.' She leaned a little closer, saying quietly, 'Well? Have you been to Florence House?'

He squeezed her hands.

'Yes. You may be easy. I have seen Tyler and given him the money. He will begin the new work next week.'

Susannah gave a little sigh of relief, her smile growing.

'Thank you, I can never tell you how grateful I am to you.' She tucked her hand into his arm and led him further into the room.

'I see my cousin is here,' he remarked. 'Would it—?' He stopped, looking about to make sure he could not be overheard. 'I do not like to keep things from him. May I tell him where I have been, why I am so late?'

'Oh good heavens, no!' she gasped, horrified.

'But Jasper is a great gun. I am sure he would understand—'

'And I am sure he would not.' She laid her hand on his sleeve, saying urgently, 'Please, Gerald, on no account would I have the viscount know anything about this.' When he looked uncertain she added, 'You promised. When I explained to you about Florence House, you gave me your word that you would not tell a soul.'

'Oh very well, Susannah, if you insist.'

'I do.' She squeezed his arm. 'Thank you, Gerald. Now what can I do to reward you? Shall we play at macao together?'

Jasper watched the little scene from across the room. There was no doubting her pleasure in seeing his cousin, and the boy was as besotted as ever. He had noticed when he had kissed her hand that she wore no rings— why should they keep their betrothal a secret? They were both of age and Gerald's nature was so open, so honest, that he would abhor any subterfuge. His eyes narrowed. It must come from the lady, then. She had secrets, and in his book that made her an unsuitable match for his young cousin.

He looked around for Charles Camerton and saw him sitting at a small table with Mrs

Logan. From the pile of coins at his elbow Jasper guessed that he was winning. That was very good. Now he, too, must continue with his plan.

'How goes it, Aunt?'

Susannah took advantage of a break in the play to speak to Mrs Wilby. The lady shook her head, making the lilac ostrich feathers on her turban tremble.

'Badly,' she muttered as she collected up the used cards. 'Lord Markham has taken two hundred off me already.'

'And Kate tells me she has just lost fifty pounds to his friend.' Susannah frowned.

'I have never known luck like it,' continued Aunt Maude. 'I admit I am loath to have the viscount play at my table again.'

'Then what do you propose I do with him?' Susannah felt the smile tugging at her mouth, despite the gravity of the situation.

'I do not know, my love, but I pray you will come up with something. He has made me so nervous that I cannot think clearly, and that, you know, is fatal to our success.'

Susannah was well aware of it. One needed a clear head if one was to succeed at card games. She hoped he would play at whist with Major Crommelly and the Sansteads, at least then any losses would not be hers, but the viscount seemed determined to play against Aunt

Maude. Susannah watched as he won another game of loo and pocketed his winnings. A few pounds—a hundred at most. A paltry sum to Lord Markham, but Susannah was well aware that the losses this evening were mounting up. Thus, when the viscount asked if he might take her down to supper she agreed, reasoning that anything she could do to keep him away from her aunt would give that lady some welcome relief. However, as soon as he pulled her hand on to his arm she began to have doubts about the wisdom of being alone with him.

'Perhaps we should ask Mrs Logan and Mr Camerton if they would like to join us...'

'I have already ascertained that they would not.' Something of her disappointment must have shown in her face for he smiled. 'I vow, ma'am, I begin to think you are afraid of being alone with me.'

'Nonsense. Why should that be?'

'My reputation, perhaps?'

'I know nothing of your reputation, Lord Markham. Is it so very bad?'

'Perfectly dreadful,' he replied cheerfully. 'At least it is in London. I am relieved that no one here knows of it.'

She stopped as a sudden worry assailed her.

'And just what is your reputation *for*, my lord—gambling?'

'No. Breaking hearts.' Again his smiling eyes

teased her. He covered her hand with his own
and held it on his sleeve. 'Do you wish to run
away from me now?'

Susannah's chin went up.

'I do not run away from anything, my lord.'

It was still early and the supper room was
empty save for the servants. The viscount
guided her to a table at the far end of the room.

Where we will not be overheard.

She stifled the thought. This was her house,
her staff were in attendance. No harm could
come to her here. The viscount insisted she sit
down and went off to fill a plate for her. Susannah looked at the table, playing with the napkins and the cutlery. She would not watch him:
she was all too aware of the graceful power of
his movements. She would be better gathering
her wits. The viscount had an uncanny knack
of disconcerting her, she must be on her guard.

Susannah kept her eyes lowered until he returned and placed before her a plate filled with
little delicacies.

'I congratulate you, Lord Markham. I gave
you leave to choose for me, and I believe there
is nothing here that I do not like.'

He slipped into the seat opposite and picked
up his napkin.

'I took the opportunity to ask your estimable
butler for his advice.'

She chuckled at that.

'I give you credit for your honesty, at least, sir.'

She applied herself to her food, gradually relaxing. Lord Markham was the perfect companion, asking nothing impertinent, amusing her with little anecdotes. As her nerves settled so her appetite improved and when her plate was empty she looked at the single syllabub glass on the table.

'Is that for you or for me?'

'For you.' He picked up the spoon. 'But I hoped you might let me share the enjoyment.'

She sat back, scandalised.

'No, that is an outrageous idea.'

He glanced around.

'Why? The room is empty at present. Even the servants are not attending.' He scooped out a small spoonful of the syllabub and held it out to her.

Susannah stared at it. She must not. She dare not. Yet she sat forwards, her eyes on that tempting spoonful.

'Go on,' he murmured, his voice low and inviting. 'While no one is watching. Tell me how it tastes.'

He held the spoon closer and automatically her lips parted. She took the sweet, succulent mouthful, felt the flavours burst upon her tongue. Nothing had ever tasted so delicious. Heavens, was this how Eve felt when she had tried the forbidden fruit?

* * *

Jasper watched, entranced. He saw the flicker of her eyelid, the movement of her throat as she swallowed. She ran her tongue across her lips and he felt the desire slam through him. By God, no wonder Gerald was besotted. He tore his eyes away and sat back. He was meant to be seducing *her*, not the other way around.

'Well, Miss Prentess, did you enjoy that?'

She would not meet his eyes. That was perhaps as well. He was not at all sure he could sound so cool if she was looking at him.

'Yes…no.'

'Another spoonful, perhaps?' He dug the spoon into the syllabub again but she lifted her hand.

'No! There are too many people now. We will be seen.'

'But you would like to do it again?'

Her blush gave him the answer but she said hurriedly, 'Of course not. You are quite outrageous, my lord. We will forget that happened, if you please.'

Her voice was perfectly steady but he noted that her hand shook a little as she picked up her napkin and touched her lips. Good. She was off balance, which had been his object. That he, too, was shaken by the moment was unfortunate, but it would not happen again.

'As you wish. But there is something else I

want from you, something that is not at all outrageous.'

'What is that?'

'To play picquet with you.'

'Out of the question. You have already won more than enough from my aunt.'

'I am giving you the chance to win it all back.'

'No.' She rose and shook out her skirts. 'I must return to the drawing room.'

'As you wish.' He held out his arm. The fingers that she laid upon his sleeve trembled a little. He fought down the impulse to put up his free hand and cover them, to protect her. That was not his purpose at all. As they left the room he asked his question again.

'And shall we now play picquet?'

'I have told you, no, my lord.'

He threw her a teasing glance.

'After such a meal do I not deserve some reward?'

The look she gave him was indignant.

'After such a meal you deserve I should not speak to you again!'

Charles Camerton and Mrs Logan were descending the stairs and they waited to let them pass.

'We were just coming down to join you,' Charles addressed them cheerfully. 'Mrs Logan hopes the luck will change after a break.'

Jasper noted the rueful look the widow gave to Susannah as they passed.

'It seems your aunt and your friend are not doing so well this evening,' he commented as they went up the stairs.

'We shall come about.'

'You could recoup everything with a single game of picquet.'

'Or lose even more.'

'Not necessarily.' He had her attention. 'We need not play for money.' He glanced up and down the staircase. They were alone. 'I will wager my diamond pin against...' He paused.

'Yes?'

'Dinner,' he said at last. 'You will join me for dinner at York House on Thursday night.'

Chapter Seven

Madness.

Susannah wanted to shake her head, to tell him she would not countenance such a wager, but her eyes were fixed upon the diamond. It winked at her. It was worth a king's ransom. It would more than pay for the repairs to Florence House. She could recover the jewels she had sold today and there might even be sufficient to cover the running costs of the house until she came into her inheritance. She was silent as they made their way to the top of the stairs and when they reached the landing she allowed him to draw her to one side.

'Well, madam, will you accept?'

She ran her tongue over her lips.

'Dinner, you say?'

'Yes.'

'Alone?'

'Of course.'

It was not to be thought of. To have dinner with him, unescorted, would ruin her reputation.

Only if it was discovered.

As if reading her thoughts he continued, 'You need have no fear. The hotel is very quiet at present and you may come veiled. My man will serve us and he is very…discreet.'

'It seems you have thought of everything, my lord.'

'I like to think so.'

'If I win you will give me the diamond.'

'I will.'

'And if I lose, I will have dinner with you at your hotel. Nothing more.'

'Nothing more.'

'We will play the best of three games,' she declared.

'If that will suit you.' The viscount bowed.

'Perfectly.' Having made her decision, she led the way into the drawing room and headed for the empty table in the corner, collecting several new packs of playing cards on her way.

Susannah unwrapped the first pack, thankful that she had taken only a small glass of wine with her supper. She drew the low card and shuffled, holding out the cards for the viscount to cut.

She could do this. It was merely a case of steady nerves and keeping a mental note of all the discards. She had done it hundreds of times before. As dealer she knew she must be on the defensive in the first game, but she had a strong hand and after making her discards she was slightly ahead on points when play started. Her optimism was dented when the viscount won the final trick.

'You were unlucky.' He reached for a new pack. 'But you showed some skill. You may do better this time.'

'I shall indeed.'

She studied her hand and chose her discards carefully. By the time play started she felt sure she had the stronger hand. Winning the first trick boosted her confidence and she played with conviction, narrowly winning the second game. The third, however, started badly and ended worse. The viscount won every trick.

'Capotted,' she declared, carefully putting down her cards. She sank her teeth into her bottom lip. She must admit defeat gracefully. 'Congratulations, my lord. You have won.'

'You play very well, Miss Prentess. I think you deserve one last chance.' He drew the diamond pin from his neck cloth and placed it on the table between them. 'What say you we play one more game, winner takes all?'

She laughed. It sounded a trifle reckless, even to her own ears.

'What do I have to lose?'

She reached out to take the pin between her thumb and finger. The viscount's hand closed over hers. A sudden flicker of candlelight made his eyes gleam with a devilish glow.

'There is one minor alteration to the terms of our wager.' His voice was smooth, as cold and deadly as steel. 'If I win this game you come to the hotel for dinner and you stay. All night.'

With a gasp she drew back. Unmoved, he continued.

'You have my word I will not seduce you. I will not even touch you without your permission. But you will stay in my rooms *until morning*.'

'What is the point of your assurances?' she challenged him. 'I shall be ruined whether you touch me or no.'

'Only if word of it gets out. And I shall tell no one.'

She sat up very straight, staring at him.

'Why are you doing this? Why force me to dine with you and stay in your rooms if you do not want to…to seduce me?'

His smile sent a shiver running down her back.

'Oh I want to seduce you, madam, but I have never yet forced any woman to accept my advances. So what do you say to the wager, Miss Susannah Prentess? A diamond worth thousands against a night with me?'

Susannah stared down at the glittering gem.

She had beaten him once, and only lost the third game by ill luck. She had his measure now. Surely it was worth the risk. She realised that she was more of a gambler than she had ever known.

Slowly and deliberately she unwrapped a new pack.

'My trick, I believe, Miss Prentess. And my game.'

Susannah put down her cards. It had not even been close. The viscount had started with the strongest hand, and although she had recovered a couple of tricks the outcome had never been in doubt. She swallowed, suddenly feeling very numb. When she managed to speak, her voice seemed to belong to some other creature, someone calm and not at all shaken by the thought of what she had agreed.

'What time do you want me to join you on Thursday?'

'Shall we say seven o'clock? My man will meet you at the entrance, you will not need to announce yourself at the desk.'

She raised her chin.

'What if I do not come? What if I refuse to honour the wager?'

His eyes rested upon her. There was no hint of blue in them now. They were slate grey, dark and implacable.

'You will come. It is not in your nature to go back on your word.'

The little flicker of defiance died.

'You are right.' She put her hands on the table to steady herself as she rose to her feet. 'If you will excuse me, I have neglected my other guests long enough.'

'Of course.' He stood, his bow the perfect mix of deference and respect. 'Until Thursday, Miss Prentess.'

When she had gone Jasper resumed his seat. He took up the diamond pin and carefully secured it amongst the folds of his neckcloth. He had never before pursued a woman who was so reluctant to succumb to his advances. For an instant his conscience pricked him. He could be ruining an innocent woman.

No. He was *saving* his innocent cousin. Susannah Prentess must never marry Gerald. How that came about was up to her—if she refused to give him up, then Jasper would make sure Gerald knew about her visit to York House. His cousin might be naïve, but he would not countenance marriage to a woman who had been unfaithful to him.

'Your visitor, my lord.'

Peters ushered the veiled figure into the small

parlour that doubled as a dining room and went out again, shutting the door behind him.

'Welcome, ma'am.'

Jasper went towards her. She stood unmoving, and at last he reached out and lifted the veil from her face. She allowed him to remove her cloak and bonnet. He noted the pleated muslin around her shoulders, ending in a fashionable neck ruff. Chosen deliberately, he suspected, to hide her charms. Her gown was a deep sea-green silk, with a matching silk cord tied in a bow beneath her breasts. The ends of the cord hung down almost to the hem and were decorated with silk tassels that bobbed and shimmered whenever she moved, drawing the eye towards the matching shoes and the occasional glimpse of a dainty ankle. Her hair was caught up in a knot on her head, from which a few golden curls dangled enticingly over her ears and glinted in the candlelight. She had never looked more beautiful, or more frightened.

He took her hand.

'You are ice-cold,' he remarked, drawing her down on to a sofa before the fire.

'I took a chair. I did not want any of my people to know my destination.'

'What of Mrs Wilby?'

'My aunt has gone to the Fancy Ball at the Upper Rooms with Mrs Logan. I told them I was...unwell.'

Again he was obliged to crush a prickle of conscience. He was doing this for Gerald. There need be no adverse consequences of this evening, as long as the lady agreed to his terms.

'There is no need for anyone to know you are here, except my man, Peters, and I can vouch for his discretion.' He smiled, hoping to dispel some of the anxiety in her face. 'I have sent him off for the night. There will be no one to disturb us.' He pointed to the table on the far side of the room. 'You see your dinner; everything is there so we may serve ourselves, when you are ready.'

'I am ready now. Let us get on.' She tugged off her gloves. 'I have urgent business that takes me out of Bath early tomorrow morning.'

She stalked to the table. Her whole demeanour indicated that she wanted to get this over with as quickly as possible. She was not intent upon flattering him, Jasper thought ruefully, as he poured wine into two glasses.

'Miss Prentess, we have a long evening ahead of us. It would pass much easier if we observe the basic civilities.' He handed her a glass. 'Will you cry quits with me, at least until we have finished our meal?'

There was a stormy look in her eyes, but after a brief hesitation she gave a little nod.

'By all means, my lord.'

'Good.' He held out her chair, his eyes drawn to the smooth curve of her neck between the frilled edge of the ruff and her upswept hair. He resisted the temptation to bend and plant a gentle kiss there—she was not to be won by such a liberty.

Susannah remained upright on her chair, her nerves at full stretch. She did not understand the man. The air was thick with tension, every word, every gesture, seemed loaded with meaning. When she had taken her seat all she could think of was his hands on the chair behind her, just inches from her shoulders. It made her skin tingle. He had not touched her, and when he took his own seat he looked cool and at his ease. From the soup to the syllabub he served her with skill and courtesy, carving for her the most delicate slices from the roast duck, helping her to a portion of the sole in red wine, a sliver of the potato pudding. There was never a hint that she was anything more than an honoured guest, but all the time she was aware of him sitting across the table from her. She kept her feet tucked beneath her chair lest they should accidentally brush his.

She watched his hands as he served her, remembering how he had held out the syllabub when he had taken her down to supper at Royal Crescent, his long fingers holding the spoon to her lips, the wonderfully decadent sweetness of the soft mixture on her tongue. Of course she would not allow him such outrageous freedom again, but there was no denying that the syllabub set before her this evening was dull and lifeless in comparison.

Her lips were dry, but she would not run her tongue across them. That would show weakness and might rouse in him the desire she suspected was just below the surface. Yet he insisted he did not wish to seduce her, that he would do nothing without her permission. She sipped thoughtfully at her wine. Was this tension, the awareness, only within her? A surreptitious glance across the table showed that he was watching her, a faint smile on his handsome face.

And he *was* handsome. Sinfully so. She thought back to when they had danced together, remembering the covetous looks of the other ladies. How they would envy her, here alone with him. It must be the dream, the fantasy, of so many females. Yet Susannah knew it should remain as nothing more than a fantasy—the reality of what could lead from such an encounter as this was too horrendous, too devastating to consider. She must be on her guard against the feelings he aroused in her. How many times had she heard a poor, misguided girl say, 'I could not help myself'?

* * *

'If you have eaten your fill, ma'am, shall we retire from the table? It would be more comfortable to sit before the fire.'

The viscount's words dragged her back from her reverie. He came around the table and held out his hand to her. Not by the flicker of an eyelid would she admit to the flash of awareness that shot through her when she placed her hand in his. She refused to lean upon him, even though her knees threatened to give way beneath her and her whole body was tingling and alive in a way that she had never known before. Her breasts were hard, pushing against the thin silk of her bodice and there was an ache of desire low down in her belly. She felt as if she was caught in some giant web. It wrapped around her, easing her closer towards her escort. When they reached the sofa it took all her effort to push against that invisible web and place herself at the very end, as far from that disturbing presence as it was possible to be.

The viscount did not appear to notice. Susannah held her breath, ready to leap up should he seat himself too close, or press himself up against her, but instead he stood a little to one side, looking down at her.

It was unbearable. If he had pounced, leered or directed lewd innuendo towards her she would have known how to react, but there was nothing lover-like or menacing in his behaviour. They might have been the best of friends, enjoying a meal together. Save that they were not friends. They were strangers, and they were totally alone in his suite of rooms in the most expensive hotel in Bath. Taking her courage in her hands, Susannah forced herself to look up and ask him a direct question.

'Why are you doing this?'

He hesitated a heart's beat before replying.

'I want to make sure you do not marry my cousin.'

She blinked at him. Was that all? Relief brought the first real smile of the evening to her face.

'Then you have gone to a great deal of trouble for nothing, my lord. I have already told you I do not mean to marry him, and I am pretty sure Gerald has told you the same.'

'I saw you,' he said. 'Coming out of the jewellers on Milsom Street.'

She raised her brows.

'And that convinced you we are to be married? You are very quick to jump to conclusions.'

'Then tell me what you were doing there.'

'I will not.'

'Then tell me where you go almost every morning, when you drive out of Bath in your carriage—and pray do not try to fob me off, I have seen you.'

'Very well, I will say nothing then.'

'You are an extremely obstinate woman, Miss Prentess.'

'And you are a fool,' she retorted. 'I told you at the outset I had no designs upon your cousin. Gerald has come to terms with that, so why cannot you?'

'You make use of him unmercifully.'

'He is happy to be of assistance to me.'

'You sent him off on an errand—'

'I did.'

'Where did he go?'

'That is none of your business.' She waved her hand. 'I doubt you would approve, if you knew.'

'But it might have stopped me from going to these extraordinary measures to prevent your liaison.'

His retort merely made her shake her head at him, smiling.

'You have led yourself a merry dance, have you not, my lord?'

He sat down beside her.

'It seems I have been well and truly bamboozled.'

He looked at her and his lips twitched. The corners of his mouth turned up. Susannah stifled a giggle, he tried not to chuckle, but the next moment both of them were laughing so hard they could not sit upright, but leaned against each other, helpless with mirth. He put his arm around her to support them and, still giggling, she turned towards him.

The laughter died away, but Susannah found she was still smiling, still looking into those dark, dark eyes that held nothing now but warmth and good humour. Without thinking she put up her hand to cup his cheek.

'How foolish you were to doubt me,' she whispered.

He turned his head to press a kiss into the palm of her hand and as he did so his arms slid around her. It seemed the most natural thing in the world to look up a little more, to invite his kiss and when his lips met hers it was as if the whole world relaxed with a sigh. She leaned into him, her lips parting under the soft pressure of his mouth. His tongue dipped into her, drawing on the ache that reached right through her body, down to her groin.

She wound her arms around him and kissed him back, tangling her tongue with his, pressing herself closer. Every inch of her skin was alive to the feel of his hands through the thin layers of her gown. When he stopped kissing her and slid one hand beneath her knees, lifting her effortlessly into his arms, she did not protest, but pressed her face against his neck, breathing in that faint, familiar scent she had come to associate with him and planting gentle kisses on the pulse beating beneath his skin.

He carried her through to the bedroom. A fire burned in the hearth, and candles flickered in the wall sconces, giving the room a warm, welcoming glow. He did not pause but made straight for the bed where he laid her on the covers. Her arms were still around his neck and she drew him to her, impatient to feel his mouth on hers again. He obliged, covering her mouth as he stretched out beside her, measuring her length with his body, arousing in her feelings she could not control.

She was almost swooning, transported to another world by the sensations he was creating in her. He had removed her ruff and was now kissing her throat, his hands unfastening the drawstring on her bodice so that he could caress her breasts. They were taut and hard, pressing against his questing fingers and when he began to circle one tender nub with his thumb she groaned aloud, her head going back as the pleasure of it surged through her whole body.

Susannah reached out for him. She did not know when he had cast off his jacket and waistcoat, but there was only the thin linen shirt between her hands and his flesh. She could feel the hard outline of his back, the contours of his shoulders, his spine. It was all so new, so exhilarating. She gasped as his mouth replaced the thumb at her breast and her body responded, softening, the very bones liquefying. His hand smoothed over her silken skirts, pushing them aside to stroke her thigh. She was drowning in the pleasure of him, opening, turning towards his questing fingers, inviting him to go further, to explore her fully.

Susannah moved sensuously against the covers. She had not known it could be so wondrous, this attraction between a man and a woman. That she could feel so alive, so at one with another person. Was it always like this? Was this how it had been for...

Memories and cold fear returned.

'*No.*' She was seized by panic and tried to push him off. 'No, please. Please, don't do this.'

Immediately he stopped and drew away. Instead of relief she felt merely chilled and bereft.

'Susannah? What is it, my dear, what is wrong?'

She rolled away from him and scrabbled to sit up, hugging herself.

'I never meant— I should never— I am so ashamed.' She buried her face in her hands as hot tears burned her cheeks. Trembling, she waited for him to curse her roughly for her wanton behaviour, to swear, maybe even to lash out at her.

After a deathly silence broken only by her

muffled sobs she felt his hand on her shoulder. A light touch. Soothing, not threatening.

'I beg your pardon, Susannah. This is all my fault. I never intended… Oh, hell and damnation, what a coil!'

His gentleness made her cry even harder. He shifted until he was sitting beside her and gently pulled her against him.

'I promised you I would do nothing without your consent, my dear. If I misunderstood—'

She shook her head, unable to speak, unable to tell him how much she had wanted, *relished* every touch, every caress.

'I must go—'

He held her tighter.

'No, not yet. It is not yet midnight, there are too many people abroad. Someone might recognise you.'

'Then what shall I do?'

'You must stay here until dawn and I will find you a chair.'

'I cannot stay here, with you.'

'To leave my chambers now would be to risk being seen. You would be ruined.' He exhaled, a long, drawn-out sigh. 'I think I have misjudged you. We must talk.'

'No, not yet.' She held her head in her hands. 'I feel so tired.'

He pulled her unresisting on to the bed.

'Then lie here and sleep.' He added quickly,

'You will be perfectly safe. I promise I shall not molest you again. The bed is wide enough for us both to lie on it without touching.'

Susannah turned away from him and curled herself into a ball. Molest her? He had not molested her. He had awoken her to the delights of her own body. He had seduced her and she had succumbed most willingly. Oh heavens, she was no different from those poor unfortunate girls at Florence House. They too had been seduced by fine words and soft caresses, before they had been abandoned. How could she have been so weak? No wonder young ladies required a chaperon to be with them constantly. She had not known how it could feel, had not realised how wayward her own body could be. She thought of the man lying beside her. There was no doubt he was kind and gentle, but it made him no less a seducer.

She felt the bed move as he slid off it, heard him pad across the room. A moment later there was the soft click as the key turned in the lock. Her worst fears were realised. She was his prisoner. Hot tears pressed against her eyes. It was clear now that his gentle assurances were worthless. He had not kissed her because he wanted to, because he was attracted to her. It was a cold plan devised to protect his cousin. The tears spilled over, burning her cheeks. What a fool she was.

* * *

Jasper came back to the bed and lay down again, keeping very still. He listened to the quiet snuffling beside him. Sympathy put his desire to flight. And he *had* desired her, so much so that he had forgotten his planned seduction, forgotten all about Gerald Barnabus. When he had taken Susannah in his arms he had thought only of possessing her fully, wholly, for himself. Her distress made him realise that somehow he had got it badly wrong. Whatever secrets she had they did not involve marriage to his cousin, he would stake his life on that now.

When she was calmer he would talk to her, assure her that if there was the faintest hint of scandal resulting from this evening then he would do the honourable thing and marry her. But that would come later. For now she needed to sleep, as did he. At least, having locked the door, there was no danger that they would be discovered in this compromising situation by some over-zealous chambermaid coming in early to light the fire.

He dozed, his dreams filled with images of Susannah. He was even aware of the faint trace of flowery perfume he had noticed on her skin when they had kissed. In his dreams she was standing beside him and he reached for her. He sighed when she caught his hands and held them. The fog of sleep lifted and he realised that Susannah really *was* standing beside the bed, but she wasn't holding his hands, she was binding them together.

'What the—?'

'Please do not struggle, my lord, that will only make the bonds tighter.'

He blinked away the final remnants of his dream. She had used the silk cord from her gown to bind his hands together and had tied the cord around the bedpost. He tried to sit up, but his arms were yanked awkwardly towards the post and he collapsed back again.

'What the hell do you think you are doing?'

'I am leaving, and I am making sure you cannot prevent me.' She watched him tug hard against his bonds. 'It is silk, you know, and incredibly strong. I doubt you will break it.'

'There is no need for this. I told you I would not stop you.'

'You also told me you would not touch me,' she retorted.

The candles were guttering in their sockets but there was still sufficient light to see that she looked incredibly desirable with her flushed cheeks and those golden curls in disarray.

'Susannah—'

'Miss Prentess to you.'

'You cannot leave.'

'Oh, yes, I can.' She picked up the key. 'You

should have hidden this, my lord, if you really wanted to keep me your prisoner.'

'Prisoner be damned! I locked the door to protect your honour.'

'Hah!'

He was not surprised as her scathing response, but he tried again.

'Please, Susannah. Think. It is not light yet. It is not safe for you to go out alone.'

'That is not your concern.'

As she walked away to the other room he pulled again at the silk rope, feeling it tighten on his wrists. There was no chance of freeing himself quickly. Frantically he searched his mind for any argument to stop her from leaving.

'But you promised, the wager—'

She returned with her cloak about her shoulders and her bonnet in one hand.

'I have dined with you, and it wants only an hour until dawn, so I have stayed with you until morning. I think you will agree I have fulfilled my part of the wager.' She put on her bonnet and tied the strings. 'I will bid you *adieu.*'

'Good God, woman, you cannot leave me tied up—'

'I can, and I will. Do not worry, your valet will be back in an hour or so. Of course, you might try calling for help, but this could be a little embarrassing to explain, don't you think?'

'Damn it all, Susannah—'

She drew herself up to her full height, and despite the tumbled curls that escaped from her bonnet she was as haughty as any aristocrat.

'You have said quite enough, my lord. Our acquaintance is at an end. You are no longer welcome in my house and I shall not acknowledge you, should we meet in public.'

With that she swept out of the room.

Chapter Eight

Jasper stared at the closed door. One of the candles guttered and went out, increasing the gloom. With a growl of frustration he strained against the silk rope. He was not worried for himself, as Susannah had said, Peters would be back soon, but he did not like to think of her out in the darkened streets alone.

However, there was little he could do about it at present, so he tried to make himself comfortable. The fire had died away to a sullen glow and the air was growing chill, so he wriggled himself under the bedclothes. It took some time but at last he managed to cover himself sufficiently and he settled down to wait for morning.

Susannah kept her veil pulled over her face as she ran through the deserted streets. The ground was covered with a fine dusting of snow and the cold seeped through her thin slippers, numbing her toes. She had always disliked the way the silk tassels knocked against her when she moved, but now she was painfully aware of their lack. It had been her plan to use the cord tonight, if it should become necessary, and it had worked exceedingly well. She felt a twinge of guilt when she thought of leaving the viscount a prisoner. He would never forgive her for that.

A scuffle made her start and look around nervously, but although she saw shadowy figures in the alleyways and heard the occasional bark of a dog as she hurried on, no one approached her and she reached the Crescent without being accosted. She ran down the area steps and used her key to enter through the servants' door, which she had instructed Dorcas to leave unbolted. A single lamp burned in the small servants' hall, and Susannah saw her maid dozing by the dying embers of the fire. She stirred as Susannah secured the door.

'Ooh, mistress, thank the Lord you are back safe.'

'Thank heaven indeed,' murmured Susannah, sinking into a chair.

'My dear ma'am, you are shaking like a leaf.'

'Y-yes. I d-didn't realise how frightened I was.'

Dorcas was wide awake now, and approached her mistress anxiously. 'Heaven help us! If that rascally viscount has harmed you—'

'No, no, it was not Lord Markham,' said Susannah. 'It was coming back alone through the dark streets. And he is not rascally,' she added with something of her old spirit. 'He was merely trying to protect his cousin.'

'Well, 'twasn't right for him to go bullying you to dine alone with him. What Mrs Wilby would say if she knew...'

'It was very wrong of me, I know that.' Now that the danger was over, Susannah felt a great desire to weep and had to fight back the tears. 'It is done, and no one is any the worse.' She glanced out of the window, where the darkness was giving way to the first grey light of dawn. She hoped very much that Peters would return soon and free Lord Markham. Resolutely she turned her thoughts away from the viscount. 'Come along, Dorcas. I must sleep. My carriage is ordered for eight o'clock.'

'Never tell me you are going to Florence House in the morning.'

'You know I must. I have arranged to call for Mrs Logan. We want to see how they go on with the new housekeeper.' She crept up to her room, thankful that the early hour prevented Dorcas from voicing her opinions as they made their way through the silent house.

* * *

When Peters entered the viscount's sitting room at York House Jasper greeted him with an angry bellow. Peters rushed to the bedroom and stopped abruptly in the doorway.

'Well don't stand there gawping,' roared Jasper. 'Untie me!'

'Yes, m'lord, at once, but, what, who—?'

'I should think that was obvious,' growled Jasper, curbing his impatience as Peters struggled with the knots in the silken rope. 'Thank God the maid did not find me like this.'

'Knowing the nature of your engagement last night, I informed the staff that you were not to be disturbed,' replied Peters calmly.

'The devil you did. What time is it?'

'Nearing seven, m'lord.'

'Good. Then we are not too late.' At last he was free and Jasper sat up, rubbing his wrists. 'I want you to send a message to the stables. Have Morton come here. Now.'

'My lord?'

'I want him to go to Royal Crescent as soon as maybe.'

'Sir, if I may be so bold, if the lady is reluctant…' Under his master's frowning gaze the valet shifted uncomfortably from one foot to the other, finally saying in a rush, 'It's not like you, sir, to pursue a woman if she ain't willing.'

Jasper shook his head.

'Willing be damned. That has nothing to do with it. Miss Prentess said she was going out this morning. I want to know where she is bound. I'll find out what her secret is if I have to tear Bath apart!'

By nine o'clock the viscount was washed and dressed in his green riding coat and buckskins. His heavy caped driving coat was thrown over a chair and his hat and gloves rested on the table in readiness. He strode impatiently up and down the sitting room, stopping occasionally to look out of the window, where large feathery flakes of snow could be seen floating down. At last he heard a hasty footstep approaching. Morton entered upon the knock.

'Well?' Jasper barked out the word.

'I saw the carriage setting off, my lord, and followed it, as you ordered. It went as far as a house just this side of Priston. On the Wells Road.'

'And you can find it again?' demanded Jasper, shrugging himself into his driving coat.

'Aye, my lord. The curricle is at the door now, but the weather's turning bad. The snow is beginning to settle.'

'Then the sooner we get started the better.'

The horses were fresh and Jasper had to concentrate to keep them in check as they trotted through the quiet streets. It was early yet, and the snow was keeping all but the very hardy indoors. Once they had crossed the bridge and were settled upon the Wells Road he gave them their heads and they rattled along at a cracking pace. It was snowing heavily now, coating the ground and hedges and making it difficult to see far ahead. Beside him, Morton hunched down into his coat and muttered occasionally about the folly of travelling in such weather. Jasper was beginning to agree with him and was contemplating abandoning his journey when the snow eased and the dense cloud lifted a little.

'There, we shall go on easily now.'

'Aye, my lord, 'til the weather sets in again,' retorted Morton with all the familiarity of an old and trusted retainer. 'I mislike the look of that sky. If you was to ask me we should turn back now.'

Jasper looked up. The grey, sullen clouds matched his mood exactly.

'Well I am not asking you,' he snapped 'You applied goose-fat to the horses' feet, didn't you, to prevent the snow from balling? So we should be good for a few hours yet. We shall turn back once I have discovered Miss Prentess's secret and not before.'

The journey had done much to cool Jasper's temper but nothing to quell his determination to find out what could persuade Susannah to drive out on such a morning. This had nothing to do with Gerald, it was purely for his own satisfaction. His wrists were still sore from that silk rope, but he was not a vindictive man, he bore her no grudge for that... Well, not much of a grudge. The woman intrigued him. She had rejected him, and he was not used to that. On the contrary most women were only too willing to accept his advances.

When he and his twin had entered society as young men they had the advantages of being wealthy and handsome. The ladies had literally fallen at their feet and they had learned to take such adulation as their due. They had flirted outrageously and become known as the dark and notorious Coale twins. Now, Jasper had the added advantage of a title. He had never had to fight for a woman in his life. He had only to cast his discerning eye upon a female and in most cases she would fall eagerly into his arms. If a lady showed any reluctance then he shrugged and moved on. No rancour, no regret.

He wondered if he had become too complacent, arrogant, even, where women were concerned. He had never had to work for their good opinion, merely taken it for granted. He had always assumed that when he eventually fell in love the lady would feel the same and it had come as something of a shock three years ago when he had proposed to Zelah Pentewan and been refused. However, she was head over heels in love with his twin and he could understand that, only berating himself for not discovering the state of the lady's affections before offering her his hand.

Zelah had taught him a salutary lesson and Jasper had been content to leave his heart behind when he returned to town to continue his bachelor lifestyle. The women in London were as eager as ever for his attentions, but somehow the attraction of such a carefree life had palled. Perhaps it was seeing his twin so happily married, but for the past three years Jasper had felt a curious restlessness. He had hidden it well, continued to flirt with all the prettiest ladies, was the most obliging guest at any party, but knowing his heart to be safe at Rooks Tower with his sister-in-law he had never felt the least inclination to offer marriage to any one of the beautiful débutantes paraded before him, much to the chagrin of their hopeful parents. Not one of them had made any impression upon him, had stirred him to make the least effort. Yet here he was, risking his precious team on snow-covered roads to pursue a woman who had made it abundantly clear that she did not want his attentions.

But this was nothing to do with the fact that she was a woman, and a very beautiful one at that. She had got the better of him, and that rankled. Lord, what an arrogant fool he had become!

'Beggin' yer pardon, m'lord, I don't see there's much to laugh at,' grumbled Morton, sinking his chin deeper into his muffler.

'I am laughing at myself,' Jasper told him, still grinning.

'You'll be laughing yerself into the parson's mousetrap if you ain't very careful.'

'What?' Jasper's head whipped round and he stared at his groom. 'I have no interest in the woman in that way. Marriage to such a virago? Good God, I can think of nothing worse.'

'Seems to me you are putting yerself out a great deal over her.'

'Fustian! It's just that there is something smoky about Miss Prentess, and I am determined to find out what it is.'

Jasper gave his attention to his driving. Perhaps he *was* being foolish. He could have paid someone to find out everything about the woman and saved himself the trouble.

'Turning's up here, sir,' said the groom. 'On the right.'

And if this outing did not solve the mystery that is what he would do, he decided as he turned into a narrow lane,

The snow lay inches deep and unbroken through the lane. Jasper proceeded cautiously. There could be deep ruts beneath the snow, waiting to catch the unwary. The track was descending into a wooded valley and the groom pointed out their destination on the far side. Jasper slowed and peered through the trees at the collection of buildings.

'It looks like a gentleman's house, my lord. What will they say to us turning up uninvited?'

'I shall use the weather as my excuse.' Jasper gave a little flick of the whip to move the team on.

Ten minutes later they drew up in front of the house. No one came out to greet them and apart from the smoke spiralling up from a couple of the chimneys there was no sign of life. Jasper jumped down and went to the door. The weathered oak panels shook as he forcefully applied the knocker. A biting wind had sprung up and when a flustered housemaid opened the door he immediately stepped into the hall.

'Good day,' he said pleasantly. 'Pray tell your master or mistress that—'

He got no further. Standing in a doorway at the far end of the hall, and holding a baby in her arms, was Susannah.

Chapter Nine

'Miss Prentess. Good day to you.'

Jasper made his bow, his brain reeling. Whatever he had expected, it was not this. He had seen Susannah's horrified look when he had appeared, but she recovered quickly.

'Lord Markham.' She hesitated and glanced down at the sleeping baby. 'Will you not come in, sir?'

He could see behind her a comfortable parlour with a cheerful fire.

'I would be delighted, madam, but first I must look after the horses, I do not like to leave them standing in this weather.'

He let the words hang and watched her expression carefully. She would like to send him to the rightabout but she knew he would not go quietly. Her gaze shifted to the housemaid still hovering by the door.

'Bessie, direct my lord's groom to the stables, if you please.'

'Thank you.' Jasper followed her into the parlour and shut the door.

As soon as they were alone she turned on him.

'What are you doing here?'

'I followed you.' He stripped off his gloves, surprised to find his hands were shaking slightly. 'I am curious to know what you are about.' There was an odd lightness in his chest, but he dare not ask the question that was now uppermost in his mind. He must be patient. Now he was here she would tell him everything. She must.

She was looking uncertain and his surprise and anger gave way to concern. He said gently, 'Will you not sit down?

She did so, gently settling the baby more comfortably in her arms before fixing her eyes upon him once more.

'My lord, why do you persist in this? I can assure you this has nothing to do with you, or your cousin. Is that not enough for you?'

'No. I want to know what is this place, and why you are here. I will not leave until I have answers.'

With a sigh she sank back in the chair.

'Very well. You are in Florence House, sir. A home for…distressed gentlewomen.'

'And the child in your arms?'

'The son of one of our…guests. He is only a few weeks old. His mother is very tired and the babe was crying so I brought him downstairs to see if I could settle him.'

Jasper realised he had been holding his breath until that moment.

'But why have you kept this so secret?'

Her lip curled.

'You were in Royal Crescent when the Magdalen Hospital was discussed with Amelia Bulstrode and Mrs Farthing. I am sure you overhead the whole. It is considered quite…improper for an unmarried lady to have any interest in such matters. That I have strong views about it is considered shocking enough. If they knew the extent of my involvement—'

'And what *is* the extent of it, Miss Prentess?'

She put up her chin and looked at him defiantly.

'This is my house, one of the properties my uncle left me in his will. When I came to Bath last year I met up again with Mrs Logan. During one of our conversations it emerged that a young lady she knew was with child. She had eloped, left her home and her friends to run off with a man who had sworn to marry her, but later he abandoned her. She could not go back to

her family, and fortunately Kate—Mrs Logan—
came upon her and took her in. When she told
me of it, I too was keen to help the poor girl,
and others like her, so we decided to open up
this house to give them refuge.

'At first we had no idea other than to take
them in and give them somewhere safe to stay
until the baby was born, but it soon became
clear that more was needed. These are gently
bred girls, they are not educated to be anything
other than a gentleman's wife. They need more
skills than that before we can turn them out into
the world again. We teach them housekeeping—
some are good with a needle and can earn their
living as a seamstress, others have a talent for
lacemaking.' She raised her eyes to his. 'We
give these young ladies hope, my lord, and the
opportunity to be independent.'

'And their families, their parents?'

'Most of these girls have been abandoned by
their kin—some are in danger of being packed
off to an asylum, as if…as if their predicament
is some kind of mental affliction. When they
come to us they are assured of anonymity. They
come here and we treat them as guests, not inmates to be punished. At present only those involved in Florence House know of its existence,
and I need that to continue for now, until I have
control of my inheritance and can set up a trust
fund to support it.'

'But if that is the case, how do those young ladies in need know where to find you?'

'We find *them*,' said Susannah. 'After that first unfortunate case, Mrs Logan heard of two more. And household servants gossip a great deal. A maid will know her mistress's situation almost as soon as the lady herself. My own maid is always ready to listen to the gossip, and if a young lady's family is not prepared to support her, then she offers an alternative. We have already helped about a dozen young women.'

'I did not know Bath had so many.'

'Word spreads, my lord. Some of them come from surrounding villages.'

'All very laudable,' he remarked. 'And how successful are you at finding employment for your, ah, guests?'

'Very. That first young lady had a remarkable eye for fashion. Kate and I purchased a house in Henrietta Street. She is now able to pay her rent and is quickly becoming established as a modiste.'

'Ah, would that be Madame Odesse?'

She nodded, smiling a little. 'The very same. I wear her gowns and the fashionable of Bath flock to copy me, but of course that will only continue as long as I maintain my place in Bath society. Odesse employs several of our young ladies as milliners and seamstresses, and she purchases lace from a little group we have es-

tablished in another little house in Bath. They
all earn enough to make a modest living.'

He looked about him.

'But a house like this does not come cheap.'

'No, indeed. And it is in need of repair. We
have made a start, but much more is required.
Once I have control of my uncle's fortune I will
be able to do more, but for now...'

There was a knock at the door and Morton
looked in.

'Beggin' yer pardon, m'lord, but it's started
to snow again, and the wind is picking up. We
had best be going.'

'Yes, very well.' Jasper looked at Susannah.
'Shall I order your carriage to be prepared?'

'I cannot leave.'

Jasper looked at the window. For the first
time he noticed the howling wind rattling the
frame and the soft white flakes swirling around
outside.

'You must, I think, or risk being stuck here,
possibly for days.'

She shook her head.

'There is no one here to look after the girls.
Mrs Gifford, the housekeeper, was obliged to go
away on Tuesday to nurse her sick sister. We engaged a temporary housekeeper, but I am afraid
we were sadly deceived in her. When I arrived
this morning I learned that she had packed her

bags and left yesterday, as soon as the weather began to turn.'

'But *you* cannot stay—surely that was not your intention when you came here today?'

'No, I planned to visit with Mrs Logan.' She frowned a little. 'Only when I called for her I was told she was not at home. These young ladies—girls—are my responsibility, my lord. There are only three of them in the house. The eldest is but nineteen. I cannot abandon them.'

'What of the other servants?'

'There is Bessie, the scullery maid who opened the door to you.'

'That is all, no manservant?'

'Only old Daniel, who lives next to the stables and does a little of the outside work. We decided that the girls would feel more at ease if there were no other menservants in the house.' She glanced at the window. 'You had best be gone, my lord. I would not have you snowbound on my account.'

Susannah shifted in her seat, no longer facing him. She had enough to think about without the viscount being here to distract her. The defection of Mrs Jennings was a blow and she had arrived at Florence House to find the household all on end. Jane had opened the door to her, looking desperately tired. She explained that Lizzie and Violet were too frightened to sleep in their own rooms, so they had spent the night huddled together in one big bed, with Lizzie's baby in its cot beside them. Susannah had helped Bessie to prepare a simple breakfast for them all before sending the girls back upstairs to rest and bringing the baby downstairs to make sure Lizzie's sleep was not disturbed. She had been walking up and down the little parlour, trying to decide what to do next, when she heard the imperious knocking on the front door and looked out to find Lord Markham standing in the hall, his broad shoulders made even wider by the many-caped driving coat so that he appeared to fill the small space.

For one dizzy, heart-stopping moment she thought he had come to rescue her, before common sense reasserted itself. She did not need rescuing, and Lord Markham was more her nemesis than a knight in shining armour. The sooner he left the better, then she could concentrate on the problem of what to do here.

'If you are staying, then so, too, am I.'

'Nay, my lord!'

'You cannot do that!'

Susannah's voice and the groom's protests were immediate but had no apparent effect upon the viscount.

'Morton, go back to the stables and make sure the horses are bedded down for the night.

I take it there is space for my groom to sleep somewhere?'

He addressed this last question to Susannah, who answered distractedly, 'Yes...yes, there is plenty of sleeping space above the stables—my coachman will show him where to find straw to make a comfortable bed—and Daniel will arrange to feed him, too, but...my lord, I cannot, *cannot* put you up here.'

He dismissed his groom before turning back to her.

'You have no choice.' He looked faintly amused at her consternation. 'Pray do not look so alarmed. I am not expecting you to wait upon me.'

'But, last night—'

'We will forget that, for now.'

His smile grew, and with it her embarrassment. The baby stirred in her arms and she got up, murmuring that she must take him back to his mother. The viscount opened the door for her and with a mutter of thanks she fled from the room. The young ladies were gathered in the upstairs sitting room, but Bessie had informed them of the viscount's arrival and they looked anxiously to Susannah for an explanation.

'Who is he, Miss Prentess?' asked Lizzie as Susannah gently handed over the baby. 'Has he come to fetch you away?'

'He s-spoke to me at the ball once.' Violet

Anstruther's voice quavered. 'Perhaps Papa sent him to fetch me...'

'You may all be easy, the viscount has not come to take anyone away. He is an acquaintance of mine and a perfect gentleman.' Should she have crossed her fingers against the lie? Despite all that had happened between them it felt like the truth. 'He is stranded here in the snow, as are we all now.' She hoped she sounded suitably reassuring. 'You are at liberty to come downstairs and join us, if you wish.'

This suggestion was quickly rejected, the girls declaring that they would prefer to remain above stairs.

'Very well, I believe there is a little soup left, so I will ask Bessie to heat it through and bring it up for you. I will ask her to bring more coal upstairs, too, so that you may keep the fire built up in here. Then we must think what we can do for dinner tonight.' She looked at the three girls. Lizzie was confined to her bed and had her baby to nurse. Jane was leaning back in her chair, her hands rubbing over her extended stomach. Only Violet Anstruther looked fit enough to help with the cooking, but when Susannah suggested it, she immediately shook her head and admitted that she did not know how to do anything more than boil a small kettle to make tea. She looked so frightened at the prospect of venturing into the kitchen that Susannah did not press her.

'I will help,' offered Jane, 'when my back has stopped aching.'

'No, you must stay here,' said Susannah quickly. 'Bessie and I will manage.'

'At least the larder is full,' observed Jane. 'I made sure Mrs Jennings sent Daniel for the supplies yesterday before she left the house.'

'I cannot forgive the woman for leaving you all in such a way,' declared Susannah. 'As soon as I can get back to Bath I will make arrangements for another housekeeper to come in to look after you until Mrs Gifford returns.'

She went downstairs to find that the viscount had built up the fire in the parlour. A patch of melting snow near the hearth caught her eye.

'Did you send Bessie out to find my footman? I meant to do it before I went upstairs, and charge him with bringing in coal for the fire.'

'No, I brought it in myself.' He laughed at her shocked countenance. 'As Gerald told you, Miss Prentess, I am not at all high in the instep.' He pointed to a tray on the side table. 'I also found the coffee pot, so I have made some. I thought we might sit by the fire and take a cup together.'

'Why, thank you, sir. But I should really be looking out what we can eat for dinner...'

'There will be time for that presently. Sit down and talk to me.'

She allowed herself to be escorted to a chair and handed a steaming cup. She had to admit that after the trials of the morning it was pleasant just to sit, even if she was determined it could not be for long.

'I have been thinking about the cost of running this house,' he began. 'I take it Mrs Wilby's card parties help to pay for it.'

'Yes.'

'And you encourage the gentlemen of your acquaintance to attend, upon your aunt's invitation, of course.'

She shot him a defiant look.

'And why not? It is the *gentlemen* who have made this place necessary.'

Jasper sat back, surprised.

'Is that what you really think?'

'Of course. They court the young ladies, flatter and cajole them into allowing them to…' She paused to put down her cup, using the moment to gather her thoughts before continuing. 'These are young, innocent girls who have fallen for a seducer's lies, heedless of the consequences.' A dull flush coloured her cheeks as she remembered her own weakness. 'It is too easily done, I fear.'

'So you invite the men to your drawing room and fleece them.'

'I do not *cheat*, sir. It is merely that we—Aunt Maude, Mrs Logan and I—we are all better at cards than most of our guests. And we never take more than fifty guineas at any one sitting.'

He ran a hand through his hair.

'Susannah, it does not matter if it is fifty guineas or five thousand, you are still taking money off these people.'

'It is not illegal.'

'No, but it is not *right*. You are in effect running a gaming house.'

She crossed her arms, as if in defence.

'It is for a good cause.'

'Then tell your guests what you are about. Let them choose whether they want to support you.'

She gave a bitter laugh.

'Support a house for fallen women? You have seen the reaction when one mentions such a subject. They would not give so much as a sou.'

'You should set up a committee, get some of the Bath tabbies on your side.'

'No. I prefer to do it my way.'

Jasper sat forwards, frowning.

'But why? Why do you want to punish the young men so? Not all of them are wild and reckless, you know. Gerald Barnabus, for example.' He saw the flash of consternation in her eyes, before the lashes swept down to veil them and a new suspicion hit him. 'Does Gerald know about this place?'

There was a brief hesitation before she replied.

'Yes. I let something slip and was obliged to tell him. He has been very helpful.'

'And that is why you took two hundred guineas from him last year.'

'Yes. We needed extra funds urgently, to set up the house for Odesse.'

He kept his eyes on her face.

'Why was he escorting you to the jewellers the other day? You may as well tell me. If you do not I shall find out from Gerald when I get back to Bath.'

She was twisting her hands together in her lap and he remained silent, waiting for her to speak.

'I needed money to pay the builder. I asked Gerald to come with me to the jewellers, to sell some of my aunt's jewels.'

'Your inheritance.'

She hung her head.

'I thought the money could be better spent here.'

'And just what did you sell?'

'An emerald set, necklace, ear-drops, aigrette—totally unsuited to me.'

'While you are single, yes.' Jasper imagined how well the stones would look against her creamy skin, accentuating the green flecks in her eyes, and nestled amongst those glowing curls. 'Once you are married—'

'I shall never marry.'

The words were uttered with such force,

such conviction, that Jasper's brows snapped together.

'That is a bold statement.'

'It is true, nevertheless.' She rose, shaking out her skirts. 'I have seen how men treat women. It shall never happen to me. Now if you will excuse me—'

'No, I will not.' He jumped up and caught her arm. 'You are very harsh upon our sex.'

'And with some reason, my lord. Witness your own behaviour last night!'

'No,' he said slowly. 'I think it goes beyond that.'

She looked alarmed and tried to free her arm.

'Can you wonder if I am harsh, when the girls here tell me such tales? Now let me go, sir.'

'Not until you tell me.' He pulled her round to face him. 'I saw it in your eyes last night. You were terrified.'

Her eyes flashed.

'You flatter yourself!'

'Not of me, but something has occurred. Something in your past.' She stopped struggling and turned her head away, her lip trembling. He said gently, 'Will you not tell me? Susannah—'

He was interrupted by a hasty knock on the door and he released her arm just as Bessie rushed in. She did not appear to notice them stepping apart, too caught up in her own news which she uttered in a scared, breathless voice.

'I beg your pardon, Miss Prentess, but—Miss Jane sent me. She says…she says the baby is coming!'

Susannah did not exclaim or cry out. She stood for a moment, hands pressed to her cheeks as she dragged her thoughts to what the maid was saying.

'We must send for the midwife.' She went to the window. 'At least we must try.'

Bessie peered over her shoulder.

'But the snow is very thick, ma'am, and 'tis drifting.'

'My footman, Lucas, should go. He is young and strong.'

'It would be safer if there were two,' said Jasper. 'Morton shall go with him. Give me the midwife's direction and I will go out to the stables and tell them.'

Susannah did not hesitate. Instructions were given and even before the viscount had left the house she ran upstairs. Jane was leaning against the wall, clutching at her stomach.

'Mrs Gifford told me these pains would come,' she gasped. 'Slowly at first, but then more frequently.'

'And how do they seem to you?' asked Susannah.

Jane gave her a strained smile. 'They are coming very quickly. I hope we can wait for the midwife.'

'Oh my heavens, what shall we do?'

Susannah turned at the anguished cry to find Violet Anstruther standing in the doorway. Quickly she ushered the girl out of the room, telling her to look after Lizzie and her baby, then she turned her attention back to Jane, who was pacing up and down, her face very pale.

She calculated that the midwife could not be here for at least another hour and she busied herself with preparing the room, bringing in a crib and blankets and clothes for the new baby, then she helped Jane out of her gown. All the time she kept up a cheerful dialogue which was punctuated by Jane's gasps each time the contractions took hold.

The heavy cloud had brought an early dusk and Susannah had given orders for the lamps to be lit. It was with relief that she heard the thud of the outer door and the low rumble of voices in the hall. She ran down the stairs. The chill of the air as she descended confirmed that the front door had been opened, but there were only three figures in the hall: the viscount, his groom and Lucas, her footman.

The two servants were covered in snow.

'I beg your pardon, miss, but we didn't make it.' Lucas blew on his hands and his teeth chattered when he spoke. 'The snow is breast high across the road and we couldn't get through.

And we daren't risk crossing the fields for the snow is falling so thick 'tis impossible to see more than an arm's length in front of you and we wouldn't have known which direction we should go.'

Susannah tried hard not to let her disappointment show.

'Very well, thank you for your efforts. If you go into the kitchen Bessie will find you something hot to drink.'

'If you don't mind, miss, we'll head back to the stables,' put in Morton. 'The old man said he would keep a good fire and have a kettle of something ready when we got back.'

'Yes, yes, you had best go then, and get yourselves warm.' The viscount waved them away and turned to look at Susannah. 'This is bad news,' he murmured, drawing her into the warmth of the parlour. 'What will you do now?'

'I must go back upstairs, I fear Jane is very near her time.'

'Is there anything I can do?' His readiness to help was comforting, but she shook her head.

'Not unless you are a man-midwife.'

'I regret I cannot help you there, my only experience of such things is when my favourite pointer whelped at Markham.'

Despite her anxiety she smiled at that.

'Then you know less than I do. I was here last year when one of the girls was in labour. She was very frightened and the midwife asked me to sit with her, to calm her.'

'So you are not totally inexperienced.'

Susannah clasped her hands together.

'On that occasion the midwife had very little to do. The baby came into the world quite easily. If Jane's birth is like that then there is nothing to worry about, but if not—'

She broke off, the horrors of what might happen crowding in on her. The viscount took her hands; the steady strength of his fingers around hers was oddly calming.

'We have no choice but to try our best.' A faint cry from above made him lift his head. He squeezed her hands. 'Do you feel up to this?'

She met his eyes.

'As you have said, there is no option. I must do what I can.'

'Then go back upstairs. If you need me you only have to call.'

The hours ticked by. Susannah sat with Jane while the contractions continued. She had heard that sometimes these pains could die away, and the baby might not come for days. For a while she hoped that perhaps this would be the case and they would be able to send again for the midwife in the morning, but as the evening wore on Jane grew more restless and the pains more frequent. Susannah fetched a bowl of warm water to bathe Jane's face and hands, and later Bessie came up with a tray, saying the viscount had ordered her to bring up tea and bread and butter for them both.

Susannah did not touch the food but she sipped gratefully at the tea, while Jane refused everything. She shifted uncomfortably on the bed, becoming more and more restless until eventually she was gasping and straining. Susannah knew the crisis must be very near now and she held Jane's hand tightly, praying that nothing would go wrong.

The birth, when it came, was mercifully brief. Jane was crying out with the pain while Susannah stood by her, feeling helpless as she could do nothing but wipe her brow and murmur inadequate words of comfort. Jane's anguish was growing by the moment and Susannah was on the point of calling for help when she saw with a mix of terror and delight that the baby was coming. Tentatively she reached out to cradle the head while she continued to encourage Jane. She watched, entranced, as the little body gradually emerged and she found herself crying with relief. The tiny form looked perfect and its angry cries were oddly reassuring. With infinite care she wiped the baby and wrapped it in a soft cloth before lifting it into its mother's arms.

'Look, Jane,' she whispered, her voice hushed with awe and wonder. 'You have a little girl.'

Chapter Ten

~~~~~~~

While Jane reclined against a bank of pillows and sleepily watched her baby taking its first, tentative feed, Susannah summoned Bessie to help clear up, then she went to tell Violet and Lizzie that all was well. The hour was advanced by the time she made her way downstairs once more and there was no sign of the viscount in the parlour. She followed the rumble of voices through to the kitchen, where she stopped in the doorway, staring in amazement.

A black range had been installed in the huge fireplace and the viscount was standing before it, stirring the contents of a saucepan. He had removed his jacket, rolled back his voluminous shirt sleeves and tied an apron over his pristine white waistcoat. He glanced round.

'Ah, you are come down at last. Do come in

and shut the door. Bessie told me the news. How are your patients?'

Susannah smiled at the term.

'They are not *my* patients. I did very little, and we still need the midwife or a doctor to visit them as soon as the weather improves. But for now mother and baby are both well and resting.' She looked towards the scullery, where Bessie was cleaning dishes. 'You have had dinner, then. I am glad.'

'There was a leg of mutton in the meat safe, so I have made collops for everyone.' He reached for a frying pan and settled it over the fire. 'Bessie and the ladies above stairs have already dined, but I was waiting for you to come down so that I could cook yours fresh for you.'

'Oh, but there is no need, I am so tired, a little soup will do...'

'Nonsense, you need to eat.' He came across and took her arm, guiding her to the cook's armchair at the head of the table. 'Sit down there and do not move, save to drink the glass of wine I have poured for you.'

She gave a shaky laugh. 'I do not think I *could* move if I wanted to, I am quite worn out.'

Outside the wind was buffeting the house and hurling icy pellets against the windows, but the kitchen was warm and comfortable, and Susannah was content to sit back and relax. She watched, entranced, as the viscount moved around the kitchen with all the assurance of an accomplished chef. Bessie, too, was completely at home, pottering between the kitchen and the scullery, responding to his instructions as if it was the most natural thing in the world to be directed by a peer of the realm.

'I did not realise how hungry I had become,' murmured Susannah as the viscount slid a plate in front of her.

'No, you have been far too busy.' He brought his own plate to the table, along with his glass and the decanter of wine. Before he sat down he went to the scullery.

'If you have finished those dishes you may go to bed, Bessie. The rest can wait until the morning.'

'Very good, m'lud. Goodnight, ma'am.' The scullery maid bobbed an awkward curtsy and hurried away. Susannah stared after her, shaking her head.

'I am amazed. You have fed everyone, with only Bessie to help you?'

'I have indeed. Her understanding is not great, but knowing everyone else was occupied upstairs, she was only too willing to help where she could. She showed me where to find everything, including Mrs Gifford's secret store of wine and cider, something I understand she did *not* share with Mrs Jennings! I hope you don't mind, but I used almost a whole bottle of claret to make the sauce for the collops.'

'Violet told me Bessie had brought them dinner, but she did not say... that is, I thought she had served them up a little bread and ham.'

'Oh, I think we did better than that.' Meeting her wondering gaze, he laughed. 'I had an eccentric uncle. When we were younger, my twin and I used to stay with him at his hunting lodge in Leicester, where we would fend for ourselves. We would hunt and fish and cook whatever we could find. My uncle was firmly of the opinion that a man should never be wholly dependent upon his servants, neither his valet nor his cook.'

'Then I am greatly indebted to your eccentric uncle,' she replied, savouring the delightful combination of flavours on her plate.

He grinned as he refilled their glasses. 'You were otherwise engaged and it soon became clear to me that if I did not do something we would be obliged to call in old Daniel to feed everyone.'

'You did very well. I am impressed by your abilities, my lord.'

'As I am with yours. Not many ladies of my acquaintance could have taken on the role of midwife.'

'And I am convinced no other gentleman of

my acquaintance could have taken on the role of cook,' she replied, smiling.

He lifted his glass.

'Perhaps we should congratulate ourselves, then.'

She raised her own, meeting his eyes with a shy smile. All the old enmities were forgotten, for now.

The meal was delicious and she could not help comparing it with the elaborate dinner he had given her the previous evening. Then he had been aiming to impress and she had been far too anxious to enjoy it but now, this simple meal served in such lowly surroundings was by far the best thing she had ever tasted.

Better a dinner of herbs...

The old proverb came to mind but she banished it quickly lest it spoil the comfortable atmosphere they were sharing.

By the time they had finished their meal the kitchen fire was dying and the cold was beginning to creep back into the high-ceilinged room. Susannah pushed her plate away and gave a little shiver.

'Let us move to the parlour,' suggested Jasper, putting on his coat. 'I left the fire banked up in there. Unless, that is, you would like to retire to your room?'

It was at that point Susannah realised that

in all the confusion she had made no provision for herself, or the viscount. With so much of the house uninhabitable due to the leaking roof and the unsafe chimney stack, it would not be easy to find two free bedchambers. She decided she would think about that later. For now the lure of a warm fire was much more seductive.

After the cavernous kitchen the parlour was snug and welcoming. The viscount used a taper to light a single branched candlestick while Susannah went to the window.

'The snow is still falling,' she said. 'I do not think I can ask Lucas to make another attempt to reach Priston until the morning.'

The viscount was bending over the fire, stirring the coals into a blaze.

'I agree. As soon as it is light we can send them out again.'

'We? I should have thought you would be anxious to return to Bath, my lord.'

'Not until I know all is well here.'

'That is not necessary...'

She trailed off as he regarded her, one dark brow raised.

'You cannot be nurse, housekeeper *and* cook, Miss Prentess, and from what I have seen of the other inhabitants of this property they are all incapable of helping you, for one reason or another.'

'It grieves me, but I have to agree with you.' She sank down on to a chair, trying not to sound too disheartened. 'Both Lizzie and Jane have young babies to look after, and Violet is quite unused to nursing or domestic work of any kind.'

'And your scullery maid, willing as she is, can only work under instruction.' The viscount pulled the spindle-legged sofa closer to the fire and sat down. 'Tomorrow we will send Morton and your footman to Priston with instructions to fetch the midwife and try if they can to find a good woman who is prepared to live here and run the house until your own housekeeper returns.' He held up his hand as she opened her mouth to speak. 'Please do not argue. If that fails, as soon as the road is clear, Morton shall drive into Bath and find a suitable female through the registry office.'

'You seem to have thought of everything, my lord.'

'I know very well that you will not leave here until you know your guests are provided for.'

'True.'

'Then if we have settled that point, perhaps it is time we retired.'

'Ah. That might be a slight problem.' Susannah stared at her hands clasped in her lap. 'I did not think to have Bessie prepare rooms for us. I imagine Mrs Gifford's room will be usable, but the other three bedrooms in this part of the house are already occupied by the young ladies. If I had thought of it earlier I would have had a truckle bed made up in Violet's room for myself—'

'Out of the question. I shall sleep here on the sofa.'

She sighed with relief.

'That is very good of you. I will go and find you some blankets.'

'Not necessary,' he said. 'The fire and my driving coat will suffice to keep me warm.'

With a chuckle she rose and went to the door.

'Oh, no, I must show some respect for your position, Lord Markham.'

The corners of his mouth lifted.

'Why change now, Miss Prentess? So far in our acquaintance you have shown no regard for my position at all!'

With a laugh gurgling in her throat she whisked herself out of the room, returning a few minutes later with blankets and a pillow.

'Brrr, it is cold once you step outside this room,' she said, putting the bedding down on a chair. 'I looked in on the others while I was upstairs; everyone is sleeping peacefully, even the new mother and baby.' Jasper was kneeling by the hearth, stirring the contents of a large pewter jug. 'Cooking again, my lord?'

'Mulled cider,' he said. 'Watch.'

He pulled the poker out of the fire and carefully lowered the red-hot tip into the jug where it sizzled and hissed, sending a spicy aroma into the air. Susannah breathed it in, appreciating the scent of apples and spices. He filled two rummers with the fragrant, steaming liquid and held one out to her.

'Perhaps you would join me?'

Susannah knew she should retire, but she had peeped into Mrs Gifford's bedchamber. It was cold and unwelcoming, with no cheerful fire burning. She was loath to return to it, so she accepted the glass and sat down beside him on the sofa. They were enveloped in the warm glow from the fire and Susannah found the dancing flames strangely soothing

'Why are you doing this?' she asked him suddenly.

'I told you, my eccentric uncle…'

'No, I mean, why did you stay here today, why are you showing such kindness to me? After last night…'

He waved one hand, the heavy gold signet ring glinting as it caught the firelight.

'Last night I thought you were leading Gerald astray. I did not know he was a party to all this. Silly cawker, why did he not tell me?'

'Pray do not blame Gerald, I made him swear to tell no one.'

He said quietly, 'That was almost your un-doing.'

She felt the colour stealing into her cheeks, and it had little to do with the cider. She thought it best to keep silent and after a moment he continued.

'This place must be very important to you, to risk coming out on such a day.'

'It is.'

'More than just charitable goodwill, I think. I noticed the new sign as we came in. Have you changed the house name? Was that your idea, or Mrs Logan's?'

The cider was dispelling the chill inside, just as the fire was warming her skin. She felt very mellow, and comfortable enough for confidences.

'Mine.'

'Will you not tell me?' His voice was gentle. 'Who was Florence?'

'She was my sister.'

Jasper caught his breath. At last she was prepared to tell him the truth.

'Was?'

He waited while she sipped at her drink. She was staring into the fire, a faraway look in her eyes.

'She died five years ago.'

'I am very sorry.' Instinctively he reached out

and covered her hand. She did not draw it away. 'Will you tell me about it?'

She sat up a little straighter but she kept her eyes on the fire, as if reading her words in the flames.

'When my father died in Gibraltar we—my mother, sister and I—went to live with his sister in London. My aunt was a strict Evangelical and when my mother died of the fever a year later we were left to her care. Our family was not rich, but respectable enough, and very soon after my mother's death my sister Florence was courted by a young man who promised to marry her.

'He was very dashing and handsome, a very fashionable beau and Florence believed his promises enough to...' He felt the little hand tremble in his. 'He disappeared, leaving her pregnant. When my aunt learned that Florence was with child she threw her out of the house. I was forbidden ever to see her again. I smuggled money and food to Florence, who managed to find lodgings nearby. My aunt discovered what was happening and she stopped my pin-money and kept me locked in my room. I think she must also have spoken to the landlady, too, because Florence left her lodgings and I heard nothing more of her.

'After six months my aunt thought it would be safe for me to go out alone again, and at the market one day a woman approached and told me Florence had died in childbirth a few weeks earlier. This woman was a milliner, earning appallingly little and living in the same house as Florence, close to Drury Lane. She said her landlady had a kind heart and had taken my sister in when she found her on the street. Florence would not say how she had got there, or what she had gone through, but she was very near her time so they gave her a bed and did what they could, although there was no money to pay for a midwife.

'I went to the house where Florence died, I had to see it for myself. It was very squalid, but the landlady was a kindly soul, and it was a comfort to know Florence had not been quite alone at the end. The landlady told me there were hundreds of women like my sister, gently bred girls who were pursued and courted by fashionable men who took their virtue and then abandoned them. It is the way of the world. Neither she nor the milliner would take any money for their trouble, but they said Florence had begged them to get a message to me, to let me know what had become of her.' Her mouth twisted and she added bitterly, 'By that kindness they showed more mercy to my sister than her family had ever done.'

She pulled her hand free and wiped a tear from her cheek.

'The letter from my Uncle Middlemass came soon after. If only he had come back to England a year earlier! As it is I left my aunt's house very willingly. It was too late to help Florence, but I vowed then that I would do something to atone for her death. That is why I set up Florence House, and using the money from those arrogant rich men goes some way towards making them pay for their cruelty.'

'Cruelty is a very strong word.'

She lifted her head.

'Not strong enough, I think.'

'But not all young men are cruel, Susannah. Some may be wild, yes, and thoughtless—this young man who courted Florence, you say he disappeared. Surely it is possible that he did not know of your sister's condition, or mayhap circumstance prevented him from coming back to her.'

'Believe me, my lord,' she said slowly, 'I know that man was an out-and-out scoundrel.'

In the dim light he saw a strange look flicker across her face—revulsion, horror, anger. Jasper's brows drew together. What was it she was not telling him? Before he could frame another question she gave a tiny shake of her head.

'This is a drear conversation when we should be celebrating having come safely through a most trying day. Is there any more of the mulled cider?'

She held out her glass

'I do not think I should give you any more. You will accuse me of trying to befuddle you with drink.'

She laughed. 'No, that was last night, when you were trying to seduce me. Today you have been a true friend, my lord.'

A friend. He smiled ruefully. No woman had ever called him friend before.

'If we are friends then surely you should not be calling me my lord.'

She turned her head to give him an appraising glance from those clear hazel eyes. They twinkled now with mischief.

'What should it be, then—viscount? Or perhaps Markham?'

His smile grew.

'Try Jasper.'

'Jasper.' He liked the sound of it on her lips, the slight hesitation in her voice as she tried it out. She nodded, apparently satisfied. 'And you must call me Susannah.'

'Thank you.'

She leaned back on the sofa and sipped at her drink, comfortable in his company, not worrying when her shoulder brushed his.

'No, you have been most gentlemanly—' A giggle escaped her. 'Perhaps that is the wrong word—I have never known a gentleman prepare a meal before. And it was delicious. The baby is safely delivered and peacefully sleeping with her mother, the other girls are resting. Did I tell you the meal was delicious, sir? All is right with the world.'

'A good day's work, Miss Prentess.'

'Yes indeed.' She smiled, and as he watched her eyelids began to close. Deftly he reached across and took the rummer from her fingers as she dropped into a deep sleep.

Susannah opened her eyes. She was lying on the sofa, her head cradled on a pillow, and she was tucked around with blankets. She shifted her head and saw the viscount stretched out in the chair opposite, his feet resting on a footstool and his many-caped driving coat thrown over him. He stirred in his chair.

'Good morning, Miss Prentess.'

She sat up and immediately put one hand to her head as it began to pound in the most unpleasant manner.

'I did not sleep in Mrs Gifford's bed, then.'

'I did not like to disturb you.'

'I brought this bedding downstairs for you...'

'There was plenty for two.' He rose, throwing off the coat and the blanket beneath it. His hair was a little tousled and stubble shadowed his cheeks, but she thought he looked remarkably well after spending the night in an armchair. 'I shall see if Bessie has built up the fire in the kitchen. I think we should have some coffee.'

Susannah said nothing as he went out. She remembered sitting here last night, talking to him. She remembered drinking the cider but then... nothing. She looked down. She was still fully dressed, neither she nor anyone else had made any attempt to disrobe her. Her hand crept to her neck. She had been alone, asleep and in the company of a strange man—a nobleman, moreover, with a reputation for breaking hearts— and he had made no attempt upon her honour. In fact, he had given her his own pillow and wrapped her in the blankets she had brought down for his comfort.

She stood up and was relieved to find her head did not feel any worse for the effort. Walking to the window, she drew back the curtains to let in the morning light. It was still early and the sun had not yet risen but its effects could be seen in the clear blue sky with its scattering of blush-pink clouds. A movement caught her eye and she saw Jasper step out on to the drive.

When had she begun to think of him as Jasper? A memory surfaced. She recalled declaring that they were friends now. With a groan she put her head in her hands. Had she been drunk last night? What else had she said to him? She raised her head to watch him striding towards the stables. He was hatless, his thick black hair gleaming and he moved with an easy grace that made her pulse stir. Quickly she turned away from the window. It was madness to think of a man in that way. It was frightening.

She bundled up the bedding and carried it upstairs, taking the time to wash her face and hands and re-pin her hair before returning to the parlour, where she busied herself relighting the fire. She wanted the coffee Jasper had promised and he did not disappoint her. He entered with a tray balanced on one hand and looking so assured that she laughed.

'You add the accomplishments of a waiter to your many skills, my lord.'

'Obviously a misspent youth.' He put the tray down on the small dining table and held out a chair for her. 'I'm afraid there are no fresh-baked muffins but there is some toast, if you would care for it.'

She joined him at the table and helped herself to a piece of toast while Jasper poured coffee for them both.

'I suggested Morton and your menservants should take the shovels and try to force a path to drive the carriage to the village. I think you would like the midwife to come here as soon as possible?'

'Yes, thank you. I did check on Jane. She and

the baby are well but I shall be happier once the midwife has seen them.'

'Of course. I have given instruction that if the midwife is not available then they must bring the doctor.'

She murmured her thanks, once more shaken by his kindness.

Susannah was relieved to feel a little better once she had broken her fast and the rest of the morning passed quickly. She coaxed Violet Anstruther down to the kitchen and showed her how to prepare breakfast for the others, then she busied herself with household duties until the noise and bustle at the front door heralded the arrival of the midwife. She was accompanied by a cheerful-looking woman who introduced herself as Mrs Ibbotson and said she had come about the position of housekeeper.

'I am a widow, you see, Miss Prentess,' she explained, when Susannah took her aside to interview her. 'All my children have flown the nest, so there is nothing I would enjoy more than to be looking after the young ladies until Mrs Gifford returns. The viscount's man told me what is expected and a few extra shillings is always welcome. I took the liberty of bringing a bag with me in the hope that you would agree to me starting immediately, which I am free to do.'

With a recommendation from the midwife and Bessie's statement that she had known Mrs Ibbotson for many years and knew her to keep an excellent house, Susannah felt it safe to think of returning to Bath.

'The men say the main road is passable,' Jasper informed her. 'I will follow you in my curricle, to make sure you come to no harm.'

'Pho, I have my coachman and footman to look after me, I shall be safe enough,' she declared, but she was pleased to know he would be there, all the same.

Suddenly it was time to go. Susannah said goodbye to the girls, forbade any of them to come outside to see her off and found herself being handed into her waiting carriage by the viscount.

'I will take another route once we reach Bath,' he announced. 'There may be talk.'

'I suspect the weather is providing the Bath residents with plenty to discuss for the moment.'

'Nevertheless, we should avoid giving them fuel for gossip.' He stood back as the servant put up the steps and closed the door. 'It may be best if we do not meet for a few days, just to be on the safe side. You may rely upon me to say nothing of Florence House, or of our being here together.'

'Thank you.' It was too soon, there was more she wanted to say, but she had to content herself with a small wave. Jasper raised his hand in salute and was lost to sight as the carriage pulled away.

Chapter Eleven

Susannah found her aunt and Mrs Logan waiting for her in Royal Crescent when she returned. Kate's immediate greeting included an apology for not accompanying her to Florence House.

'I admit I was concerned when you were not at home,' remarked Susannah.

'I had business I was obliged to attend to.'

'At eight in the morning?'

She was surprised to see her friend looking a little ill at ease, but she had no time to reflect upon it for her aunt was already fussing over her.

'With Edwards driving you, and Lucas in attendance I was not overly worried,' declared Aunt Maude, hugging her. 'And when the snow set in I guessed you would be obliged to put up at the house overnight.'

'Knowing how few habitable rooms there are in Florence House perhaps it was a good thing I was not with you,' remarked Kate. 'I said to Charles—'

'Charles?' Susannah turned to her. 'You were with Charles Camerton? Was that the reason you could not come with me.'

She had never seen Kate blush before. Could it mean that her friend was truly attracted to the gentleman? Susannah tried to be happy for Kate, but she had to acknowledge a slight disappointment, a vague feeling that somehow her friend had let her down.

Susannah kept them occupied for the next hour discussing the snow and the situation at Florence House. She did not mention the viscount's presence in the house, salving her conscience with the thought that do to so would give rise to unnecessary speculation. At length she escaped to her room to dress for dinner, only to suffer an uncomfortable half-hour as Dorcas bemoaned the loss of the tasselled cord from her mistress's green-silk gown. She was scandalised by Susannah's airy admission that she had never liked the cord and had thrown it away. Her declaration that she was going to send the gown back to Odesse to be fitted with a ribbon tie instead met with even more condemnation.

'Never did I think you would be guilty of

such extravagance, Miss Prentess,' declared her maid, shaking her head. 'Why, as high and mighty as a viscountess you are getting.'

'No, I am not,' declared Susannah, blushing hotly. 'Why on earth should you say such a thing?'

Dorcas turned to stare at her.

'It's just a saying, miss, as well you knows. And I'm sure if you want a gown altering then 'tis no business of mine.'

Susannah quickly begged pardon and sat meekly while her maid dressed her hair, fervently hoping that she would be able to get through the rest of the evening without blushing again over the events of the past few days.

By Sunday the snow was melting, leaving the ground waterlogged and the sky grey and overcast. Susannah wondered if Jasper had left Bath, now that he knew she had no intention of marrying Gerald. She realised she would be very sorry if she did not see him again. Then she remembered his final words to her—*it may be best if we do not meet for a few days.* Her hopes rose. Surely that could only mean he was remaining in Bath? With this in mind she took particular care over her choice of walking dress for the Sunday morning service in the Abbey. A watery sun broke through the clouds as she descended from the carriage, prompting her aunt to hope that they had seen the last of the winter weather.

The walk to the Abbey doors was a short one, but Susannah was aware of the frowning looks that were cast her way as she accompanied her aunt. A *frisson* of nerves tingled down her spine. Did they know about her meetings with Lord Markham? To dine with him in York House had been a risk, but that was compounded by being stranded with him at Florence House the following night. Head high, she tucked her hand in Aunt Maude's arm and accompanied her into the Abbey. A quick look around convinced Susannah that the viscount was not present. She was disappointed, but considering the looks she had received, she thought perhaps it was for the best.

The service seemed interminably long and Susannah was impatient to be outside again where she could confront those who were casting such disapproving stares in her direction. Better to know the worst immediately. At last they were making their way out through the doors and into the spring sunshine. Aunt Maude had been blissfully unaware of the frosty looks and now sailed up to Mr and Mrs Farthing, who were conversing with Amelia Bulstrode.

'Oh, Mrs Wilby, I did not see you there.' Mrs Bulstrode stopped, flustered, her eyes flickering to Susannah and away again. 'Heavens, I did not expect—that is, with all the talk, I thought you might prefer not to come here today.'

'Talk?' Aunt Maude glanced at Susannah, a crease furrowing her brow. 'Perhaps I have missed something. I have not been outside the house since Thursday.'

'Then you will not know that everyone is talking about the new establishment you have seen fit to create,' Mrs Farthing's strident tones cut in. She turned to Susannah, her rather protuberant eyes snapping angrily. 'I suppose you think yourself superior, Miss Prentess, to be setting up your own house for fallen women. Our establishment in Walcot Street is not good enough for you. I wonder what your uncle would think if he knew you had put one of his houses to such use.'

So it was Florence House that had started such a fluttering in the dovecotes. Relief allowed Susannah to respond mildly to the accusations.

'I beg your pardon, ma'am, but you said yourself the Walcot Street home cannot cope with the number of applicants. My own small attempt to help distressed gentlewomen…'

'Gentlewomen!' Mrs Farthing snorted. 'Trollops, they are. Wanton hussies, flaunting themselves before the young men. Is it any wonder that they find themselves in difficulties? Rather than trying to set up your own establishment, you should contribute to ours. I do not know why you want to pander to these females, setting them up in their own house out of town with a cook and a housekeeper and treating them as guests. Guests! They should be made to work, to understand the error of their ways. And if she were *my* niece, Mrs Wilby—' she turned her attack towards Aunt Maude '—I would strongly counsel her to leave these matters to those who understand them.'

'I'm afraid she is right,' added Mr Farthing, smiling at Susannah in a very patronising way. 'You young ladies like your worthy causes, I know, but my dear wife has the right of it. You should not be associating with these creatures, lest you become tainted.'

Susannah's temper reared at that, but Aunt Maude nipped her arm. Somehow she managed to hold her peace while Mrs Wilby smiled and nodded and said all that was necessary before leading her away.

'Tainted!' Susannah almost ground her teeth in annoyance. 'Why, Aunt, if anyone is to talk of arrogance—'

'I know, my dear, but few people are as liberal as you.' Aunt Maude patted her arm as she guided her firmly towards the waiting carriage. 'It is the reason we told no one about your little scheme, is it not? How on earth did word get out?'

Susannah wondered this, too, and she considered the matter during the short drive back to Royal Crescent.

'I do not believe it could have come from the servants, I pay them very well for their discretion.'

'Mrs Farthing did seem to be particularly well informed,' mused Aunt Maude as the carriage pulled up at their door. 'I suppose the truth was bound to come out at some point.'

'But not yet,' muttered Susannah. 'Not now.'

She followed Aunt Maude into the house, where they divested themselves of their coats before repairing to the drawing room.

'It could be very damaging if the connection between Odesse and Florence House is known,' said Aunt Maude. 'She is not yet well established, and the knowledge might affect her business. If that happened we would have to find another market for the lace, too. But who could have let it slip? Apart from the servants only you, me and Kate Logan know the truth.'

Susannah walked to the window and stared out. Suddenly the spring sun did not seem quite so bright.

'There is another,' she said slowly. 'Lord Markham knows the truth.'

'What?'

Susannah turned from the window. She could not bring herself to meet her aunt's astonished gaze.

'He followed me on Friday morning. I was obliged to explain to him. Everything.'

'Oh heavens!' Aunt Maude fell back in her chair, one hand pressed to her breast. 'Why did you not say earlier, my dear? I suppose you thought it not worth a mention. And when I recall how bad the weather was on Friday, I suppose we must think ourselves lucky that he was not snowed up with you.'

'Well, actually, ma'am…'

It took all Susannah's reassurance and the judicious use of her aunt's silver vinaigrette bottle to bring Mrs Wilby back to a semblance of normality. She would not rest until she had heard the whole story. She was shocked, scandalised, not least when Susannah told her that the viscount had cooked dinner for them all.

'Well he is a very odd sort of man,' she declared, fanning herself rapidly. 'To remain in the house while you were all at sixes and sevens with the birth. And you say he did not insist upon taking the best bedchamber? Very odd indeed.'

'He was content to sleep in the parlour and leave Mrs Gifford's room for me.' Susannah was relieved when her aunt accepted the inference. She feared that not even the vinaigrette would help if she had to confess to spending the night in the same room as the viscount.

'Oh good heavens, what a tangle,' declared Mrs Wilby. 'It is bad enough that everyone knows you are involved in Florence House. If they should discover that you spent the night there, alone, with Lord Markham—'

'I was hardly alone, Aunt,' objected Susannah. 'There was the scullery maid, three other ladies and two babies in the house, too.'

'As if that makes it any better! I suppose it is too much to hope that the viscount has left Bath. He was not at the Abbey.'

'Neither was Mr Barnabus.'

'That is true.' Mrs Wilby sighed. 'Perhaps we should attend the ball in the Upper Rooms tomorrow night, after all, to make a show of indifference.'

Susannah shook her head.

'We agreed we would go to the Fancy Ball on Thursday this week. We mentioned it to several of our acquaintances. I do not see that we should change our plans because of a little talk.'

'Then we must wait until Tuesday to see what effect this has upon our card party.'

Susannah was inclined to be optimistic.

'It is a matter of little importance to anyone but ourselves. I hope we will find our rooms as busy as ever.'

But when Tuesday arrived several of their usual guests sent their apologies and there was a depressing number of empty tables in the room. Susannah was relieved to see Gerald Barnabus arrive and several other young gentleman came in shortly after, but Susannah heard them telling her aunt that Mr Warwick would not be joining them.

'He said he had a prior engagement, but we think otherwise,' declared Mr Edmonds, grinning at his friends. 'Your links with a certain house in the country appear to have upset him badly.'

'Aye, guilty conscience, most likely,' added William Farthing with a grating laugh that reminded Susannah very much of his mother.

Mrs Wilby raised her brows. The young man coloured and immediately begged pardon before moving off quickly with his friends to find amusement at one of the card tables. Susannah turned away, pretending to be busy until they had passed. Their amusement was almost worse than the disapproval of the older members of Bath society. She hoped her aunt's obvious displeasure at their laughter would prevent the matter being raised again, but when several of them joined Susannah at the loo table, she discovered that they were more than ready to tease her about Florence House. She tried to keep her temper, but their constant gibes made her call a halt.

'I pray you will say no more, gentlemen. This

is a cause that should be supported by every Christian, not ridiculed. You at least should realise that, Mr Farthing, since your own mother is so closely involved with Walcot Street.' She handed the cards to the gentleman on her right and rose from the table. 'Pray continue the game for me, Mr Edmonds, I have had enough for tonight.'

She walked away, trying to calm herself. She should have known what to expect.

'Miss Prentess.' She turned to find Gerald beside her. He gave her a rueful smile. 'So Florence House is no longer a secret.'

'And the subject of much merriment,' she said bitterly. 'The jokes and winks, the innuendo—'

'They are young and thoughtless,' he said pacifically. 'It is unusual for an unmarried lady to be involved in such a charity. You know yourself most young ladies would deny all knowledge of such matters.'

'I would very much like to know how the secret got out,' she said. 'I don't suppose it was you…'

'Good Gad, Susannah, you know I would not say anything! I did not even tell Jasper about it.'

'No, of course not.' She smiled, and after a few moments he went off to join in a game of whist.

Susannah moved to a corner table, ostensibly

to trim a flickering candle, but this was only an excuse to have a few moments to herself.

'You are very pensive.' Mrs Logan approached her.

'Kate,' Susannah kissed her cheek. 'I did not see you arrive. How are you?'

'Well, thank you.' Kate searched her face. 'But you are looking pale, Susannah. What is wrong?'

'Oh, nothing.' She tried to dismiss it with a smile. 'I am merely wondering how everyone knows about Florence House. I have spoken to the servants, and I am convinced not one of them has said anything about it. Gerald, too, swears he has not said a word.' She bit her lip. That left only Jasper.

You may rely upon me to say nothing of Florence House.

In her mind's eye she saw his image again, standing at the carriage door, solid, secure... and unreliable. He had let her down, and it hurt all the more because she had been so sure she could trust him. Giving herself a mental shake, she dragged up a smile.

'Well, it cannot be helped. We must do what we can to continue. Will you play *vingt-et-un* tonight, Kate? The winnings from the table are badly needed. I have paid Mr Tyler for the moment, but there will be more bills.'

'Of course, although only until Char—I mean, Mr Camerton arrives.'

'Oh, will he be coming then? Is be bringing the viscount?'

'I can only vouch for Mr Camerton,' replied Kate, a heightened colour in her cheeks. 'I do not think he has seen Lord Markham at all this week.'

'My biggest problem with Mr Camerton is that he wins far too often.' Susannah said it lightly, but she was half in earnest. She had noticed that when Charles Camerton was at the table, Kate's attention was not given fully to the game, and she could ill afford more losses.

The following morning Susannah's worst fears were confirmed. Their rooms had been only half-full, and when Mrs Wilby totted up the figures she reported sadly that they had made only thirty pounds.

'Hardly enough to pay for the supper.' Aunt Maude put down her pen. 'And nothing from Kate. She was playing picquet with Mr Camerton for most of the evening. One can only guess what her losses must be. I cannot understand why she continues to play against him.'

'Can you not, Aunt?' Susannah rubbed her arms. 'I think she is in love with him.'

'Kate? I do not believe it. She has completely forsworn men.'

'That is what I thought, too. I thought she felt as I do.'

'But if she is in love...'

'I know,' said Susannah in a hollow voice. 'Everything has changed. And it is all Lord Markham's fault, damn him!'

'Susannah!'

She coloured and quickly begged pardon. 'But it was the viscount who brought Charles Camerton to our rooms, and he betrayed me—us.'

'I am inclined to be philosophical,' her aunt responded. 'Florence House could not remain a secret for ever, and I cannot be sorry if Kate has found a man to love her.'

'Her first husband was a brute,' declared Susannah. 'In Gibraltar his viciousness was the talk of the regiment. I only hope she will not be hurt again.'

'My love, not all men are undeserving scoundrels,' said Aunt Maude gently. 'I was happily married to a good, kind man for fifteen years. Why, even Lord Markham may have his good points. At least he does not appear to have told anyone about Odesse.'

'He should not have told anyone *anything*,' retorted Susannah. 'He promised me—' She broke off, determined not to give in to the dull aching misery inside her. 'Enough of this. We shall come about, so let us not be too despondent.

The sun is shining, Odesse has just delivered my new walking dress, so I shall take a stroll in Sydney Gardens. Will you come with me?'

No more was said about the card party and Aunt Maude was content to accept Susannah's assurances that all would be well. A visit to Odesse confirmed that her business was still doing well. In fact she reported that the number of customers was increasing, but despite that, Susannah felt the leaden weight inside. It was not that the secret of Florence House was out, but the fact that she had trusted Jasper, and he had let her down.

As they made their way to the Upper Rooms for Thursday's ball Aunt Maude wondered aloud how many of their acquaintance knew about her patronage of Florence House, and how many would show their disapproval. Susannah made a brave response, but she was secretly relieved to find that they were not completely ignored when they entered the ballroom.

A short distance from the door a group of young bucks stood talking. Susannah knew them all, but as they approached one of them looked up. For a moment he glared at her, then turned and strode off.

'Dear me, it appears we have indeed offended Mr Warwick,' murmured Aunt Wilby.

She spoke quietly, but a young gentleman

making his bow to Susannah overheard and grinned.

'Take no notice of Warwick, Miss Prentess, he's been like a bear with a sore head recently. Probably worrying over some female.' He laughed heartily, then he leaned closer, saying confidentially, 'We've told him, ma'am, that if it's *that* sort of trouble...' he tapped his nose '...then the gal might be glad of your little, ah, charity.' With a knowing grin he linked arms with his companions and walked away.

'I suppose we shall have to accustom ourselves to such talk,' remarked Mrs Wilby in a tone of long-suffering. 'It will die away soon enough, once there is some other juicy gossip to replace it.'

Susannah knew this to be true, but it angered her to think all her careful preparations for Florence House might be jeopardised because the secret had been revealed too soon, and by a man who assured her she could trust him.

She had convinced herself that she never wanted to see Lord Markham again, that she could shrug her shoulders and put him from her mind, but when she saw him conversing with Gerald Barnabus all the pent-up anger of the past few days came flooding back.

As if aware of her eyes upon him, the viscount looked up. He touched Gerald's arm and the two men approached. Susannah watched in growing anger and amazement as Jasper made his bow to her aunt. He was completely at his ease. She glared at him, but it had no effect. When he addressed her she quickly turned away from him, causing her filmy muslin skirts to flounce around her. How dare he think he could betray her and get away with it!

'Miss Prentess, are you not well?'

'Perfectly, thank you.' She wanted to ignore him but he took her elbow and in the confusion of the crowded room he adroitly moved her away from her aunt.

'Are you cross with me for staying away for so long?' he said quietly. 'I beg your pardon, but I had business to attend to, and thought, in the circumstances—'

'In the circumstances, my lord,' she interrupted him savagely, 'it would be better if you stayed away for good.'

'What is this? What have I done to offend you?'

'As if you did not know!'

His brows snapped together.

'No, I do not know. When we parted on Saturday—'

'On Saturday you promised not to mention Florence House to anyone.'

'And I have not done so.'

'Why, then, is everyone talking of it? Why

have I been subjected to cold stares and even been snubbed by my erstwhile acquaintances?'

'Susannah, I give you my word—'

'Don't you dare use my name,' she shot back at him. 'How dare you even *speak* to me!'

She went to move away but his fingers tightened on her arm.

'I do not know who has given away your secret, but it was not me.'

She shook off his hand.

'Everyone else who knows about Florence House has been party to the secret for months and not a hint of it has leaked out. But only days after I tell you, it is common knowledge.'

'However that may be, it is not my doing, and not my groom's either. He knows better than to talk out of turn.'

'I do not believe you.' Her lip curled. 'Pray leave me, Lord Markham. I have no wish for your company this evening.'

Susannah turned away and this time he made no attempt to prevent her. She made her way back through the crowd to her aunt's side, prepared to explain the angry flush on her cheek, but Aunt Maude merely gave her a distracted smile.

'Mr Barnabus has gone, Susannah, but he said to remind you that you promised to dance with him later. Oh dear, I have received the cut direct from at least two ladies, and Mrs Sanstead says I should persuade you to distance yourself from Florence House if you are not to be ostracised by Bath society.'

'Really? How dare these small-minded matrons think they can dictate to me!'

'Now, Susannah, pray be careful,' Aunt Maude begged her. 'Do not let your temper carry you away. We need the good offices of these ladies. How else are we to fund Florence House for the rest of this year?'

'I neither know nor care,' Susanna ground out furiously.

'Perhaps we should close the house, until we have more funds.'

Aunt Maude's tentative suggestion brought Susannah's outraged eyes upon her, but after a moment her fury died down.

'No, I will not do that, unless there is no other way.' She looked around. 'I expected to see Kate here.'

Mrs Wilby tutted.

'Oh, my dear, it completely slipped my mind. She sent a note to say she was going out of town for a few days.'

'That is a pity, I would have liked her support tonight. Never mind.' Susannah put on a brave smile. 'We shall stand our ground, Aunt. One or two may turn away from us, but our true friends will stand by us, and I hope once the gossip has died down we shall recover.' She smiled mischievously. 'Besides, I cannot leave yet. Odesse assured me this latest gown she has created for me will look its best when I am dancing.'

There was no lack of partners for Susannah, but the numbers soliciting her to dance were sadly diminished, and the high-nosed stares she received from a group of matrons standing with Mrs Farthing suggested that many of them were shocked to learn of her involvement with Florence House. Keeping her head high, Susannah smiled and laughed with her dance partners, but by the time she rejoined her aunt after a series of lively country dances her cheeks ached with the effort.

'Heavens, I never thought dancing could be such a chore,' she muttered, following Aunt Maude to a space where they might not be overheard, but when asked if she wanted to go home, she quickly disclaimed, 'I beg your pardon, Aunt, I should not be complaining. There are still many here who do not care a fig for my association with Florence House.'

'Yes, my love, but they are not the high sticklers who can make a difference to our long-term plans. If the cream of Bath society should turn against you, then your patronage of Odesse could count against her—' Aunt Maude broke off and gazed past Susannah, a wary look in her eye.

'Miss Prentess, would you do me the honour of standing up with me for the next dance?'

Jasper's cool voice brought the angry flush back to Susannah's cheeks. Had he not understood what she had said to him? Without turning, she said coldly, 'No, my lord, I will not.'

Aunt Maude gasped in horror, but Susannah merely hunched one white shoulder. Instead of moving off, the viscount stepped closer. She was aware of his presence, the heat of his body at her back. She could feel his breath on her cheek as he spoke quietly in her ear.

'Think carefully about this, madam. Your credit in Bath is sadly diminished. Can you afford *not* to dance with me?'

She bit her lip. He was right. It did not take Aunt Maude's beseeching stare to tell her so. Slowly she turned around. He smiled and held out his arm, but the steely glint in his eye told her he was not in the mood to be refused. Reluctantly she placed her fingers on his sleeve.

'That is better. Let us see what we can do to repair the damage.'

'I am doing this under sufferance,' she muttered as he led her on to the floor. 'I have not forgiven you.'

'Since I am not at fault there is nothing to forgive,' he retorted. They took their places facing one another, more duellists than dancers. He bowed to her as the music started, and as they passed in the dance he continued, 'Do you know, you are the most stubborn female I have ever met.'

'It must be a novel experience for you, my lord, to find a woman who will not toady and flatter you.' She bit the words off quickly as they circled about the other dancers. Angry as she was, Susannah did not wish anyone else to hear their argument. When Jasper took her hand again he carried on the conversation.

'Not at all—' they separated, circled, returned '—there are many such, but few who would be as ungrateful as you.'

Susannah's eyes flashed, but she was obliged to hold back her retort until they were once again holding hands.

'Oh, so I should be obliged to you, should I, because you deign to stand up with me?'

'No, you tiresome wench, because I am trying my utmost to prevent you from becoming a pariah. My attendance upon you may persuade those ladies whose support you need to think better of you.' His lips curved upwards as he watched her struggle. He reached out and took her hand as the last notes of the music died away. 'You know I am right,' he murmured as he bowed over her fingers. 'I can make you or break you tonight.' He straightened and bestowed on her his most charming smile. 'Well,

Miss Prentess, what is it to be? Shall we stay for the cotillion?'

The fact that he was right did nothing for Susannah's temper. In any other circumstances she would have swept off and left him standing alone on the dance floor, but she was well aware that such an action would only increase the disapprobation already surrounding her. She cared nothing for her own standing in Bath, but at present Florence House could not survive without the extra revenue she could provide. In the future she hoped there would be sufficient money from Odesse and the lace-makers to help maintain the house, but this was a critical time. She needed the viscount's support.

With enormous effort she forced herself to smile at him, saying through her clenched teeth, 'With the greatest of pleasure, Lord Markham.'

'Well, that passed off exceeding well,' declared Mrs Wilby as she waited for Susannah to extricate herself from her chair in the hallway of Royal Crescent. 'Lord Markham's timely intervention had a profound effect on everyone. Even before you had finished the cotillion Lady Horsham and Mrs Bray-Tillotson came up to speak to me, and I have received no more than a nod from either of them before.' She took Susannah's arm and led her into the morning room on the ground floor, where candles burned and the

fire had been built up for their return. 'And then
to join Mr Barnabus in escorting us to supper.
Why, even Mrs Farthing and her cronies could
not quite snub us after that!'

'No' Susannah moved towards the fire to
warm her hands. 'His lordship was most ac-
commodating.'

'Indeed he was. I think he must regret letting
slip our secret.'

'He maintains he said nothing.'

'Well then, it was even more considerate of
him to give us so much of his time tonight.'

It was clear to Susannah that her aunt had
been very anxious about their reception at the
ball and her relief now took the form of contin-
uous chatter. Susannah let it wash over her for
a few minutes before making her excuses and
fleeing to her bedroom.

She was obliged to be grateful for the viscount's attentions but she would have preferred
a simple apology. In that he was no different
from most men, so arrogant that he would not
admit he had been at fault, that he had made
known her connection with Florence House. His
refusal to do so had quite spoiled her evening.
Jasper was a good dancer and in other circumstances she would have revelled in standing up
with him for the cotillion, holding his hands,
laughing up into his face, but his perfidy hung
between them like a cloud. She had kept her

smile in place, concentrating on the intricacies of the dance and determined not to allow her anger to be visible to the constantly changing partners, but it had been difficult.

The viscount had been most attentive at supper, too. Outwardly Susannah had been serene and smiling, but he had not been deceived, and once Dorcas had undressed her, brushed out her hair and departed, Susannah slipped between the sheets and relived her brief, final meeting with the viscount.

They had been waiting for their cloaks when Jasper came up to take his leave. He had taken advantage of the noisy, bustling chatter to speak to her alone.

'You will not cry friends with me?'

'I am, of course, grateful for what you have done tonight, my lord…'

'Well that is something, I suppose.' He took her hand. 'I have much ground to make up, but I will come about, Susannah, believe me.'

But, of course, she could not believe him. She could not trust him ever again.

When Jasper awoke the following morning his first conscious thought was of Susannah Prentess. How she had ripped up at him when she thought he had broken his word to her. She had looked quite magnificent, those hazel eyes flashing with emerald-green sparks of anger. It would take time and patience to convince her he had not been to blame but it would be worth it. For the present he hoped he had deflected some of the disapproval away from her—surely the attentions of a viscount would count for something with the Bath harpies.

He jumped out of bed and rang the bell. He was eager to see Susannah again—it surprised him a little to realise how much he wanted to see her—but he must allow her a day or two. At present she was too angry to listen to reasoned argument. There was plenty to do. He had letters to write to his man of business, and he and Gerald had discussed plans for a riding party with Charles Camerton and a few of the other gentlemen of their acquaintance, so perhaps he should talk to Gerald about that. Still, he might take a walk this morning, and if he should happen to bump into Miss Prentess, well....

He made his way to the Pump Room, stopping off on his way to call at the White Hart, where he was told that Mr Camerton was gone away.

'We are expecting him back in a day or so, though, m'lord,' said the servant, pocketing the coin Jasper pressed into his hand. 'He's left his bags here.'

With an inward shrug Jasper left the inn. His plans to form a riding party must wait, then.

He crossed the road to the Pump Room, but a quick tour of the crowded room informed him that Susannah and her aunt were not present. However, having ventured into the busy meeting place, he could not leave before speaking to a number of his acquaintances and listening to the latest gossip. He was pleased that this no longer centred on Susannah—she had been supplanted by the news that the Dowager Countess of Gisburne was in Bath.

Jasper received the information with interest, and set off for Laura Place, where he was shown into the countess's drawing room by her stately butler.

He found himself in the presence of an elderly lady dressed in black satin. She was sitting in a large, carved armchair, her back ramrod straight, and the bright eyes that watched him cross the room were remarkably piercing.

'Markham...' she held out her hand '...I did not expect to find you here, but it is a pleasant surprise. You will take wine with me? Good.' She paused while he bowed over her fingers and did not object when he then leaned forwards to kiss her cheek. 'You can tell me how your family go on. I saw your sister in town, looking radiant, as ever. And how is Dominic, my godson? I wanted to get to Rooks Tower for the christening, but the weather...' She waved one beringed hand. 'I would have risked it, but Gisburne and my doctor were adamant.'

'And quite right, too, ma'am,' Jasper agreed, pulling up a chair and sitting down. 'Dominic would never forgive you for knocking your-self up with such a journey. He is inordinately happy, you know.'

'Having met his wife I can believe it,' replied the dowager. 'Zelah Coale is a very sensible gel, and a reliable correspondent, too.'

'Yes, she has won all our hearts.'

Even as he uttered the words, Jasper realised with a slight jolt of surprise that Zelah had not been in his thoughts for some weeks now.

'And how are you, my boy—still leading the young ladies a merry dance?'

'Rather the reverse, ma'am,' he replied, think-ing of Susannah. 'But tell me, what brings you to Bath?'

'The winter left me a trifle fagged and my doctor thought it would do me good to take the waters.'

'As long as it is nothing serious.'

'Not a whit, although I don't doubt Gisburne and his wife would like it to be. They must wish me at Jericho.'

Jasper grinned, too well acquainted with the dowager's easy-natured son to believe any such thing.

'You know he would dispute that, and your

many charities would miss you, too.' He paused, gazing down at the large signet ring on his finger. 'And talking of your charities, I think you may be able to help me.'

'Go on.'

Jasper took advantage of the servant's entrance to consider his words. Once the glasses had been filled and they were alone again he began.

'A friend…' He hesitated, knowing that in her present mood Susannah would object strongly to the term. 'An acquaintance has set up a home for young ladies of gentle birth who have been abandoned by their families for, ah…'

'For being pregnant,' she finished for him. 'There is no need to be mealy-mouthed with me, Markham.'

He smiled.

'I beg your pardon. Let me explain…'

When he had finished telling her about Florence House, the lace-makers and Odesse, Lady Gisburne nodded slowly.

'Exemplary.' She put down her empty wineglass. 'What is it you want from me?'

'Ostensibly all this was set up by Mrs Wilby. Now it is known that her unmarried niece is closely involved with Florence House and the Bath tabbies are sharpening their claws Some have already cut the acquaintance. If they learn of the connection with the modiste it could destroy the small income that keeps the house going.' He refilled the glasses and held one out to the Dowager. 'The niece is an heiress and I believe she intends to fund the scheme, once she comes into her inheritance, but that will not be for a year or two yet. I would like to help them.'

She looked at him over the rim of her glass.

'Repenting past sins, Markham?'

'Certainly not,' he replied, in no way offended. 'Seducing innocents has never been my style, and despite my reputation I have always been alive to the consequences of my actions. I am tolerably certain there are no bastards of mine in the world. No, it is purely altruistic.' He found he could not meet that searching gaze and studied the contents of his wineglass instead. 'Any offer of assistance from me would be rejected, but you could tell Mrs Wilby there is an anonymous benefactor who wishes to invest in some worthy cause.'

The dowager sipped at her wine, a slight crease furrowing her brow. Jasper waited patiently, knowing better than to disturb the old lady. At last she looked up, a glimmer of a smile on her sharp features.

'Very well, I will do it. If only to confound the Bath tabbies!'

Chapter Twelve

When Saturday dawned wet and windy, Susannah and Mrs Wilby decided to remain indoors. They settled quietly to their sewing, although Susannah's work remained untouched on her lap for most of the time. Her thoughts kept going back to the viscount and his refusal to admit he had spoken to anyone about Florence House. She had seen too many of the young men in Bath bluster and boast. One could not rely on any of them, but it surprised her how much it hurt her to know the viscount was one of their number. She had thought him different from the rest. She had hoped—quickly she stifled her half-formed thoughts. She would think no more about it. When Mrs Wilby addressed some remark to her she replied briefly and bent her head over her tambour frame once more. She had thought herself quite content with her lot, but recently she had to admit that the future as an unmarried lady seemed rather a lonely one.

Susannah was surprised out of this melancholy train of thought by Gatley coming in to announce a visitor.

'The Dowager Countess of Gisburne?' Aunt Maude dropped her sewing in amazement. 'But we do not know—I saw her name in Mr King's visitors' book, but—oh, show her up, Gatley, show her up! Good heavens, what on earth has brought a dowager countess to our door?'

'I have no idea, Aunt, but we shall soon know.' Susannah quickly put away the sewing things while her aunt patted her cap and straightened her gown.

The Dowager was a thin, formidable-looking figure, her severe black gown relieved by a vast quantity of white lace. Her dark, bird-like eyes rested for a moment on Susannah as she entered the room, before she turned her attention to Aunt Maude.

'Mrs Wilby, we have not been introduced, but I hope you will forgive the intrusion when you know my business.'

Murmuring, Aunt Maude rose from her curtsy and begged the dowager to be seated.

She moved to a sofa and sat down, saying in her forthright manner, 'I believe you are responsible for an establishment near here. Florence House.'

Susannah looked up.

'Goodness me, ma'am, however did you hear of that?'

Those sharp eyes flickered over her again, and Susannah saw the gleam of amusement in their depths.

'The rumour mill in Bath is quite inexhaustible, Miss Prentess. You may know, Mrs Wilby, that I am very interested in such causes. I would like to help you.'

Aunt Maude threw an anguished glance towards Susannah, who replied cautiously, 'That is very gracious of you, ma'am, but I am not sure...'

'Oh come, ladies, I have not been in Bath long but one visit to the Pump Room was sufficient for me to know that your little scheme has set up the backs of the Walcot Street committee. Will you deny that your present funding is inadequate?'

'No, we will not deny that,' replied Susannah.

'Good.' The dowager put down her cane. 'Then let us discuss it!'

When at last Lady Gisburne had been shown out, Mrs Wilby fell back in her chair.

'Heavens, my head is fairly spinning.'

'I admit she is a very forceful personality,'

agreed Susannah, smiling slightly, 'but her patronage—and her money!—will be most welcome.'

'But can we believe her when she says she will leave the control of Florence House in our hands?'

'Oh, I think so, but that is something we can go over once the papers are drawn up.' Susanna stood by the window, watching the dowager being helped into her carriage. 'I liked her plain speaking. She is very knowledgeable about how we should proceed. With Lady Gisburne as patroness I think the future of Florence House is assured.'

'And Odesse,' added Mrs Wilby. 'My lady agreed we should not make her connection with Florence House public knowledge, but she was keen to see her work.'

Susannah chuckled.

'From the prodigious amount of lace on the dowager's gown, her patronage alone should bring plenty of work for the modiste and the lace-makers.' She turned back to her aunt. 'It is a great relief to me,' she admitted. 'I do not mind if Bath society shuns me, but the thought of not being able to support the house, or the girls—' She broke off, shaking her head to dispel the tears that threatened.

'Well,' declared Mrs Wilby, taking up her sewing again. 'I believe with the Dowager

Countess of Gisburne as an acquaintance, Bath society will not dare to shun us!'

And so it proved. On Sunday the Dowager had attended the morning service at the Abbey and once she had acknowledged Susannah and her aunt, others followed suit, even Mrs Bulstrode and Mrs Farthing, although it was clearly an effort. A visit to Henrietta Street on Monday was also encouraging.

'I have had no one ask me about Florence House,' said Odesse, going to fetch a large box from a shelf. 'And this morning, I received a visit from a most superior personage: a dowager countess, no less. She has ordered a new morning gown and hinted that she might place even more business with me, if I can turn it round quickly. Thank goodness I stayed up last night to finish this for you, Miss Prentess, otherwise heaven knows when I would have time to do it.'

She opened the box and pulled out a new evening gown of apricot silk.

'Oh it is beautiful,' exclaimed Susannah.

'I hoped you would like it.' Odesse held up the gown for Susannah's inspection. 'The flounced skirt is hemmed with lace, like the neck and the puff sleeves, and I have found a pair of long gloves that match the colour exactly.'

'Quite exquisite,' declared Mrs Wilby. 'You

must wear it at the ball, my love.' She beamed at the modiste. 'It is quite the finest gown you have made yet, Odesse.'

'Thank you, ma'am. And the walking dress with the lilac-sarcenet petticoat that you ordered for yourself is ready now, if you wish to take it, Mrs Wilby, but I'm afraid I have not had time to finish the green pelisse, I am very sorry.'

'Oh, never mind about that.' Mrs Wilby happily waved aside her apology. 'I do not need the new pelisse yet and would much rather you satisfied your other customers.'

'Lady Gisburne has lost no time in seeking out Odesse,' remarked Susannah, when the ladies were once more in their carriage, surrounded by their purchases. 'I have every confidence that she will be well satisfied with her services.' She put her hand on the box beside her and chuckled. 'Perhaps now I can stop buying so many new gowns!'

That same evening, Susannah smoothed the long gloves over her arms and stood back to look at herself in the glass. There was no doubt that the apricot silk was most becoming. Dorcas had dressed her hair à la Madonna, with a centre parting and the curls falling from a topknot so that they would bounce and shimmer about her head when she danced at the ball tonight.

She wondered if Jasper would like it, but resolutely stifled the thought. He was still not forgiven, so it was of no odds to her at all whether he liked it or not. With something like a toss of those guinea-gold curls she picked up her shawl and hurried downstairs to join Aunt Maude.

Their reception at the Upper Rooms was noticeably warmer than it had been the previous week. There were smiles and bows from most of the matrons as they entered, and more than one lady promised Mrs Wilby an invitation to drink tea with her the following week.

Aunt Maude caught Susannah's eyes, a glow of triumph in her own, and Susannah was forced to bite back a smile. A sudden commotion at the door was followed by a reverent hush. Susannah and her aunt stood back as the Dowager Countess of Gisburne was announced. The old lady progressed regally and Susannah noticed that although she carried a stick she rarely leaned on it as she made her way through the crowd with a nod here, a word there. When she reached Susannah she stopped.

'Miss Prentess.'

Susannah rose from her curtsy to find the dowager was regarding her through her quizzing glass.

'Hmm. Elegantly turned out, as always. I think you are in a fair way to becoming the best-dressed lady in Bath, my dear.' She had not raised her voice, but her words carried effortlessly around the room.

'Thank you, ma'am.'

Susannah inclined her head to acknowledge the compliment but she was almost startled into a laugh when the old lady winked at her before continuing her regal progress towards the ballroom.

Gerald Barnabus had begged her to keep the first dance for him and he came to find her when the orchestra began tuning up. He too cast an appraising eye over her.

'I have never seen you looking lovelier,' he declared, pressing a fervent kiss upon her gloved fingers.

Susannah laughed.

'I am immune to your compliments, Gerald, you give me too many of them.'

'That is because I am violently in love with you,' he replied gallantly.

'I fear you have just fallen into the habit of saying so,' she retorted, shaking her head at him.

'How can you say so? I have been your most loyal suitor.' A faint frown marred his boyish countenance when he spotted a group of gentlemen at the far side of the room and he added quietly, 'At least I am not one of those fair-weather suitors, who abandon you at the first hint of adversity. Most of that crowd over there have not been to one of your card parties since it was known that you are the patroness of Florence House.'

'We are grateful for your constant support, and Lord Markham's,' she added conscientiously. 'Is, um, is the viscount coming tonight, by the bye?'

'Oh, yes, we dined together. He is here somewhere,' said Gerald carelessly. 'He agrees with me, your support for Florence House is to be applauded.'

'Thank you, I am glad to know that. However, we have another patroness now, although she does not wish to be named yet. It means the house's future is much more secure. Our card parties are less important now. We may even discontinue them.'

'I should be glad of it,' he replied earnestly. 'While I understand the necessity I have always thought—' He broke off, flushing. 'But never mind that. The first set is forming. Shall we join them?'

Susannah stood up for the first two dances with Gerald, and after that there was no lack of partners. The music lifted her spirits. She no longer needed to worry about Florence House, she could relax and enjoy herself. As she was waiting for another dance to begin she saw Jasper at the side of the room. He looked very handsome in his dark coat, his black hair gleam-

ing in the candlelight. Perhaps she was being
unfair to him. Mayhap he had not intended to
tell anyone about Florence House. Surely she
could forgive such a slip?

By the end of the dance she had made up
her mind she would speak to him. She gracefully excused herself and moved off the dance
floor. The crowd was so thick it was impossible to see very far and Jasper's dark head
was not visible in any direction. On one of the
higher tiers of benches she could see her aunt,
part of a large crowd gathered around Lady
Gisburne. Susannah had no desire to join that
throng and she decided she would sit out on the
lower benches until the dancing stopped and
tea was served, then she would join her aunt
in the tea room. Perhaps she would find Jasper there. She began to make her way through
the crowd. Ahead of her she could see Mrs
Bulstrode and Mrs Farthing at the centre of a
little group of ladies. Susannah had no wish
to push past them and endure their insincere
greetings so she stepped to one side, where
she was shielded from their view by two large
gentlemen deep in conversation. However, she
was close enough to hear Mrs Farthing's sneer-
ing tones.

'I see Miss Prentess is wearing yet another

new gown. I wonder she can afford so many, with her little "interest" to keep up.'

Her cronies laughed. Susannah's lip curled slightly and she was about to move away when she heard Mrs Bulstrode give an angry titter.

'My dear, she can afford anything she wants now she has Markham in her pocket. I wager we will be calling her "Viscountess" before the end of the summer.'

Susannah froze. She folded her arms across her breast, hugging herself. Markham in her pocket? Nothing was further from the truth and yet…perhaps that is how it looked, to those who had been watching them at the last ball. Jasper had been very attentive. The blood that had earlier drained from her body now returned in an angry rush. How dare they! How dare they couple her name with anyone, least of all the viscount?

She remembered their last meeting. His insouciance, his confident assertion that he would *come about*. Perhaps Jasper himself had started these rumours, perhaps he was misguided enough to think that the hint of such a liaison would protect her from the disapproval of Bath society.

Fustian, she told herself savagely. *Only a nodcock would believe it would do anything other than make me look foolish!*

She looked about her. She must find Jasper and have it out with him. Now.

Another perambulation of the ballroom convinced her that the viscount was not present and she made her way to the Octagon. That, too, was crowded, but still no sign of him. Her last hope was the tea room. That was the least crowded of all, for the dancing was still going on and the waiters had not yet completed setting out the refreshments. One or two couples stood about the room and Susannah was about to give up and return to the ballroom when a movement on the balcony at the far end of the room caught her eye. Someone was on the upper level, and even in the shadows she recognised the familiar form of Lord Markham.

Susannah hurried up the stairs to the landing. The light from the three grand chandeliers did not reach this far and the soaring pillars threw further bands of shadow across the narrow gallery.

'Lord Markham. I have been looking for you.'

He turned at her voice and she saw the flash of white teeth as he smiled at her.

'Really? I came up here to escape the crowds. I am honoured that you have sought me out.'

'You should not be. I have come to pick a crow with you!' She began to pace up and down, too angry to keep still. 'Do you know that everyone is saying we are betrothed?'

'Are they?'

'Yes, they are,' she said furiously. 'Perhaps you can tell me how that rumour came about?'

'Your spending the whole evening with me at the Fancy Ball, perhaps?'

'That was to protect Florence House. You should have scotched this rumour.'

He spread his hands.

'I beg your pardon, but I was not aware of it.'

'Well you are aware of it now, and I demand you put a stop to it.'

He caught her hand as she went to pass him.

'Pray do not put yourself into a passion over such a little matter, Miss Prentess.'

'It is not a little matter,' she flashed at him, tearing her hand free. 'It is—it is a slur on my good name!'

His black brows went up.

'That you should be considered a fit wife for a viscount? I see no slur there.'

'This is all your fault,' she railed at him, too furious for reason. 'First you betray a confidence and then—'

With a growl of exasperation he caught her arms and turned her towards him, giving her a little shake.

'How many more times do I have to tell you I did *not* give away your secret? And no more

have I set it about that we are to be married.
Thunder an' turf, what would I want to do such
a thing for?' His hands slid up to her shoulders,
she could feel their heat through the thin silk of
the tiny puff sleeves.

'I don't know—to make mischief, perhaps!'

His thumbs moved gently over her collar
bones, caressing the bare skin. It was strangely
arresting. Her mind might still be angry with
him, but her limbs were locked, she was unable
to move away.

'I am not in the habit of making mischief of
that sort.'

His low voice resonated through her body. A
tingle ran down the length of her spine. Gently he pulled her back against the wall, where
the shadows were deepest. She should protest,
push him away, run back to the safety of the
crowded ballroom.

She did none of these things. His hands continued to hold her shoulders. He was standing
so close now that she could smell the spicy tang
of cologne on his skin. Her breasts seemed to
swell and pull her forwards, responding to the
attraction of his lean, muscular body.

He put the fingers of one hand beneath her
chin and forced her to look up at him. His face
was in shadow, but she could sense his eyes on
her face, feel them burning into her very soul,

laying it bare. It was as much as she could do not to whimper in fear.

'S-stop this,' she stammered. 'Let me go.'

In response he lowered his head and touched her lips with his own. She found herself reaching up, standing on tiptoe to prolong the contact.

'You may leave whenever you wish.'

The words whispered over her skin, their meaning lost. She closed her eyes, shivering with delight as his kisses strayed to her neck. Her head went back and she clutched at his jacket, a wave of dizziness washing over her. He planted kisses on her throat and along the length of her jaw before returning his attention to her mouth and then she was drowning in his kiss, opening her lips, inviting him to plunder her mouth, her own tongue tentatively flickering to meet his.

He gave a groan as his arms tightened around her. She was crushed against his body—it was every bit as hard and demanding as she remembered. She wanted to tear at his clothes but instead drove her hands into his hair, revelling in the silky strength of those black locks between her fingers. Her body was on fire, her thighs aching for his touch and when he raised his head she clung to him, trembling. Only his encircling arms prevented her from collapsing in a heap at his feet.

'Tell me you did not plan this,' he murmured into her hair.

'Plan what?'

He laughed softly.

'You bewitch me.'

Susannah took a few deep breaths and fought to regain control of her unruly body. Not just her body, her mind, too. Jasper spoke of being bewitched. Surely something of that kind had happened to her? This was not normal, rational behaviour.

Steeling herself, she pushed him away. She felt a little unsteady, but her legs did not crumple beneath her.

'Pray to not think I came up here to, to...'

'No, I acquit you of that. As you must acquit me of spreading rumours about our impending marriage. But you know, perhaps it is not such an impossible idea.'

'I beg your pardon?'

'Perhaps we *should* marry,' he said.

'P-pray do not tease me, my lord.'

'No, I am in earnest. After forcing you to dine alone with me, then our being together at Florence House, it occurs to me that I should offer you the protection of my name.' His wicked smile flashed. 'Especially if we have this effect upon each other.'

Another tremor ran through her, but this time of fear.

'No. Never.' She crossed her arms, thoroughly alarmed. 'Th-this is not natural. It is to be avoided. It leads to, to debauchery and decadence.'

He smiled. 'I am becoming more enamoured of the idea every minute.'

He reached out for her but she whisked herself away from him, putting her hands on the iron railings behind her for support.

'I c-cannot marry you.' Panic welled up inside her. 'You—I—you frighten me.'

'No, you have frightened yourself,' he said gently. 'These feeling are natural. When we are married you will see—'

'No! I have made a vow to myself never to marry.'

'Because of what happened to your sister? It is time to let that go, Susannah. It is time to live your own life.'

She gazed up at him. His words were gentle, but there was something in his eyes, a warm glow that promised much and threatened her self-control. It terrified her. A sudden burst of laughter echoed around them. Jasper looked down into the tea room.

'The dancing has ended. Everyone is coming in here now. You had best go and find your aunt.'

She took a step away from him.

'I c-can't marry you, my lord. I c-can't…'

'Yes, you can.'

He reached out and touched her cheek with his fingers. The skin burned, sending white-hot shards of pleasure pulsing through her. Did he not understand this should not be happening to her? She could not allow any man such control over her.

'I have to leave Bath for a few days,' he said. 'There are papers I have to sign at Markham, but I will be back on Wednesday evening. I will call on Thursday and we will discuss it further. You need not fear, everything shall be done properly. I shall ask your aunt for permission to pay my addresses.'

She shivered. It must not happen. She could not live in such a way, turning into a wanton, unrestrained wretch every time he came near her. She knew only too well the pain and heartache she would suffer if she allowed it to continue. Ladies were to be respected, worshipped—the way Gerald respected and worshipped her. Those baser instincts that Jasper unleashed in her must be controlled at all costs. Biting her lip, she began to back away, yet when he put out his hand she gave him hers, trying to ignore the little arrows of desire that darted along her arm as his thumb grazed the soft skin of her wrist.

'Go now, then. Until Thursday.'

He let her go and she stood irresolute. She

wanted to throw herself back into his arms, to surrender to that overwhelming passion he called up so easily within her, but that would mean disaster. He was the flame, she the moth. He would destroy her. Summoning up every reserve of energy she could find, she nodded to him and forced herself to turn and walk away.

Susannah did not go in search of her aunt, instead she wandered around the ballroom, which was deserted now save for little chattering groups that had no wish for refreshment. How had it happened? How had this man come into her world and turned it upside down? She did not need this, did not want it. She wanted only to go back to the safe certainties of the life she had known, where she was in control, in charge of her own happiness. She sank down on a chair, unseeing eyes staring at the empty dance floor. He did not want to marry her but he felt obliged to, because he had compromised her reputation. Despite that he would come to the Crescent, as he had promised. He would talk to Aunt Maude, he would propose. He would take her hand, look into her eyes and she would be powerless to refuse him.

'I can't let that happen,' she whispered. 'I c-cannot let myself be subjugated by him. No man shall ever be my master.'

She wrapped her arms about herself and

began to rock backwards and forwards. There must be a way to prevent it.

'Miss Prentess, are you unwell?'

General Sanstead was bending over her, his kindly face creased with concern. She forced herself to get up, to smile at him.

'I am perfectly well, thank you General. I, um, I need to find someone...'

She walked off, her limbs feeling strangely stiff and difficult to control. She must go home immediately. She would leave Bath, go away where no one could find her. People were beginning to return to the ballroom now, and one of the first to come through the door was Gerald Barnabus. He saw her immediately.

'Good heavens, Susannah, you are as white as a sheet. Are you unwell?'

'Yes—no—I must get away from here.' She clutched at his outstretched hand, trying to remain calm and not burst into tears.

'Yes, of course, my dear. We will find Mrs Wilby. But is there anything I can do?'

'Oh, Gerald, I have made such a mess of everything. I am afraid—'

'Afraid of what?'

She could not bring herself to tell him about Jasper. She said distractedly, 'Of being alone.'

His grip on her hand tightened.

'Well that is easily resolved,' he said cheerfully. 'Have I not asked you to marry me count-

less times? You only have to say the word and
you need never be alone again. I will protect
you from everything.'

She stared up into his smiling face. Good,
kind Gerald, who had been a friend to her and
had never asked more than to be allowed to kiss
her hand. He would protect her.

'Oh, yes, Gerald,' she said quickly. 'I will
marry you. And as soon as possible.'

Chapter Thirteen

Gerald stared at her for a long, long moment before a grin of delight broke over his face. 'Truly? Why, Susannah, you have made me the happiest of men.'

He pressed a kiss upon her fingers and she waited for the reaction, for her skin to tingle and burn, for that ache deep in her body. It did not come. She was safe.

'We must tell my aunt,' she said.

'By all means, let us go and find her.'

Mrs Wilby was sitting beside Lady Gisburne on the first row of benches. Susannah was inclined to hold back, but Gerald was eager to impart the good news, so she stood silently beside him as he made his announcement.

Mrs Wilby looked a little startled at first, but then she smiled and held out her hand for him to kiss. Lady Gisburne's congratulations were more restrained, and she gave Susannah a quizzical look.

'I did not know you were considering matrimony, Miss Prentess.'

'I have been pestering her to marry me for months now,' said Gerald happily. He turned his smile towards Susannah. 'And at last my persistence has been rewarded.'

'And when will the engagement be announced?' the dowager enquired. 'Or is it to be a private affair?'

'Of course it will be made public,' replied Susannah, frowning a little. 'Everything shall be done properly.'

The words reminded her of the encounter with Jasper and she had to force her wandering mind to concentrate upon the dowager's next words.

'And will this affect our plans for the charity?'

'Not at all, except...' Susannah hesitated as she thought of a way to delay her next meeting with the viscount. 'Perhaps we could put off our visit to Florence House until Thursday morning?'

'Very well, my dear, Thursday it shall be.'

'Thank you, ma'am.' The sudden scrape of the fiddles caught Susannah's attention. She wanted very much to go home, but to leave so suddenly after the announcement would cause comment, Instead she turned to Gerald.

'The dancing will be starting again very soon. Shall we join them?'

'Why not?' He grinned. 'And now we are betrothed I need not give you up for the rest of the evening!'

Jasper stood back, watching the dancers. He could not keep his eyes from Susannah, who skipped and twirled about the room, her bouncing curls gleaming in the candlelight. She was going down the dance with Gerald, and although she was smiling Jasper thought her enjoyment a trifle forced. He considered seeking her out for the next dance but decided against it. Their earlier meeting had flustered her. He grinned to himself. It had thrown him, too, to discover just how much he wanted her. His inner smile grew and he shook his head a little, thinking of the mull he had made of his proposal. For once his charming address had deserted him, so it was no wonder he had startled her. But she was no fool. She would know he was in earnest, so he would leave her to become accustomed to the idea of being Lady Markham.

A movement nearby caught his attention. Lady Gisburne was making her way towards the door.

'Going so soon, ma'am?'

'I am. These late hours no longer agree with me.' She paused, her eyes following his gaze to the centre of the room.

'Are you hoping to dance with Miss Prentess? You will be disappointed, I think.'

'No, let Barnabus enjoy himself. I shall be calling upon Miss Prentess on Thursday.'

'Will you now?' She paused. 'And does the lady know of it?'

He smiled.

'She does indeed.' He dragged his eyes away from the dancers and fixed them upon the old lady's face. 'Why do you ask?'

She did not reply and for an instant Jasper wanted to take her into his confidence, to tell her he intended to make Susannah Prentess his wife. But no. She was Dominic's godmother, not his. His family must be informed first, and he would tell them just as soon as he had made his formal proposal to Susannah.

The dowager waved her hand as she finally replied, 'Oh, no reason. But if you are not going to dance again, Markham, then you can make yourself useful and escort me back to Laura Place.'

He laughed at that.

'Of course, ma'am. With the greatest of pleasure.'

Jasper had never been so impatient to be done with his estate business, but at length it was concluded and he could return to Bath. On Thursday morning he rose early and dressed with particular care, honouring the occasion with a morning coat of midnight blue, a white-embroidered waistcoat and buff coloured pantaloons tucked into shining Hessians. He arrived at Royal Crescent shortly before ten o'clock. He was shown into the morning room, where he found Mrs Wilby engaged with her tambour frame. She quickly put it down when he entered, and rose to greet him.

'Lord Markham, this is a pleasant surprise.'

He bowed over her hand.

'Did Miss Prentess not tell you I would be calling?'

'No, my lord, she did not.' She waved him to a seat. 'She has gone out.'

'Oh? And when do you expect her to return?'

'Not for some time, my lord. She is gone to Florence House with Lady Gisburne.' She noticed his frown and added quickly, 'They arranged it some days ago, I believe.'

'Then she did not tell you I intended to call?'

She fluttered her hands.

'No, but with all the excitement of the past few days I expect it slipped her mind.'

'Excitement, ma'am?'

She looked at him in surprise.

'Did you not know? She is engaged to Mr Barnabus.'

It took all Jasper's self-command to get him through the rest of the interview and back out into the street. While his mouth uttered the congratulations expected of him, his mind was seething with conjecture, none of which made any sense.

So she had accepted Gerald's proposal. But why now, when she had consistently turned him down in the past? And to do so within days of their explosive encounter on Monday evening? The two events must be linked. She had said she could not marry him—was that because she had already accepted Gerald? He paused, rubbing his chin. If that was so, why did she not tell him as much?

By the time he reached York House he was no nearer an answer and he strode on to Westgate Buildings, where he was informed Mr Barnabus had not yet left his room. He took the stairs two at a time and his knock upon the door was answered almost immediately.

'Jasper, come in.' Gerald was in his shirtsleeves, his cravat hanging loose about his neck. He stood aside to let Jasper enter. 'I thought you were at Markham.'

'I returned last night. I understand I should congratulate you.' Jasper watched him carefully. There was nothing but genuine pleasure in the young man's smile.

'Ah, you have heard then. She has accepted me at last.'

Jasper forced his own lips into a smile and said casually, 'You have been very busy while I have been away.'

'It was all agreed at the Upper Rooms on Monday. I was coming out of the tea room when we met and, well…' He paused while he deftly knotted his neckcloth, then grinned at Jasper. 'Suddenly we had agreed it all.'

'Extraordinary,' murmured Jasper.

'Isn't it?' said Gerald. 'I can't tell you how happy I am.' He glanced down at his watch. 'I cannot stay longer, I am afraid. I am off to Hotwells to see my mother. I want to tell her myself and give her time to become accustomed to the idea before I take Susannah to meet her. Then we can decide upon when and where we are to be married.'

Jasper had been holding on to some faint idea that this was all a hoax, but now that hope died. Susannah would not deliberately serve Gerald such a trick. But something was wrong, he was certain of it, and if he was to prevent her making the biggest mistake of her life then he had to call a halt to this engagement, before it was too late.

He went back to his hotel and sent a note to Royal Crescent, formally begging for an interview with Miss Prentess as soon as she returned. Shortly before dinner he had his reply.

He read the words aloud. 'Miss Prentess regrets she is not at home to callers.'

With a savage curse he screwed up the paper and hurled it into the fireplace.

Susannah and Lady Gisburne's visit to Florence House took the best part of the day, but Susannah was well satisfied with the result. Mrs Gifford was now back as housekeeper, and after accepting their condolences upon the death of her sister she sat down with them to discuss the running of the house. Lady Gisburne approved of all that had been achieved and promised to provide funds to enable more extensive repairs on the house to begin immediately. Before leaving, Susannah took some time to speak to the young ladies still in residence. There were only two, Lizzie and her baby having moved to Henrietta Street. Violet Anstruther was inclined to be tearful and required a great deal of comforting from Mrs Gifford, but Jane and her baby were doing well and Susannah was touched when Jane asked permission to call her daughter Susan.

'You were wise to start on a small scale,' Lady Gisburne commented as the carriage trundled back to Bath. 'Now word of Florence House is out I expect applications to increase rapidly.'

'Yes, sadly I believe that is true. There are any number of young women requiring our support. The rent from Odesse and the lace-makers helps, but it will not cover everything. Your help is very welcome in keeping the house running.'

'The papers are being drawn up even now, and I have sent out invitations for the little party on Saturday, to formally announce my patronage of Florence House.' The dowager gave a thin smile. 'There are times when a title is very useful, Miss Prentess. I have had very few refusals.'

'I am glad to hear it, My aunt and I are very much looking forward to coming to Laura Place for the event, I only wish Gerald could be back in time, but he writes to say Mrs Barnabus needs him for a few more days yet.'

With an alarming want of tact he had also written that his mother had been thrown into strong hysterics by the news of their betrothal, but she did not intend to share this news with anyone.

'Once you are married you may not be able to play such an active role,' remarked the dowager. 'You will have a family of your own to consider.'

Susannah looked away, uncomfortable with such thoughts. She had become engaged to Barnabus because he had seemed safe, he was inclined to worship her reverently, but she was well aware that once they were married he would expect her to allow him more than a chaste kiss on the cheek.

'My aunt has always been the main player in this, Lady Gisburne.'

'Tush, everyone knows now that you are the force behind Florence House.' The dowager smiled. 'It does not matter too much. Mrs Gifford is perfectly capable of handling the day-to-day running of the charity, and we will merely be patronesses, something that you can do even if you were to live many miles from here.'

Susannah frowned.

'Why should you say that? Mr Barnabus is very happy to make his home in Bath.'

From her corner of the carriage the dowager gave her an enigmatic smile.

'Sometimes one's plans can change,' she said.

The news that Lord Markham had called was no surprise to Susannah, although she told Aunt Maude she had quite forgotten about it. The viscount's subsequent note gave her a momentary panic, but her response was soon sent back to him and she hoped that would be the end of it.

'Indeed, I am quite fatigued with all the recent excitement,' she remarked as she sat down to dinner with her aunt. 'I think, while Gerald is away from Bath, I should like to have Gatley deny all visitors.'

Aunt Maude was immediately concerned.

'My love, this is quite unlike you, you usually have an abundance of energy. Are you sure you are not sickening for something?'

'No, no, of course not. I have been trotting a little too hard, as Gerald would say. I shall come about again very soon, you will see.'

'I sincerely hope so.' Aunt Maude picked up her knife and fork. 'Very well, we shall cancel all our engagements for a few days, and do nothing more strenuous than stroll to the Pump Room, where I am sure a glass of the waters will soon restore your spirits.'

The Pump Room was always popular, but any hope Susannah had that she might lose herself in the jostling crowd soon disappeared when she saw Jasper making his purposeful way towards her.

His greeting was abrupt, and when he suggested they might take a turn about the room together she politely declined. She remained resolutely beside her aunt, conversing with friends, then she took a cup of the waters, sipping at it reluctantly and doing her best not to screw up her face at the sulphurous taste, but all the time she was aware of the viscount's dark presence, waiting for his chance for a private word with her. It could not last, however. Lord Markham was far too distinguished a visitor to be allowed to stand idle. He was soon accosted by those claiming an acquaintance and he was obliged to move away. Eventually he left the Pump Room and the tension in her spine eased. She could relax again, and when she saw Kate Logan she hurried across the room to greet her.

'My dear, where have you been for such an age?' Susannah took Kate's hands and pulled her forwards to kiss her cheek. 'To go off for such a time, and never a word to me to say where you had gone.'

'I know, and I apologise,' said Kate. 'We arrived back too late last night to call upon you.'

'Never mind that, you are here now.' Susannah took her arm. 'Let us walk about the room and you can tell me where you have been.'

'I believe you have news, too, Susannah—'

'Yes, but you must go first,' she interrupted her. 'I insist.'

'Very well.' They walked on for a few steps and Susannah watched her friend biting her lip. She looked unusually pensive. 'I have been to Radstock.'

'Radstock!' Susannah laughed. 'What on earth can have taken you there?'

'Mr Camerton's mother lives there. Mr—that is—Charles and I are to be married.'

Susannah halted.

'But I thought—' She stared at her friend. 'I don't understand. I thought you had vowed never to marry again. After the last time…'

'I know, I thought I would never meet any-one who would make me change my mind on that, but I have.'

'No.' Susannah turned to her, taking her hands and giving them a little shake. 'Kate, you are funning. You must be. Your last husband was a monster, you told me he— That no man was worth the risk...'

Kate blushed and shook her head.

'I was wrong,' she said simply. 'When I met Charles I knew I was wrong.' She looked up suddenly. 'But you are a fine one to be admon-ishing me for my change of heart! I hear you are engaged, now, to Gerald Barnabus.'

'Yes, yes, but that is different,' argued Susan-nah. 'I will not be diverted, Kate. How can you be engaged to Mr Camerton? You have known him for only a few short weeks.'

'I know, but I love him, Susannah.' The smile and the soft look that transfigured the widow's face made Susannah's heart sink. 'He is a gam-bler, like me. We fell in love at the card table, then he came to call and took me riding, and we went walking in Sydney Gardens, and...' Kate looked up, her eyes shining. 'He has turned my whole world upside down, Susannah. He sends my spirits soaring heavenwards just by holding my hand. His smile lights up my day. And he feels the same way about me. I can hardly be-lieve my good fortune. He loves me, he really does. So we are to be married, just as soon as the banns have been called.'

A cold, dark cloud wrapped itself around Susannah's heart as she listened to her friend. She thought of Gerald Barnabus, her own fiancé. She imagined him holding her hand, smiling at her and she felt nothing. Nothing at all.

Mrs Wilby was as good as her word and cancelled all their engagements for the whole week, with the exception of Lady Gisburne's party at Laura Place. Susannah was adamant that they must attend, but she was uncharacteristically nervous as she allowed Dorcas to dress her in her cream satin with the green ribbon ties.

'Stop fidgeting, miss, do,' Dorcas admonished her as she nestled tiny cream rosebuds amongst the golden curls piled up on her head. 'I've never known you in such a fret before a party.'

'Tonight's soirée means Florence House is no longer a secret, Dorcas,' Susannah told her. 'I am very anxious that it should be a success.'

But to herself she acknowledged that this was not the reason for her unease. Since her engagement to Gerald she had avoided Jasper's company, but tonight there could be no escape. She would have to face him.

'Well this is most satisfactory,' murmured Aunt Maude, looking around the crowded reception rooms in Laura Place, 'I believe all of Bath is here tonight.'

Susannah could only nod in agreement. Lady Gisburne had specifically noted on her invitations that the evening was to acknowledge her patronage of Florence House, a home for distressed gentlewomen, but only one or two people had stayed away. Everyone else was keen to congratulate the dowager upon her support of such a cause. Even Mrs Bulstrode was present, as well as Mr and Mrs Farthing, a generous donation from Lady Gisburne to the Walcot Street Penitentiary helping them to bury their resentment.

'A very different reaction to the one I received,' murmured Susannah.

'Unmarried ladies are expected to be more circumspect,' came her aunt's comfortable response. 'When you are Mrs Barnabus no one will think anything of you supporting such a cause. What a pity Gerald could not be here tonight.'

Susannah thought so, too, especially when Jasper appeared. Her heart began to hammer uncomfortably when she saw him walk in, his gleaming black hair brushed back from that handsome face. He bowed over the dowager's hand, and as he straightened his dark eyes raked the room. It was as if some second sense brought his gaze straight to her.

She squared her shoulders. It would be better to get this first meeting over, then they could be easy. Her confidence began to wane as he made his way towards her. He stopped to speak to others on his way, his easy manners and charming smile much in evidence, but when at last he stood before her there was a fierce, uncompromising look in his eye that made her want to run away. Instead she forced her knees to bend a little. She kept her hands firmly clasped about her fan.

'Lord Markham.'

'Miss Prentess.'

Aunt Maude was addressing the viscount, nervousness making her garrulous, but Susannah did not hear her and she suspected Jasper too was not attending. He was holding her eyes.

'I believe you have been indisposed, ma'am.'

'I, er, I have been resting, but I could not miss this evening.'

'I guessed as much, which is why I came.' He lowered his voice. 'You cannot avoid me for ever, you know.'

A sudden constriction in her throat made it difficult for Susannah to swallow. She kept her eyes on her fan, studying the intricate pattern on the sticks.

'I have no idea what...' Her voice tailed away when she looked up and met his hard eyes again.

Someone had claimed Mrs Wilby's attention.

For the moment no one was attending to them and Jasper made the most of the opportunity.

'We will talk, alone.'

'No, I cannot. I—'

'You can and will.' He leaned closer. 'There is a small sitting room downstairs. The door to the left of the hall table. I will meet you there at midnight.'

'No.' She cast about wildly for an excuse. 'That is…'

In the press of the crowd no one saw him grip her arm.

'Midnight,' he said again. 'Be there, madam. You owe me that much.'

Jasper moved away and Susannah was free to circulate, to talk, but even while she conversed and smiled her mind was racing. He was angry with her and she could not blame him. She tried to tell herself he could not touch her now, she was engaged to Gerald, but somehow that thought did not reassure her as it should. She took a glass of wine to steady her nerves and tried to interest herself in the proceedings. She knew most of the people present, even the various single gentlemen who attended her card parties had turned out in force. At one point she found herself face to face with Mr Warwick. He looked confused for a moment, she thought he might speak to her, but after acknowledging her with a tiny nod of his head he hurried away. She wondered why. If it was true that he was the father of Violet Anstruther's child then he should be grateful to her. Florence House would take on the responsibility that he had shirked. Hunching one white shoulder, she turned away. Her eyes strayed to the clock on the mantelpiece. Eleven o'clock. Another hour and she would have to join Jasper in that downstairs room. Alone.

You do not have to go, a little voice in her head whispered seductively. *Think of the scandal. You are promised to another man. You should not go.*

But she would go, if only because she knew that Jasper would come after her if she did not. The minutes ticked by with agonising slowness. Lady Gisburne carried her away to introduce her to Lady this, and Lord that, but she could concentrate on nothing, only the hands of the clock steadily moving towards twelve.

The noise from the reception rooms died away behind her as Susannah slipped down the stairs. The hall was deserted save for a porter dozing in his chair by the front door. She could see the hall table, flanked by two identical doors. Pausing only to collect herself, she moved to the one on the left.

Susannah closed the door quietly behind her and looked around. At first she thought the room was empty. A small fire and the single-branched candlestick provided only enough light to show her the empty satin-covered sofa and armchairs. Then a shadow moved by the window and she saw Jasper.

'I cannot stay long, my lord. I shall be missed.'

'Tell me why you are marrying Barnabus.'

She moved towards the fire, holding her hands out to the glow, more for distraction than any need of warmth.

'Is it not obvious?'

'Not to me.'

She ran her tongue across her lips. They were dry, a sign of her nervousness.

'He...he has courted me for months.'

'But you knew I was going to offer for you. Why did you not tell me then?'

'I did not think you were serious.'

'After what happened on the balcony of the tea room?' He gave a savage laugh. 'How passionate does a man have to be, madam, before you consider him *serious*?'

She did not move, keeping her attention on the hearth. She heard his hasty stride behind her.

'How passionate was Barnabus, when you accepted him?'

Her head came up at that.

'Gerald is a gentleman—'

'You mean he has not touched you.'

She fluttered her fan.

'He does not need to. We—'

'You have promised yourself to a man for whom you feel nothing.'

'That is not true!'

'Is it not?' He grasped her shoulders and turned her to face him. 'Does the blood pulse through your veins when he touches you? Does Barnabus drive you to the brink of madness with desire?'

She shrugged him off.

'I do not want that.' Her cheeks were burning and she fanned herself rapidly.

'Did you accept him to escape from me?' When she did not reply he continued, 'So that's it. You are afraid of what is between us—'

'There is nothing between us!'

He took the fan from her and threw it down on the chair. Before she could protest he pulled her into his arms and kissed her savagely. Immediately her body sprang to life. The blood not only pulsed, it positively sang in her veins. She knew she must not give in. She put her hands on his chest, resisting the impulse to cling to his coat.

'Tell me you feel nothing for me.' His breath was hot on her neck as he covered her skin with kisses, each one burning even further through the defences she had erected. 'Tell me you do not want to lie here with me now and let me make love to you.'

With a superhuman effort she pushed herself away from him.

'That is desire, my lord, but it is not *love*.'

He towered over her, his face in shadow and his shoulders rising and falling with each ragged breath.

'If it is love to know I cannot live without you, that every day we are apart is a day in hell then, yes, Susannah, I love you.'

Lies, said the voice in her head. *He is a seducer. He will say anything to bend you to his will.*

She backed away, the pain of the separation tearing at her skin.

'Well, *I* do not love *you*.'

The words fell like lead weights into the silence between them.

'Do you love Gerald?'

She hesitated.

'We have mutual affection and respect. Love will follow.'

'Are you sure, Susannah?' He was closing in again, and once more desire and panic warred within her. 'Are you sure it won't be boredom that will follow? Dull complacency?'

She gave a sob.

'You do not understand. I am *safe* with Gerald. I can live my life in comfort, I will not be forever wondering if he is faithful to me, I will not risk…' she turned away, squeezing her eyes shut, trying to hold back the tears as she forced out the final words '…breaking my heart.'

Silence. Susannah could hear only the ticking of the clock. Surreptitiously she wiped away a rogue tear.

'Ah.' He uttered the word like a sigh. 'I would offer you my hand, my heart, my *life*, Susannah, but there is an element of risk in all things. This passion we feel for one another may burn out, though I do not believe it. You would have to trust me on that, but you have never trusted any man, have you?'

'Men in the grip of passion are unreliable,' she muttered. 'Even my own father, though he swore he loved my mother and came crawling back, begging for forgiveness on more than one occasion.'

'I cannot argue against that,' he said quietly. 'I know some men are feckless creatures, but not all of us. However, if you would rather have Barnabus—

'He loves me!'

'Then let us hope that is enough for both of you, and that I have been mistaken in my own feelings.' He walked to the door. 'Goodbye, Susannah. I will not trouble you again.'

He went out, the door closing behind him. The emptiness and silence pressed in on her.

Susannah felt then that she had lost something in her life. As though some prop, something necessary to her comfort, had been taken away.

Chapter Fourteen

Jasper did not go back upstairs. He was in no mood for company so he let himself out of the house and walked back to his hotel. He was promised to escort the dowager to the Abbey in the morning, but after that he would quit Bath. He had spent far too long here already and there was work on his estates that needed his attention. That should help to keep his mind from dwelling on Susannah Prentess. He should be glad to be leaving her behind. He had found her a patroness for Florence House, he had even endured an uncomfortable night in a chair there, to say nothing of slaving away in the kitchen to feed everyone, and for what? She was not even grateful. He shook his head and swung his cane at a clump of weeds pushing up at the roadside. He did not want her gratitude, he wanted to protect her, to make her comfortable—to make her happy. And if that meant he had to disappear from her life then so be it.

Susannah and her aunt did not attend the Abbey service the following morning. Jasper sat beside Lady Gisburne during the long sermon, impatiently waiting for the service to end so that he could get back to his rooms, where Peters was packing up everything in readiness for an early start in the morning. It was not until he was helping Lady Gisburne back into her carriage that Jasper told her he was leaving, hoping to fend off any questions by adding that he had business at Markham.

'No doubt it can wait a few more days.'

'I regret it cannot. My stay in Bath has been far longer than intended.'

'Because of Susannah Prentess.'

Her shrewd gaze was on his face but he kept his countenance impassive as he took his seat beside her.

'She was a distraction, I admit.'

'Hmm. I wondered how you would take it when you learned that she was to marry. What happened last night?'

He raised his brows.

'Last night, ma'am?'

The slight note of hauteur in his tone had no effect on the dowager.

'It was obvious to me that the two of you have been playing cat and mouse. Then you both disappeared last night. What did she say to you?'

He decided not to deny it. The old lady was too astute to be fobbed off.

'She intends to marry Barnabus.' He added bitterly, 'She feels safe with him. Safe! What she means is she thinks she can keep him under her thumb, poor devil!'

'Yes, I thought as much.'

He shifted his eyes to her face.

'You knew she was engaged to Barnabus, didn't you? You knew it that night, at the ball, before I went off to Markham. For pity's sake, why did you not tell me?'

'Would it have made any difference?'

'Yes! I might have reasoned with her—'

'As you did last night? When Susannah came back upstairs she looked positively distraught.'

A dull flush crept into his cheek.

'She inflames me,' he admitted. 'I find myself attracted to her like no other, and she feels the same, though she will not admit it. That is why I am going home in the morning. There is nothing here for me now.'

'Much as it pains me to contradict you, Markham,' replied the dowager untruthfully, 'you are not leaving Bath tomorrow. Dominic and his family are on their way, and he will expect you to be here to meet him.'

'I don't believe it!'

Ignoring his exclamation, the dowager continued impassively, 'I had an express from my godson this morning, telling me they will be arriving tomorrow.'

Jasper found a similar note waiting for him when he returned to York House. Peters received the change of plan with unimpaired calm, merely enquiring if he should instruct the hotel to prepare rooms in readiness for their arrival.

'No need. The dowager has invited them to stay with her at Laura Place.' He crumpled the note in his fist. 'It means we will not be returning to Markham tomorrow after all. I must at least stay to welcome them.'

'So tell me all about your engagement to Mr Barnabus.'

Susannah was strolling through Sydney Gardens with Kate, and was half-expecting the question. She had managed to avoid the subject since Kate's return to Bath, but had known that at some point she would have to explain.

'Oh well, he has been very persistent, you know, and he is such a sweet boy.'

'I thought you had turned your face against marriage.'

'No more than you, Kate,' she countered. 'I have heard you say many times that nothing would persuade you to take another husband.'

'I know.' Kate looked down, and Susannah saw the tell-tale blush mantle her cheeks. She could not remember Kate ever being out of countenance before Charles Camerton appeared, but recently she had changed, become much…softer, somehow. Now she gave a self-conscious laugh. 'I thought myself too old, too embittered to risk marrying again, but meeting Charles has changed my mind.' She glanced up. 'I am afraid he rather swept me off my feet, so much so that I confided in him about Florence House.'

'You did?'

'Yes, and I am very sorry for it. It is entirely my fault that your secret is known. You know how it is when you meet someone and you just want to talk and talk for ever? I am afraid I was not very discreet, and since I did not impress upon Charles that it *was* a secret he spoke of it in the Pump Room and—well, it went on from there. I suspected as much when we were so thin of company at your card party, and when I asked Charles he said he had mentioned it to Mrs Bulstrode, although thankfully he said nothing about the connection with Odesse. I know I should have told you immediately, but I did not want you to be cross with Charles. I hoped it might soon be forgotten. I beg your pardon, Susannah. Can you ever forgive me?'

So Jasper had not betrayed her. A dozen disjointed thoughts raced through her brain. If she had not been so quick to condemn him they might still be friends—more than friends. No. He roused in her such uncontrollable passions that friendship was not possible. She was engaged to Gerald now. Safe, dependable Gerald. That was what she wanted. She summoned up a smile.

'Of course I can forgive you, Kate. In fact, it has all turned out very well. If it had remained a secret then Lady Gisburne would not have learned of it and wanted to become our patroness. What I find it harder to understand is your sudden decision to marry.'

Kate's mouth twisted into a rueful smile.

'I was very strident, was I not, in my condemnation of all men? It comes from my years married to one who…'

Susannah squeezed her arm.

'You do not need to tell me, Kate. I knew you then, I saw what you went through, even though I was very young and everyone did their best to keep these things from the children. Infidelity was rife in Gibraltar. Even my own father was not above taking advantage of the camp followers.'

'How do you know that?' asked Kate quickly. 'I do not believe he would tell you such a thing, nor your mother.'

'I heard them arguing one night.' Susannah

blushed at the memory. 'He said if Mama would not let him into her bed then he had to relieve his—his *passions* elsewhere.'

'Oh my dear, I am so sorry.' Kate squeezed her arm. 'Your mother had become very religious, had she not?'

'Yes, like her sister, although not quite such a zealot.' Susannah shivered. 'But that does not excuse his behaviour.'

'Do not be too hard on your father, my dear. He was a good man, in his way. Certainly not vicious, like Logan.'

'That is why I was so shocked when you told me about you and Charles Camerton.'

Kate sighed.

'I did not mean to fall in love with him, but I could not help it.' She laughed suddenly. 'I have broken all the rules I set for myself, have I not? I have listened to my heart, and not my head. But you must have done the same, my dear. Why else would you have decided to marry— Susannah, why do you look like that?'

Susannah shook her head, suddenly tears were crowding her eyes.

'Oh, Kate,' she whispered. 'I think I have made a terrible mistake.'

'Dom.' Jasper touched his brother's shoulder. 'I was told I would find you in the Pump Room, but I didn't believe it.'

Dominic turned, grinning. It was like looking into a mirror, thought Jasper. He still felt it, despite the livid scar that stretched across his twin's cheek.

'My godmother must drink the waters and my wife wants to gossip.' Dominic gripped his hand. 'How are you, Brother?'

'Well enough, thank you. I received your note yesterday, but I thought you would need the evening to recover.'

'Aye, after a whole day on the road the children were fractious and Zelah and I too tired to be good company.'

'I am pleased I did not take up your invitation to join you for dinner then! What brings you to Bath?'

Dominic's hard eyes flickered towards Lady Gisburne.

'Summoned. She told us *you* have been here for some time.'

'I came here after visiting Gloriana. She was afraid Gerald had fallen into the clutches of some harpy.'

'And had he?'

'Not at all.' Jasper spotted a speck of dust on his sleeve and flicked it away. 'The lady is an heiress. Considerably richer than Gerald, I believe.'

A soft voice called his name. Zelah was beside him, holding out her hands.

'Welcome to Bath, Sister.' He kissed her cheek. 'What brings you here? Your glowing looks tell me it is not for your health.'

'No, of course not.' She tucked her arm in his. 'Take me for a promenade about the room, Jasper.'

He glanced at Dominic, who nodded his approval.

'Aye, off you go, but don't keep her too long. I won't spend all day here.'

'Surly as ever,' commented Jasper as he led his sister-in-law away.

She laughed. 'No, no, he is much better now. When I met him he would not have dreamed of attending an assembly such as this. Now he is completely at his ease, and is not even conscious of his scars.'

'That is down to you, Zelah. We are all grateful for that.'

'Nonsense.' She blushed. 'He would have come about, in time. But this not why I wanted you to myself. Tell me about this lady who has stolen your heart.'

He stopped, exclaiming explosively, 'Who the devil—!'

'Lady Gisburne told us all about it last night.'

'Then she has been a great deal too busy!'

'Dom says he has never known you to take so much trouble over a woman.'

'Hell and damnation, I won't have my affairs

discussed in this way,' he muttered in a furious undertone.

Zelah was not noticeably abashed, and merely made him walk on.

'So is it true? I do hope so, Jasper, because I never liked the idea of your pining over me. Tell me all about her.'

That drew a reluctant smile from him.

'You have grown very forward since you married my brother. But there is nothing to tell you, since she is going to marry Gerald Barnabus.'

'He is some sort of cousin of yours, is he not? And does she love him?'

'She will drive him to distraction.'

'That does not answer my question.'

'Does it matter?' he said impatiently. 'They are to be married. Barnabus has gone off to see his mother to arrange everything. There is nothing to be done.' Zelah's questioning gaze goaded him to add, 'Yes, I had some hopes there, but nothing serious.'

'Everyone tells me she is a great beauty.'

'Matchless.'

'But you have known many beauties, Jasper. What makes this one so different?'

He considered the question.

'Her spirit,' he said at last. 'She saw an injustice and has fought to do something about it, even at the expense of her own good name. She is very courageous…' he remembered the alarm in Susannah's hazel eyes when he had reached out for her '…at least, in some things.'

'Then I hope I shall meet this paragon, very soon.'

Jasper looked up.

'You shall do so now. Gerald is here, and he has Miss Prentess on his arm.'

Introductions were performed and Jasper sensed an air of unhappiness about Susannah. There was nothing in her manner to suggest she was melancholy, she smiled and conversed with her usual ease, save that she would not look at him. Perhaps it was his imagination, perhaps he merely wished to believe she was regretting her choice.

He was too distracted to take note of the conversation and suddenly realised that Zelah had left his side and was walking away with Susannah, declaring with a smile that they were off to talk of fashion and furbelows.

'We shall not see them again for some time,' he remarked, turning to Gerald. 'When did you get back from Hotwells?'

'Yesterday.'

'And how is Gloriana? How did she take your news?'

Gerald's eyes were fixed on the ladies as they walked away and he did not answer immediately.

'Very much as I expected. She was overset

at first, but she saw I was not to be moved, and after a night's reflection she came round. I am to take Susannah to meet her next week.'

'That is good news then.' Jasper hoped his reply was sufficiently cheerful, but his companion did not respond. 'You do not seem particularly elated by your success.'

'Hmm? Oh, I am tired, I suppose.'

Jasper gave a crack of laughter.

'Tired, after a journey of just over a dozen miles? My dear boy, you should go and drink a cup of that foul-tasting water immediately.'

Gerald's smile was perfunctory.

'No need for that, it is just…' He sighed. 'I don't know if I can explain it to you. You will say that a fellow cannot be euphoric for ever, but…oh, you know how it is, Jasper. You want something so badly for a long time, then when you eventually achieve it, it is a trifle—' He broke off and gave a self-conscious laugh. 'This is all nonsense, of course. Susannah is everything I ever dreamed she would be.' He looked past Jasper. 'By Jove, is that your twin over there? I didn't know Dominic was here, too, that is famous, I must speak to him immediately.'

He dashed off, leaving Jasper to follow more slowly in his wake.

Susannah was never quite sure how Mrs Coale had managed to carry her off. One minute she was holding Gerald's arm and trying to steel herself to meet Jasper, who was watching her approach with a dark, unfathomable look in his hard eyes, the next she was promenading around the Pump Room with the slight, dark-haired lady that was Jasper's sister-in-law, telling her all about Florence House. At first she was a little wary, but Zelah's gentle manner and genuine interest soon had its effect and she found herself answering her questions quite freely.

'The dowager countess is most impressed with your efforts there,' remarked Zelah. 'That is no small compliment, believe me.'

'I am only too thankful that she thought the cause worthy of her attention.'

'Lady Gisburne loathes being bored and she was most thankful that Jasper brought your project to her attention.'

Susannah blinked.

'I did not know it was the viscount who told her about Florence House. I thought she had merely heard the gossip.'

'Oh, no, she told me Jasper argued the case very strongly. And I believe there is a good modiste here that I must visit,' added Zelah, with a twinkling look. 'I intend to order at least one gown from Odesse while I am in Bath.'

The conversation turned towards fashion and in no time at all they had completed another full promenade of the room.

'Oh dear, I can see my husband is looking out for me.' Zelah chuckled as they came within sight of Lady Gisburne's party. 'Come along, let us join them.'

'Oh, but there is no need for me to come with you,' declared Susannah, hanging back. She could see Jasper standing beside his equally tall brother and was reluctant to go any closer.

'Nonsense, I must make you known to Dominic, and I can see Mr Barnabus is with them, too, so where else would you want to go?'

Unable to withstand the pressure of that small, determined hand on her sleeve Susannah accompanied Zelah to join the little group and said all that was proper when she was introduced to Dominic Coale. She resolutely kept her eyes averted from Jasper, but it was impossible not to think of him when she looked at his twin.

Even with the livid scar dissecting his cheek, she thought Dominic Coale as heart-stoppingly handsome as his brother. They shared the same thick, glossy black hair, the same regular features, the lean cheek and finely carved jawline, and if she fancied Jasper's smile a shade warmer and the glint in his blue-grey eyes a trifle more wicked, that was surely her imagination. While Dominic spoke to her she did her best to ignore Jasper, standing so close and silent, almost within touching distance. She could feel his presence, like a tangible force drawing her closer. She told herself that since Gerald was distantly related to the brothers she would have to grow accustomed to meeting Jasper. And she would do so. She had told Kate as much when they were strolling in the gardens yesterday.

Her tears had taken her by surprise and she had found herself admitting to Kate that she did not love Gerald.

'But he loves *me*,' she had said, wiping her eyes with the handkerchief Kate supplied. 'I cannot cry off, it would break his heart.'

'Better that he should be disappointed now than he should discover it later.'

'He shall *not* be disappointed,' Susannah declared. 'I will be a good wife to him. I *will*.'

'You are in love with someone else.' Kate's shrewd eyes did not miss the tell-tale flush that immediately coloured Susannah's cheek. 'Is it Markham? Are you in love with the viscount?'

'No.' Susannah knew her hasty denial was too vehement. She added quickly, 'And if I were it would make no odds. He cares nothing for me.'

'Oh, my poor girl, you have lost your heart to a rake!' Kate's sympathy had almost overset Susannah again. 'I can see how one might easily fall in love with such a man, but it will not do. He is too much a flirt, universally charming to any pretty woman, but you could never be happy for long with such a man. He is far too insubstantial for you.'

Susannah thought back to the night she had spent with Jasper at Florence House. There had been nothing insubstantial about him there when he took charge of the cooking, his orders to Bessie echoing around the cavernous kitchen. Nor had there been anything rakish in his manner when they were sitting together later, in the parlour. Not that it made any difference now.

She raised her head and said again, 'I shall make Gerald a good wife, I promise you.'

'...my love, shall we go? We arranged to meet your aunt at the circulating library.'

Gerald touched her elbow. Susannah turned to look at him, yesterday's words still ringing in her head.

'Yes, of course.' She waited until they were out in the sunshine before she spoke again and when she did it was with studied coolness. 'I thought Lord Markham and Mr Coale were only distant relations of yours, Gerald. Do you...do you expect to see much of them, when we are married?'

'Oh, I shouldn't think so,' he replied carelessly. 'Dominic rarely leaves Exmoor and Jasper divides his time between Markham and London. By Jove, I never thought!' He stopped, clapping his hand to his head. 'Should we look around for a country house, Susannah? It had not occurred to me that you might want to live elsewhere.'

'No, I would rather stay in Bath,' she said quickly. 'I have the house in Royal Crescent, after all. My aunt has already told me she intends to find a little place for herself once we are wed.'

'That will suit me very well, although perhaps we will make the occasional jaunt to town.'

'Of course, whatever will make you happy, Gerald.'

'Good heavens, marrying you will make me the happiest of men, my dear.' He kissed her hand. 'Now, here we are at Duffields—shall we go in and find your aunt?'

Chapter Fifteen

Jasper was glad to get up after a restless night and he was putting the finishing touches to his cravat when Peters announced that Mr Barnabus wished to see him.

'So early?' He took out his watch. 'You had best send him up.'

Jasper did not turn round when Gerald came in, but one glance in the mirror showed him that the young man was looking unusually serious.

'What is it, my young friend?' Jasper fastened his diamond pin into the snowy folds before turning away from the mirror. 'Are you in dun territory, perhaps? Do you need money?'

'Good heavens, no.' Gerald looked suitably shocked. 'My fortune ain't nearly as large as yours, Jasper, but it is sufficient for my needs. No, I need some advice.'

Jasper took another look at Gerald and knew a craven desire to fob him off.

'I am engaged to ride out with Dominic this morning,' he said, picking up his coat. 'Walk with me and tell me what is troubling you.'

They were out on the street before Gerald began.

'I think I have been a little rash in asking Miss Prentess to be my wife.'

'Oh?'

'I wonder if it is a mistake, for both of us. After all, as Mama pointed out to me, Susannah is a couple of years older than I.'

'That is no reason to cry off,' objected Jasper. 'You have chosen a lady who is both beautiful and rich. An ideal choice, most people would think.'

Gerald looked even more tortured.

'I know and she is. I have even convinced my mother that Susannah is the perfect partner for me.'

'Then what is the problem?'

'I thought I was in love with her, but recently, I am not so sure. She is the kindest, most generous of women, but there is not that grand passion that I expected to feel with the woman I intend to make my wife.' He looked up, his blue eyes troubled. 'I am afraid I am making a mistake, Jasper. I am very much afraid we shall both be rendered unhappy. What shall I do?'

Jasper regarded him steadily. This was his moment. One word from him and Gerald would break off his engagement. Susannah would be free again. The temptation was extreme, but Jasper knew he could not do it. At last he said abruptly, 'I am not the person to advise you on this, Gerald. You must make up your own mind. At the very least you should talk to Miss Prentess about it.'

With that he turned on his heel and walked away.

Susannah was gazing out of the drawing-room window. The snow had mostly disappeared from the Crescent, but there was still a covering of snow on Crescent Fields. Kate stood at her shoulder. They had been going over the same subject for more than an hour.

'If you are unsure then you must talk to Gerald,' said Kate firmly.

'I cannot do that. It would wreck his dreams.'

'So you would marry him without love.'

Susannah turned away from the window.

'You are forgetting he loves me,' she said with a sad little smile. 'That must count for something.'

'But if you are in love with Markham—'

Susannah stopped her.

'Even if I were not to marry Gerald there is no hope for me there.' She thought of Jasper's frowning looks, the hard silence he maintained when she had seen him in the Pump Room. 'Lord Markham no longer cares for me. So I will marry Gerald, and at least one of us will be happy.'

'Your happiness is important, too!' Kate gave her a little shake. 'Promise me you will at least talk to Gerald. You are rich. You have no need to marry to secure your future comfort.'

Susannah gave a dispirited shrug. 'Loneliness is not comfortable.'

'It can be a great deal better than marriage to the wrong man,' returned Kate. She glanced out of the window. 'Barnabus is approaching now, another minute and he will be here.' She swept up her bonnet. 'I will leave you to talk to him alone. But remember, Susannah, treat him honestly now, or face a lifetime of regret.'

The news that the rich Miss Prentess and Mr Gerald Barnabus were *not* to be married spread even faster than the rumours of their engagement. Gossip-mongers like Mrs Farthing and Mrs Bulstrode might disapprove of Miss Prentess's fickleness, but mothers with daughters to dispose of were very happy that a genial young gentleman of independent means was once more on the marriage market.

Jasper was dining at Laura Place when the

dowager countess announced the news as they commenced upon their soup.

'This is not Pump Room gossip,' she declared, looking around the dining table. 'I saw Miss Prentess myself today, to discuss Florence House. She told me she and Mr Barnabus had agreed they should not suit.'

Her sharp eyes flickered over Jasper, who maintained his outward calm.

'Will you call upon her?' Zelah was sitting beside him and she took advantage of the dowager's conversation with Dominic to ask her question.

'No. I have no reason to do so.'

She laid down her spoon.

'Jasper, I declare you are even more stubborn than your brother! As soon as I saw you and Miss Prentess together I knew you were in love.'

'You are right in so many cases, my dear Sister-in-law, but not in this.'

'Am I not? I think—'

'No.' He gave her a warning glance. 'Pray do not meddle in what you do not understand!'

He was thankful that no more was said and engaged to join them the following day for a party of pleasure, to drive out to Lansdown.

However, when he called the next morning he was met with the news that the children were too fractious to go out, and Lady Gisburne had bethought herself of urgent business to discuss with Dominic.

'Which leaves me at a loose end,' explained Zelah, buttoning her spencer. 'I thought you might like to escort me to Sydney Gardens.'

Jasper's eyes narrowed.

'I mislike that look in your eye, madam,' he said. 'What are you planning?'

Zelah opened her eyes at him.

'Why, nothing, Brother dear, 'tis merely that I want to see the canal. I am told it is perfectly charming with its overhanging trees and pretty iron bridges.' She took his arm. 'Come along, it is such a lovely morning and a walk in the fresh air will do us both good.'

Jasper's suspicions were not fully allayed, but he accompanied his sister-in-law to the gardens. The fine weather had brought out many visitors and their progress up the sweeping gravelled walk was slowed by the need to stop and speak to their numerous acquaintances, but at last Zelah guided her escort off the main path towards a much quieter part of the gardens.

'I believe there is a grotto down here where Sheridan courted Elizabeth Linley. He wrote verses about it, you know.'

'I thought you wanted to see the canal,' objected Jasper.

'I do, of course, but let us look for the grotto first.'

Jasper's earlier suspicions began to stir again. They were roused fully when he saw Susannah coming towards them. She was accompanied by Charles Camerton and Mrs Logan, and a swift glance at Zelah's countenance convinced him their meeting was not unplanned.

Mrs Logan waved to them. 'Mrs Coale, Lord Markham, what a surprise.'

Susannah's look of shock seemed real enough.

'I did not know you were acquainted with Mrs Coale, Kate.'

'We met at the Pump Room yesterday.' Kate quickly passed on to introducing Mr Camerton, and Jasper took the opportunity to observe Susannah.

She was a little pale but otherwise composed. She looked as if she would prefer to be anywhere but in his vicinity. His inner demon took a perverse satisfaction in it. If this was a ruse to throw them together then it was not going to work. However, he had reckoned without his resourceful sister-in-law. After a few moments' conversation she clapped her hands in delight.

'Well, is this not my great good fortune? Mr Camerton is taking the ladies to see the grotto, too, and he has been regaling them with all sorts of stories about Mr Sheridan's time in Bath. It is clearly the most salacious gossip, and I am desperate to hear it!'

'Can events that happened forty years ago be considered gossip?' Jasper enquired.

Charles Camerton had the grace to look a little guilty. 'The ladies seem to like it.'

'Well, since you do not wish to listen you may give your arm to Miss Prentess for a little while,' said Zelah. 'She will not want to hear the stories again. There, now we can all be comfortable. Shall we walk on?'

The party thus rearranged they began to move, Jasper and Susannah following the others. Jasper sought for something to say to break the awkward silence.

'I fear we are the victims of two extremely managing female minds. I acquit Charles of being anything more than a pawn in their hands.'

'I beg your pardon.'

Her despondent manner wrenched at his heart.

'Come now, this is not like you,' he said in a rallying tone. 'You are more like to rip up at me.'

She gave a little shake of her head, keeping her face averted.

'I have treated you very badly. Kate told me it was Mr Camerton, and not you, who divulged the secret of Florence House.'

'To good effect, since you now have a patroness.'

She looked round at that.

'I am aware that I have you to thank for that, too.'

He raised his hand and touched her pale cheek.

'You have had a very horrid time of it recently, I think. Were you sorry to terminate your engagement?'

'No. I was more concerned for Gerald, but when he told me the true state of his feelings I knew we must call it off.'

Jasper hesitated before saying slowly, 'Perhaps you are afraid of marriage.'

'Perhaps I am, a little.'

'Because of what happened to your sister.'

'Not just that.'

Her fingers trembled against the crook of his arm and he brought his hand up to cover them.

'Will you not tell me?'

'I have tried for so long to blot it out,' she whispered. 'I have told no one.'

Jasper looked up. They had fallen some way behind the others.

'There is no one to hear us, only the trees.' He pressed her fingers. 'Have we not shared enough for you to know you can trust me with your confidences?'

'Every experience I have had has shown me that men are not to be trusted.'

'You trusted Gerald enough to become betrothed.'

'Gerald was never a town beau.'

'Yet still you cannot bring yourself to marry him.'

'I began to think, to realise. At some stage he would want to— I would have to…' She shuddered. 'I could not bear the thought of it.'

'Tell me, Susannah.'

They walked on in silence. Jasper kept his hand over hers where it rested on his sleeve. He wanted to pull her into his arms, to kiss away her sadness, but she was tense, like a filly on the edge of bolting. She began to speak.

'My Uncle Middlemass took me to London when I was eighteen. You know his money came from trade, so there was no formal presentation at court, but he had many acquaintances in town, so our society was not limited. On one evening at a party I recognised the young man who had courted Florence. He did not recognise me—even when we were introduced he did not remember the name. I was incensed. I followed him and his friends to the card room. I told him what had happened to Florence—' She broke off. A gentle wind was sighing through the trees and making the spring flowers dance around them, but she did not notice any of it, her eyes fixed upon some unseen point in the distance.

'He laughed. He said if she had been foolish enough to give herself to him then she deserved her fate. They were all laughing, all those fashionable young men with their windswept hair and elegant neckties, laughing at the fate of my poor sister. Then he grabbed me and began to... to kiss me. He said he'd wager I was as wanton as my sister. If it had not been for the timely entrance of a servant I do not think he would have stopped. And the others were standing by, watching.' She shivered. 'I managed to make my escape but I will never forget. He was laughing as I fled down the stairs. He saw women as nothing but playthings for his pleasure.'

'And then?' demanded Jasper, his temper rising. 'Surely Middlemass took action against this man?'

'No, I never told him of it. My uncle had a weak heart. I was afraid if he knew, it would make him ill.'

Susannah looked back over the years. It was all such a long time ago. She had never spoken of it, not even to Kate, but somehow, telling Jasper was a relief. Now perhaps he would understand her panic. Suddenly, walking with him here in Sydney Gardens with the spring sunshine warm on their backs, the past did not seem quite so horrific. She stole a glance at Jasper. He was scowling as he digested all she had told him. He, a man of fashion with a reputation as a breaker of hearts, was part of that set that she despised, but somehow he did not quite fit. Perhaps she was wrong. Perhaps not all men were the same.

He turned his head suddenly, his blue-grey eyes locking with hers and she was aware of that familiar breathlessness, but the panic she had felt before did not engulf her. Instead she was relieved that he was beside her. She was comfortable in his company. Thinking back, she realised it had been the same when they had been together at Florence House. Perhaps…

'I am honoured by your confidences, Miss Prentess, but I think we should catch up with the others. Mrs Logan will be anxious about you.'

How formal he was, how polite. He lengthened his stride and she was obliged to quicken her own step to keep up with him.

'I am quite capable of looking after myself, my lord.' She uttered the words almost as a challenge, hoping he would contradict her. When he did not, she tried again. 'I think you were correct, sir, when you surmised that Mrs Logan and your sister-in-law engineered this meeting to throw us together.'

'Yes, but you need have no fear, madam. I have no intention of importuning you.'

'Oh.'

Susannah's spirits swooped even further. He threw her a quick smile.

'I am well aware of your low opinion of me, madam. My actions in the past have only reinforced that, but I do not intend to repeat them.'

Susannah swallowed her disappointment. They had caught up with the others so there was no time to reply. Jasper offered his arm to Zelah as they approached the secluded grotto and did not address Susannah again until the two parties split up. Then he took her hand and saluted it before walking off with his sister-in-law on his arm.

'Well?' Kate waited only until the viscount was out of earshot before turning to Susannah, an eager question in her eyes. Susannah merely returned her look and Kate almost stamped her foot. 'What did he say to you?'

Susannah gave an exaggerated shiver.

'The wind is growing a little chill. Perhaps, Mr Camerton, you would escort us back to town now?'

'Susannah!'

Mr Camerton chuckled as he offered both ladies an arm.

'You had best tell her, Miss Prentess. She can be extraordinarily tenacious.'

'There is nothing to tell.'

'You mean he did not make you an offer?'

Susannah shook her head.

'No. He behaved like a perfect gentleman.'

Zelah was less complimentary about her brother-in-law.

'You are a complete nodcock,' she told him bluntly as they strolled back through the gardens. 'We gave you every opportunity to put things right with Susannah Prentess—'

'There is nothing to put right,' he argued. 'And I am shocked that you and the lady's so-called friends should design to place her into such a position, alone with a man and unchaperoned.'

'The lady was clearly not averse to your company,' she observed. 'You had your heads together for most of the time you were together.'

'She confided in me. I understand perfectly now why she does not wish to marry.'

'Why not, when she is clearly in love with you?'

'Do you think so?'

Zelah laughed.

'Of course. Why, her eyes followed you from the moment we met. Dear heavens, Jasper, you have never doubted your attraction before!'

It was true, but it had never mattered so much to him before. The knowledge that he was in love with Susannah Prentess had shaken him badly. Until he had actually uttered the words at Lady Gisburne's party he had not realised it.

And for once in his life he was not sure how to proceed.

'She has been hurt,' he said at last. 'Frightened very badly. I must go gently, give her time to recover. Besides…' another objection reared its head '…I am not convinced she and Gerald are not in love.'

However, a chance meeting with that young man later that day put all doubts to flight. They met in Stall Street and Gerald explained that he was off to the theatre with friends that evening.

'You are not regretting your new-found freedom then?' said Jasper, smiling.

Gerald grinned.

'Not at all, I am supremely happy about it. And the added bonus is that I don't have to go to the Upper Rooms tonight.' He took Jasper's arm and began to walk with him. 'You know I had my doubts about the betrothal, and I went to Royal Crescent to discuss it with Susannah, as you suggested, but I had hardly begun when she interrupted me to say that she had changed her mind, that we would always be friends but that she could never love me. I cannot tell you how relieved I was. In fact, we laughed over it, once we had agreed to part. She is such a darling girl, but I can see clearly now that we would never suit. The hardest part will be telling my mother. After working so hard to convince her that Susannah was the only woman for me I now have to tell her it was all a hum!' They had reached Stall Street and prepared to part. 'I am going to see her tomorrow,' said Gerald, moving away. 'Wish me luck!'

Smiling at the memory, Jasper made his way back to York House. It would appear Miss Prentess was indeed free. If Zelah was correct and Susannah did feel something for him, then why wait to put it to the touch again? He thought back to what she had told him in Sydney Gardens, the confidences she had shared. What if she was not warning him off but merely trying to explain to him her previous actions? The thought raised his spirits. He must talk to her.

Jasper took out his watch. It was nearly dinnertime, he would write to her, making his intentions perfectly clear and telling her he would call tomorrow morning. He would send the message tonight, so that it would be waiting for her when she returned from the Assembly Rooms. That would give her time to make up her mind. If she did not wish to see him a short note by return would spare her the pain of a meeting, although it would be sufficient to end his hopes. But that would be her choice. Perhaps all was not yet lost.

* * *

Susannah had no inclination for dancing, but they had promised to attend the Fancy Ball and she must keep her word. The Upper Rooms were as full as ever, and there was no shortage of partners, but she did not enjoy herself. By the time the interval came to take tea she had given up all hope of seeing Jasper, which made the evening even more dull and she was relieved when eleven o'clock struck and she could go home.

Susannah and Aunt Maude took chairs to Royal Crescent, but being a fine night they alighted on the pavement and shook out their skirts before ascending the scrubbed steps to the front door. They had barely entered the house when a body hurled itself off the street and into the hall, causing panic. Mrs Wilby shrieked as Gatley laid hands on the intruder. In the ensuing struggle they fell against the hall table, sending the silver tray clattering to the floor. Above the mayhem Susannah heard the man call out to her.

'Miss Prentess, a minute of your time, I beg you!'

She peered through the gloom.

'Mr Warwick? What in heaven's name is the meaning of this?'

'I must speak to you.'

The young man gazed at her. His hair was dishevelled and there was a wild look in his eyes, but when the butler tried to hustle him out of the door she put out her hand to stop him.

'Wait, Gatley. Let him speak.'

'I called earlier, but you were out.'

'Aye, that he did, miss,' averred the butler, panting slightly. 'About eight o'clock.'

'Goodness, and you have been waiting outside ever since?'

'Yes.' He raked his hand through his hair. 'I have been walking up and down, waiting for you to return. You are my last hope.'

Mrs Wilby tutted loudly. 'I hardly think this is the time—'

'Hush, Aunt.'

Susannah regarded her visitor with some concern. With his crumpled neckcloth and haggard eyes he looked more like a ragged schoolboy than the fashionable gentleman she had welcomed into her drawing room on countless occasions.

'Come along into the morning room, Mr Warwick. We will talk there.' She observed the shocked faces around her. 'You must come, too, Aunt, and Gatley shall remain in the hall, where we may call him if necessary.'

She handed her cloak to the goggling footman and ushered her unexpected guest into the morning room. He allowed himself to be pushed down gently into a chair and once Susannah had made sure that the door was closed and Aunt

Maude was comfortably seated, she took a seat opposite Mr Warwick and asked him the reason for his visit.

Immediately he jumped up and began to stride about the room, wringing his hands together. She waited patiently. At last he stopped and turned to her.

'Miss Prentess. I want to see Miss Anstruther!'

Aunt Maude gave a little gasp, but Susannah said merely, 'Go on.'

'I have treated her abominably.' He began to pace the room. 'I cannot eat, cannot sleep— I cannot forget her. She has been on my conscience ever since I knew—' He broke off and returned to his chair, burying his face in his hands.

'I have been to Shropshire, to visit her parents, but they told me they have no idea where she is.' He pushed his fist against his mouth. 'They abandoned her. She might be dying in a gutter for all they know! How could they be so cruel?'

'And what of your own actions, sir?' Susannah demanded, her voice icy. 'Do you hold yourself blameless in all this?'

'No, no, not at all! When she told me, I w-was frightened, I refused to acknowledge that the child was mine. I thought Mr Anstruther would call me out, that I should be disgraced.'

'As you deserved to be,' put in Aunt Maude, with uncharacteristic severity.

He turned to look at her.

'I know, ma'am. I am well aware of that. It took me a long time to come to my senses, to realise that I had to present myself to her parents, to own up to my actions and ask for Violet's hand in marriage. But then, when I arrived at the house and was told she was not there—'

'So why do you come to me, Mr Warwick?'

'I have scoured the city, I called at Walcot Street, but they denied all knowledge of Miss Anstruther. Your charity is my last hope. I have no idea where the house may be, but I remember hearing that it is a refuge for young ladies such as Violet. So I came here, hoping, praying, that she might be one of the lucky ones.' His wild, frightened eyes fixed themselves upon Susannah. 'Tell me if she is there, Miss Prentess.'

Susannah watched him. There was no doubt of his distress.

'And if she should be under my care,' she said slowly, 'what do you intend by her?'

'To throw myself at her feet, to beg her forgiveness and to make amends. I want to marry her, Miss Prentess, if she will have me. If not, I want to support her and my child. I must make some reparation for what I have done.'

Mrs Wilby sat forwards, saying gently, 'That is all very well, Mr Warwick, but we would need to ascertain the young lady's wishes in this case.'

'But that is not the end of it.' Mr Warwick was on his feet again. 'William Farthing told me that his mother had written to Mrs Anstruther, suggesting Violet might be at Florence House. He said his mother had received a reply this morning. Mr Anstruther is even now on his way to Bath, intent upon taking his daughter back to Shropshire with him. You do not know him, Miss Prentess. He is a cruel man, he will incarcerate her and force her to give up the child, if it is allowed to live. And Violet is under age— he is still her legal guardian.'

'Well goodness gracious me!'

Susannah paid little heed to her aunt's exclamation. She was thinking quickly.

'Very well, Mr Warwick. Can you have a travelling carriage here first thing tomorrow morning? I will take you to Florence House to see Violet. If she is agreeable, then my maid shall accompany you both to Gretna Green. However, the decision must be Violet's. If she does not want to go with you then I will find somewhere to hide her.'

Mrs Wilby gave a little shriek.

'But, Susannah, if her father should bring the law down upon us…'

Susannah shrugged. 'We will deal with that problem if and when it arises.' She rose. 'I suggest you go home now, Mr Warwick, and get some sleep.'

He came up and clasped her hand, kissing it fervently.

'Thank you, ma'am, thank you. I shall be here at eight, without fail!'

Chapter Sixteen

The sun streaming through the curtains roused Jasper. He looked at his watch. It was very early, but he knew he would not sleep again. Today he was going to ask Susannah Prentess to marry him. There had been no reply from Royal Crescent, and he was sure that if Susannah was going to refuse him she would have replied immediately. He got up, calling for Peters to bring hot water. He would shave now and get dressed. Not in the clothes he planned to wear for his visit to Royal Crescent, but the plain dark riding coat and buckskins that he could walk out in, to pass the hours until he could see Susannah. He strode out of the town and up on to Beechen Cliff. The wind was warm, a promise of the summer to come. Jasper smiled to himself. A good omen, perhaps? A sign that the gods were smiling upon him. He heard the distant chiming of a bell on the breeze as he headed back towards York House. As long as there was no note waiting for him, he would call on Susannah at ten o'clock. There was plenty of time for a leisurely breakfast and to change into his morning coat and knee breeches before setting off for the most momentous meeting of his life.

'Peters, Peters! Where the devil are you?' He strode through the rooms, frowning. Then he heard the scurry of footsteps behind him.

'My lord, thank heaven you are back!' Peters ran in, one hand on his chest which was heaving alarmingly as he gasped out his explanation. 'I was out collecting your best shirt from the laundrywoman. Knew you would want to wear it this morning. I was about to cross Gay Street when a travelling carriage comes down the road. Naturally I stepped back out of the way, but happened to look up as it went past me, and I saw who was in it.'

'Well, what of it?'

Jasper looked at him impatiently, he had more important things on his mind. Should he wear his white quilted waistcoat or the oyster satin with the pearl buttons?

'It was Miss Prentess, my lord. Large as life.'

Jasper forgot about waistcoats.

'*What?* Are you quite sure?'

'Yes, my lord. The carriage was forced to

slow to wait for a bullock cart to get out of the way and I had plenty of time to look.' Peters paused to regain his breath.

'And is there a note for me from Royal Crescent?'

'No, my lord. I left word at the desk that any messages were to be brought upstairs immediately.' The valet added in a colourless voice, 'She was travelling with young Mr Warwick, my lord.'

His words hit Jasper like cold water. She was running away from him. She knew he intended to make her an offer and she was too afraid to tell him to his face that she could not marry him. So that was it. Over.

Peters was still talking.

'It was a smart turn-out, my lord, four horses, no expense spared, I'd say, and a couple of trunks strapped to the roof. I've got a lad following the carriage to see which way they are heading and to report back. And I sent word to the stable for Morton to bring your curricle round.'

Jasper turned on him with and growl.

'Dammit, Peters, I have never yet chased after any woman!'

The valet gave him a long stare.

'This isn't any woman, my lord. It is Miss Prentess.'

Aye, and she didn't want to face him. First

she had used Gerald Barnabus to protect her. Now Warwick. Devil take it, why should he care?

Only Warwick was not Gerald. Warwick was not a diffident young man who would treat Susannah gently if she refused his advances. Jasper did not know the man well, but if the rumours were anything to go by he was a hotheaded young buck who had already ruined one lady's reputation.

He picked up his hat and gloves.

'By God you are right. I must go after her!'

Susannah paced up and down the parlour at Florence House, anxiously pulling her gloves through her hands. Mrs Gifford was sitting by the window quietly mending a pillowcase.

'Perhaps I should not leave them alone.'

Mrs Gifford looked up, her kindly old eyes twinkling.

'My dear, Violet was quite happy to afford the young man a private interview.'

'I know, but perhaps he is coercing her.'

'They are only in the next room. She has but to raise her voice and we would hear it.' The housekeeper picked up her scissors and snipped the thread. 'Be patient,' she said, putting away her needle and folding up the pillowcase. 'You were sufficiently convinced of Mr Warwick's sincerity to bring him here. Now let him make his case to the lady.'

Susannah stopped pacing.

'I may be wrong,' she said. 'Until very recently I would not put my trust in any man—' She broke off as the adjoining door opened and the young couple came in. One look at Violet's happy face told her that everything was well.

'Miss Anstruther has consented to become my wife,' declared Mr Warwick, following Violet into the parlour. He caught her hand and smiled down at her. 'We want to be married immediately, so that no disgrace shall be attached to my child.'

The proud note in his voice as he uttered the last two words was unmistakable. Mrs Gifford caught Susannah's eye and smiled.

'That is settled then.' The housekeeper got up from her chair and came forwards to envelope Violet in a motherly embrace. 'I wish you very well, my dear.'

'You understand what you must do?' Susannah asked Violet.

The girl nodded. 'We fly to Scotland immediately, I understand that.'

'But Miss Prentess is sending her own maid to act as your chaperon and look after you until we can be married,' Mr Warwick told her. He addressed Susannah. 'I will not risk a meeting with Anstruther until Violet is my wife, but once

I have her safe then I shall write to him. I hope he will recognise the connection.'

'And if he will not?' asked Susannah gently.

'Then I shall take Violet to my own family. I have already written to apprise them of the situation.' The young man met her gaze steadily. 'I have told them what a fool I was not to accept my responsibilities immediately.'

'Oh, no, no,' cried Violet. 'You were shocked, frightened, I quite understand.'

His arm went about her.

'Ah, sweetheart, you are an angel to be so forgiving, but I must bear some blame...'

'Yes, yes, you can discuss all this in the carriage,' Susannah interrupted them. 'If you are going to make any headway at all today then you need to be setting off as soon as may be. We know your father is on his way to Bath, Violet. It would be better if he did not find you here.'

'No indeed.' Violet's eyes darkened with fear. 'I will go and collect my things, and I must say goodbye to Jane and Lizzie, and the babies.'

She hurried away, returning a few minutes later with her meagre belongings packed in a single portmanteau and her travelling cloak around her shoulders. Mrs Gifford provided a basket of food and a flask of wine to refresh them on their journey and Susannah accompanied them to the door, where the carriage was waiting.

'I cannot tell you how very grateful I am to you, Miss Prentess.' Violet hugged her. 'Without your kindness I do not know what would have become of me.'

'You need not think of that now. You have no doubts about marrying Mr Warwick?'

'Oh, no, none at all.' Violet's eyes positively shone at the prospect. 'But how will you manage without your maid? Who knows how long we will be gone?'

'I shall miss her, of course, but she is by far the best person to look after you on your long journey,' replied Susannah, sending a laughing glance towards her servant as she helped Violet into the carriage. 'You have sufficient money with you, Dorcas? I do not want you to leave Miss Anstruther until she has hired a suitable maid.'

'Don't you worry, miss, I'll make sure she takes on someone that knows how to look after her. 'Tis you I am more concerned about, miss,' said the maid gruffly. 'Without me to dress you.'

'I shall fetch Mary upstairs to help me,' replied Susannah. 'You said yourself she has ambitions to be a lady's maid. Now go along, and look after your new charge.'

A flurry of goodbyes, a few last minute words of advice and the carriage was shut up.

'Ah, they are such children,' declared Mrs

Gifford, wiping her eyes with the corner of her apron. 'I pray they will be happy.'

'So, too, do I,' muttered Susannah fervently.

She stepped back and raised her hand in a final salute as the coachman gathered up the reins. He was about to pull away when the clatter of hooves announced another vehicle approaching.

'Oh, good heavens, who can this be?' exclaimed Mrs Gifford. 'Never say Mr Anstruther is here already!'

'No indeed.' Susannah's voice faltered as she recognised the curricle sweeping through the gateway. 'It is Lord Markham.'

He had seen her. He checked his horses and turned on to the carriage circle. Susannah looked at the coachman.

'He is not obstructing the gates, you can go. Quickly.' She turned to the housekeeper. 'You too should go inside, Mrs Gifford. I will join you presently.'

She stepped on to the drive in front of the approaching curricle. If the viscount had any thoughts of pursuing the carriage then she would at least delay him.

'Lord Markham,' she hailed him cheerfully. 'What brings you here?'

He brought the horses to a plunging halt, just feet away from her.

'I might ask you the same question.' He

waited until his groom had run to the horses' heads and jumped down. 'And *who* was driving away in that carriage?'

She knew of no connection between the viscount and Mr Warwick or Violet Anstruther, but she could not be sure. She kept her smile in place.

'There is a cold wind, my lord, and I have left my cloak in the parlour. Shall we continue this discussion indoors?' She heard his firm step on the gravel as he followed her to the house. The parlour was empty and the viscount closed the door upon them with a snap.

'Now will you tell me what the devil is going on?'

Jasper sounded angry and she turned to him, frowning slightly.

'I do not understand you.'

'You were seen leaving Bath this morning. In the company of Mr Warwick.'

'What of it?'

'You could have told me you would not be at home.'

Her frown deepened.

'Why should I do that? This is no business of yours.'

He looked as if he would argue, then thought better of it.

'So why has he left you here? Where has he gone?'

She regarded him in silence for a few moments. She did not understand him. Yesterday he had been so friendly, so understanding that she had wanted to confide in him, to have no secrets between them. But that had been a mistake. He had clearly been shocked and appalled at what she had told him, for he had left her abruptly, with no word of comfort, nothing to say he wanted to continue the acquaintance. Now here he was, frowning at her, demanding to know what she was about. Did he think because he had stayed at Florence House, helped her during the birth of Jane's baby, that he was entitled to an explanation? She tried to put aside her own hurt feelings and think logically.

'You had better sit down, my lord, and I will try to explain.'

'Thank you, I prefer to stand.'

'Very well.' She sank down into the armchair beside the fire. 'There was talk in Bath—you may have heard it—that Mr Warwick was the father of Violet Anstruther's baby.'

'What of it?'

'It is true. Mr Warwick initially denied all involvement in the case, but when Violet disappeared he had a change of heart. He has been searching for her for some time, I believe. He came to me last night to ask if she was here. He wanted to make reparation, to marry her.

He appeared to be in earnest so I brought him to see her.'

'In a travelling carriage.'

'He has taken her to the border.'

'So you were not running away with him.'

'Of course not!'

'But it was very convenient for you, to go out of Bath so early this morning, Miss Prentess.'

She blinked at the scathing note in his voice. She had cried herself to sleep last night over the loss of his friendship, but that was over. He could not touch her heart, hurt her, ever again.

'It was necessary,' she said coldly. 'Mr Warwick believes Mr Anstruther is even now on his way here to wrest his daughter away from us. May I ask why you are so interested in this case, my lord? What is it to you?'

'I have no interest at all in Warwick and Miss Anstruther.' He was pacing up and down, his black brows drawn together. 'But it is not the first time you have left Bath to avoid meeting me.'

'I do not know what you are talking about.'

He stopped pacing and stared at her.

'Did you not receive my note?'

'Note, sir? What note? What did it say?'

She fancied a dull flush tinged his cheek, but he turned away and she could not be sure.

'Nothing. It is not important. Tell me, Miss

Prentess. How do you intend to get back to Bath?'

'Do you know, my lord, until this moment I had not considered. I have no idea.'

He came to stand before her, calm and assured.

'Then I can offer you a solution, madam. My curricle is outside. I will convey you to Royal Crescent.'

Susannah might tell herself she felt nothing for him, but when Jasper was standing over her, the capes of his driving coat making his shoulders look so impossibly broad, it was difficult to ignore his powerful presence. Her heart was thudding painfully in her chest but she tried to think sensibly. It was a perfectly logical solution. A dignified, graceful acceptance was all that was required, but her nerves had been at full stretch the whole morning and she could not control the torrent of words that poured forth.

'Thank you. Unless perhaps I should remain here in case Mr Anstruther should appear. What do you think? I do not consider it at all likely that he will arrive today, and I have every confidence that Mrs Gifford will be able to convince him that his daughter was never here—we keep a record of all our residents of course, but she enters false names for them, you see.'

Susannah listened to herself, horrified, knowing she had only stopped because she had run out of breath.

'I believe you can leave Mrs Gifford to deal with Mr Anstruther, if he should arrive,' replied Jasper. 'You should come back to Bath with me, now.'

'Very well.' She rose and went to the table to collect her bonnet and gloves. 'I must say that your arrival is very convenient. I would have had to ask old Daniel to take me home in the gig.'

His lips twitched.

'I fear that a common gig would never do for you, Miss Prentess.'

He picked up her cloak and put it around her shoulders. The touch of his hands, fleeting though it was, instantly brought a reaction. Her body tensed, every nerve on end, anticipating the next contact. Dear heaven, she must get over this! She quickly stepped away from him.

'I shall take my leave of Mrs Gifford and our guests, and join you outside.'

Jasper stood on the drive and breathed deeply, taking the cold, clear air into his lungs. She had not seen his message. She did not know he had intended to make her an offer. The mixture of frustration and rage that had consumed him during his headlong dash to Florence House was still simmering within him. She was the most infuriating woman he had ever met. He could not pin her down, she was constantly surprising him.

Perhaps he should not propose to her. He never knew where he stood with Susannah from one moment to the next. And the emotions she aroused in him—would he ever be in control if he allowed her into his life? He turned in time to see her coming out of the house, tying the ribbons of her bonnet beneath her chin as she walked towards him. The bonnet was not the frivolous, over-decorated confection preferred by most fashionable ladies, but its stylish simplicity was very becoming. The pale satin lining of the wide brim gave her countenance an added glow, and the jaunty angle of the bow drew attention to the dainty chin and those cherry lips, just waiting to be kissed.

No! After what she had told him yesterday he dare not indulge in such fantasies. No wonder she was so afraid of his embraces. He schooled his features into what he hoped was a polite smile and waited to help her into the curricle. The hesitation she showed before allowing those slender fingers in their kid glove to touch his hand was confirmation that she was still wary of him.

He set the team in motion, waiting for Morton to scramble up behind him before settling them into the swift, comfortable pace that would carry them all the way to Bath. She made an innocuous comment about the weather. He responded with a monosyllable. Jasper kept himself rigidly upright, trying not to react when the jolting of the curricle threw her against him. The silence between them seemed to grow more awkward as the miles passed. Finally he cleared his throat.

'I shall be leaving Bath tomorrow.'

'I am surprised you have stayed so long, my lord.'

Her cold response disappointed him. Not even a polite word of regret. He retorted bitterly, 'It was not my original intention.'

'I hope you do not blame me for that.'

'Who else should I blame? It was my cousin's interest in you that brought me here in the first place.'

She stared at him.

'I told you at the outset I had no intention of marrying Gerald.'

'And then you became engaged to him.'

She turned away again, but not before he had seen the shock in her eyes. He might as well have struck her. Remorse flayed him, but it only added to his frustration.

'You know that was an error.' She added, with something of her old spirit, 'But it is not one I intend to repeat.'

'I am glad to hear it. I pity any man who falls into your clutches.'

He regretted the words immediately, but they had reached the old bridge leading into Bath and the sudden appearance of a barouche made his team shy. He was obliged to give his attention to preventing a collision before he could reply.

'I beg your pardon, Susannah. I—'

'Do not *speak* to me,' she commanded him in arctic tones. 'I will not spend another moment in your company. You will set me down immediately, if you please.'

'The devil I will. You cannot walk alone through this part of the town.'

'I can do whatever I want!'

'Do not be so foolish. No lady should walk near the docks, and beyond that are the poorest stews of Bath. Heaven knows what would become of you if I set you down here.'

'If you will not stop I will jump down.'

'Oh, no, you won't.' He reached out and grabbed her wrist. 'You are in my care and I shall deliver you to your house.'

'Your *care*, my lord, has almost resulted in my ruin on at least two occasions.'

Jasper glanced behind. Morton was sitting in the rumble seat, wooden-faced. He would stake his life on Morton's discretion, but she must be very angry with him, to speak so in front of a servant.

Susannah tried to shake off his iron grip.

'Let go of me!'

His hold on her wrist did not weaken. The heat from his fingers burned through her sleeve.

'Only if you promise that you will not try to jump down. Quickly,' he growled. 'I cannot control this team with one hand and if you will not give me your word then I shall instruct Morton to hold you in your seat.' He showed his teeth. 'Only think how that would look.'

'You wouldn't dare!'

'Morton—'

'Very well!' Hastily and with a burning look of reproach she made her promise. How could she have ever thought him a gentleman!

'Good.' He released her and she cradled her wrist in her other hand, convinced she would see a bruise there if she were to peel back her sleeve. 'Now you will sit still until we reach Royal Crescent. If you move so much as a finger then Morton will lay hands on you, is that understood?'

She sat upright, staring rigidly before her as they picked up speed. The sense of injustice was fanned by the ensuing silence.

'You are a monster,' she told him. When that elicited no reply she added, 'A brutish beast. You should be locked up.'

Still he did not reply. She tried again.

'I have never known why everyone thinks you so charming. You are a fraud, Lord Markham. You are nothing but a rake. A—a libertine. A wolf in sheep's clothing. A seducer of innocent females.'

His frown grew blacker with every word she threw at him, but he said nothing until he had guided the curricle into the Crescent and pulled up at her front door.

'We will continue this conversation inside.'

'If you think I am going to allow you into my house after this—!'

With a total want of decorum she scrambled out of the curricle and ran up the steps. Unfortunately Gatley had not been prepared for their approach and she was obliged to hammer upon the knocker. Behind her she heard Morton addressing his master.

'I'll take 'em back to the stables, shall I, m'lord? You're in a fair way to ruining their mouths, the way you've been jerking at the ribbons.'

Glancing back, she saw that Jasper had jumped down and was even now on the pavement. The door opened and she ran inside, but before she could order Gatley to deny him, Jasper had followed her into the hall.

'I am afraid Mrs Wilby is not at home,' offered the butler. 'She left a message to say she is visiting Lady Gisburne today and after dinner they are going on to a concert at the Lower Rooms.'

Ignoring him, Susannah confronted Jasper.

'Get out of my house. Immediately!'

'Not until we have had this out. You have hurled every insult at me and I think you owe me the opportunity to reply!'

'There is a note for you, madam,' Gatley went on. 'The maid found it beneath the hall table when she was cleaning this morning. I have put it on the mantelshelf in the morning room.'

She paid no heed to him but continued to glare at Jasper. It was like confronting a wild animal. If she took her eyes off him he would pounce.

'Well?' His own eyes narrowed, anger darkening them to slate-grey.

'I have nothing to say to you,' she threw at him.

'But I have plenty to say to you.' With a growl he caught her wrist and dragged her towards the nearest doorway.

Gatley dithered beside them.

'Madam—'

The viscount turned upon him, saying imperiously, 'We are not to be disturbed!'

He dragged Susannah into the morning room, closed the door and turned the key in the lock.

Chapter Seventeen

'No, do not shut the door on us, Gatley,' Mrs Logan called out to the butler as she trod up the steps to the house. 'Mrs Coale and I have come to see if Miss Prentess has returned yet.'

He held the door wide to admit them and as Zelah followed Kate into the hall she cast another glance at the butler. He was definitely looking a little flustered.

'Miss Prentess has come in, madam. She is in the morning room. With Lord Markham.' He stood before them and if he had not been a most stately personage, Zelah would have sworn he was hopping from one foot to the other. He continued, as if the words were wrenched from him, *'They have locked the door.'*

Kate's eyes widened and the look she cast at Zelah was positively triumphant.

'Well, this is a most interesting development,' she murmured.

Gatley cleared his throat. 'I was wondering if I should call Lucas…'

'No, no, if you will be advised by me you will leave well alone,' said Zelah.

'I agree,' said Kate. 'We will come back another time, will we not, Mrs Coale?'

Zelah was having difficulty concealing her smile.

'We will indeed,' she managed. They stepped out of the door and she paused as a final thought occurred to her. 'And, Gatley, I suggest you fetch up a bottle or two of your finest claret. For a celebration.'

A rare gleam entered in the butler's eye and a smile broke over his usually austere features.

'I will indeed, madam!'

Susannah tore herself free, saying furiously, 'You cannot give my staff orders!'

He stripped off his gloves and threw them on a side table.

'You could have told him to throw me out.'

'I should not need to. It should be perfectly clear to him that you are unwelcome in this house.'

The angry light faded and he grinned.

'I doubt if your butler has ever been called upon to eject a peer before.'

She bit her lip, fighting back an answering smile. He was standing in front of the door so she could not escape, but she was not prepared to forgive him so easily.

'Very well, my lord, say what you have to and be gone.' Rather than look at him she removed her bonnet and cloak and set them carefully over a chair.

'When I heard you had left town with Warwick I thought you were running away from me again.'

'I never run away,' she told him haughtily, then spoiled the effect by adding, 'but it would be understandable if I should do so, after the way you have treated me. You tried to seduce me. You used me shamelessly.'

'I did,' he agreed. 'And you gave me my own again for that, did you not, madam? Leaving me tied to the bedpost.'

She grew hot at the memory. Her cheeks burned.

'I am not proud of my actions that night.'

'You should be.' He paused. 'You are a woman to be reckoned with, Miss Prentess.'

Embarrassed by his praise she turned away.

'Nonsense. I did what was necessary to protect myself.' As she was doing now, closing her mind to the attraction she felt for him. After all, he would soon be gone and she would be alone again. She had a vision of the bleak, cold years stretching ahead of her and felt the sudden sting of tears.

Susannah rubbed her eyes. She felt incredibly despondent. If Jasper did not leave soon she knew she would begin to cry. She summoned up every ounce of energy to say angrily, 'If that is all, perhaps you will go now, and leave me in peace.'

'No, it is not all,' he retorted. 'You have thrown a great many accusations at my head, madam. I demand the right to defend myself.' He walked to the window and stood looking out, his hands clasped behind his back. 'You accused me of being a rake. I am not, madam. I admit I have indulged in many a flirtation, but the women have never been unwilling.'

'Hah!' She curled her lip. 'Would they have been quite so willing if you had not had a title, and a fortune?'

'I would like to think there is more to me than that, but you are right, Miss Prentess, I cannot be sure.' He added quietly, 'Since meeting you, madam, I am not sure of anything.'

She had to steel herself not to crumble at this sudden diffidence. To distract herself she went to the mantelpiece and picked up the note that was resting against the clock. She said, as her fingers broke the seal, 'Your doubts will fade once you are gone from Bath.'

'Oh, you may be sure I shall do my best to forget this,' he retorted.

She paid no heed to his words, her attention given to the paper in her hands.

'This is the note you sent me yesterday?'

He gave a quick look over his shoulder. 'Yes, I—'

'Oh, heavens.' One hand crept to her cheek, she could *feel* the colour draining from her face. 'You were g-going to, to—'

'Yes,' he interrupted her. 'I was going to offer for you.'

'B-but why?' She felt almost dizzy.

'I have already told you, I love you.'

She lifted her hand.

'No, no, that was an error. You don't even *like* me.'

He laughed harshly.

'You are quite right. You are the most maddening, exasperating woman I have ever encountered, but it has not stopped me falling in love with you.'

She could only stare at his back, groping for words that would not come. After an uncomfortable silence he continued.

'Oh, pray, don't be alarmed, madam. I may love you to distraction but after what has passed this morning I will not put you to the trouble of refusing me. You have made your sentiments perfectly clear.'

She shook her head.

'No. You do not understand. I—I cannot allow you to be near me...'

'I *do* understand,' he said gently. 'You honoured me with your confidences and they made me realise how repugnant my advances must have been to you.'

He still had his back to her, his gaze fixed on the view over Crescent Fields. Her heart was beating so hard it was difficult to speak, even to *think*, but she knew she had to try, and she must get it right, or she would never see him again.

'N-not repugnant,' she whispered, moving closer. 'I cannot allow you to touch me because of what happens to me when you do.' She reached out and put her hand on his shoulder. 'I want you so much it terrifies me.' He turned at that and with his eyes upon her it was twice as hard to go on, but continue she must. 'I have never felt such an overwhelming desire for anyone, for anything in my life before. When you kiss me I am in danger of forgetting everything, my fear of men, of losing control, of falling in love...' her voice faded until it was little more than a breath '...of you breaking my heart.'

He raked his fingers through his gleaming black hair, saying unsteadily, 'Oh my dear, I swear I will never do that. But you have to trust me.'

'I do, Jasper, I do trust you.' She put her hand

up and touched his cheek. 'Do you see what this means, Jasper, do you know what I am asking? I *want* you to seduce me.'

Still he did not move. Placing her hands on his shoulders, she reached up and touched her lips against his. Immediately his arms came round her and with a sigh she leaned against him, twining her arms about his neck. Their kiss was long and languorous and incredibly gentle, but when at last he broke away she rested her head on his shoulder, aware that not one of her bones felt strong enough to support her.

'Oh dear.' She clung to him, murmuring the words into his neckcloth. 'I do not think I can stand.'

With a laugh he swept her up and carried her across to the sofa, where he sat down with her on his lap and began kissing her again. She responded eagerly, her lips parting to allow his tongue to roam wherever it would. She drove her fingers through his hair, revelling in the silky feel of it. Every nerve was alive and aching for his touch. She wanted to feel his skin against hers and she began to tug at his cravat. He stopped kissing her and put his hand up over her fingers.

'Susannah, I cannot do this.'

Cold fear clutched at her heart.

'Have I offended you, have I been too forward? I know some men do not like that in a woman…'

He gathered her into his arms and held her close, his cheek resting against her curls.

'No, sweetheart, that is not it, but I do not want to do anything you might later regret.'

'No…' she ran her tongue over her lips '…I won't regret this. It is what I want. Truly.'

'Then I won't seduce you.' His smile was warm. 'But I will make love to you, if you will let me?'

The burning look in his eyes sent a shiver of anticipation through her.

'Oh yes, yes, please.'

With a look that promised everything he slid her from his lap on to the sofa and knelt on the floor beside her.

'First we must dispose of some of these garments.'

He divested himself of his driving coat and jacket then slowly, and with infinite gentleness, he removed her walking dress, pausing occasionally to kiss the newly exposed skin.

Susannah lay back against the satin cushions, her eyes closed, revelling in the touch of his hands as they roamed over her body. He pressed kisses on her breasts where they rose up from the confining corset, his tongue flicking over the soft flesh and causing her to moan softly. When he stopped she opened her eyes and saw that he had transferred his attention to her feet. Gently he untied her ribbon garters and rolled down each stocking, caressing her calves as he did so. He kissed her ankles and toes, nibbling at their rosy tips while his hands slid up to her thighs. Her body tightened as his fingers moved upwards and immediately he stopped.

'Tell me if you don't want this,' he murmured.

In response she reached out for him, pulling him down on the sofa with her, capturing his mouth and kissing him with a ferocity that left them both gasping. Susannah kissed him again while his gently roving fingers caressed her inner thighs until she was arching against his hand. She heard him groan and even as she was swooning with the new and delightful sensations he was rousing in her, he covered her with his body. Her hips rose up to welcome him She gave a little cry but when he hesitated she gripped him even tighter.

'No, no, don't stop,' she murmured, her mouth against his cheek. 'I want this, I *want* this.'

She sought his mouth again and they kissed, their bodies moving as one, faster, harder. She clung to him, her fingers tracing the hard muscles of his shoulders while she matched his movements, delighting in their union. It was too much. She threw back her head, dragging air into her lungs while her limbs bucked and twisted, beyond her control. She felt rather than heard Jasper's muffled cry and held on as he tensed above her, and she gave herself up to the delicious sensation of flying and drowning at the same time.

As their bodies relaxed together he held her closer.

'Oh, my dearest love. I hope I didn't frighten you.'

Her heart swelled with the words. She reached up and stroked his hair.

'Now I know what they mean by taking one's pleasure,' she said, smiling. She grew still and he raised his head.

'What is it?'

'Did you mean what you said?' she asked him shyly. 'About loving me to distraction?'

'Of course. Have I not just proved it is so?' After another kiss he helped her to sit up. 'I am afraid we will not be able to marry immediately. It will have to be a big ceremony, at Markham, with all the family and tenants as witnesses. I hope you do not object—' He broke off. 'What is it? What have I said?'

She looked away.

'It is what you have *not* said. You have not yet asked me to marry you, my lord.'

With a growl he pulled her back into his arms.

'On the contrary, I suggested it some time

ago, but you refused me. However, I am taking what has just happened as a sign that you have changed your mind. Well, strumpet?'

She lowered her eyes, saying provocatively, 'I suppose I *must* marry you now, even without a formal proposal.'

Her teasing provoked just the reaction she had hoped for. She was swept up into another passionate embrace and within minutes Jasper had once more carried her to such ecstatic heights that afterwards she could only lay docile and compliant in his arms, agreeing with all his plans for the future.

'We must buy you a ring,' he decided. 'We will do that tomorrow. And while we are in Milsom Street we will retrieve the emeralds you sold.'

'If they still have them. The manager said it was a very fine set.'

His grin was pure wickedness.

'It is and they do still have it. I purchased it and asked them to put it aside for me. I had meant to give it to Lady Gisburne to return to you, once I had left Bath.'

She shook her head, distressed.

'Oh, how can you be so good, when I have treated you so abominably?'

He gave a soft laugh and kissed her again.

'You have made up for all that now.'

'No, this has pleased me, too.' She cast another shy look at him. 'I did not realise being in love could be—'

His arms tightened.

'Is that true?' he demanded. 'You love me?'

'To distraction,' she said, smiling. 'I would have told you sooner if I had realised how wonderful it would be to have you make love to me.' She cast a glance at her stays and chemise. 'And we have not yet removed all our clothes.'

'Your morning room is not the place for that.' He dropped a kiss on her forehead. 'But believe me, my darling, when I finally undress you, I shall make love to you even more thoroughly.'

Three months later Jasper was as good as his word, when he carried his new bride to the marriage bed at Markham. The costly linen nightgowns were soon thrown off and they lay together, exploring and enjoying each other until their mutual passions could no longer be denied and they gave themselves up to the consummation that carried them to new and exhilarating heights.

Later, in the first flush of dawn, Jasper knelt beside Susannah, gazing at her perfect, creamy body. She lay on the silken sheets, her hair spread across the pillow like a golden cloud.

'My viscountess,' he murmured. 'When will I ever grow tired of looking at you?'

'Never, I hope.' She opened her sleepy eyes and reached for him. 'My darling husband, seduce me again.'

* * * * *

A sneaky peek at next month...

HISTORICAL

IGNITE YOUR IMAGINATION, STEP INTO THE PAST...

My wish list for next month's titles...

In stores from 1st February 2013:

- ❑ Never Trust a Rake – Annie Burrows
- ❑ Dicing with the Dangerous Lord – Margaret McPhee
- ❑ Haunted by the Earl's Touch – Ann Lethbridge
- ❑ The Last de Burgh – Deborah Simmons
- ❑ A Daring Liaison – Gail Ranstrom
- ❑ The Texas Ranger's Daughter – Jenna Kernan

Available at WHSmith, Tesco, Asda, Eason, Amazon and Apple

Just can't wait?

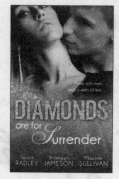
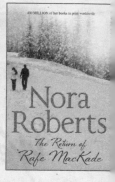

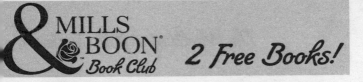

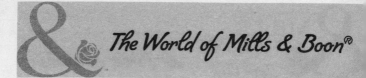

The World of Mills & Boon®

There's a Mills & Boon® series that's perfect
for you. We publish ten series and, with new
titles every month, you never have to wait
long for your favourite to come along.

Scorching hot, sexy reads
4 new stories every month

By Request
*Relive the romance with
the best of the best*
9 new stories every month

Cherish™
*Romance to melt the
heart every time*
12 new stories every month

Desire™
*Passionate and dramatic
love stories*
8 new stories every month

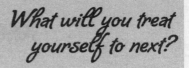